THE BLOODMIST ENVELOPED HIM

Aonghus felt a terrible passion. Cellach, son of the High King, was now sprawling back in his chair, openly smiling with mocking self-assurance. A vision swam before Aonghus' eyes: his violated and slain sister, the scorched ruins of Dún Gorm and the bodies of his brutally murdered father and his retinue. A red mist began to form in front of him. His temples throbbed. He had no control over the wave of anger that swept through him.

"Gods of justice!" he found himself crying. "This evil will not go unpunished!"

One of the Fianna moved forward, spear across his chest, as if to protect Cellach. The throbbing in Aonghus' temples became unbearable. He reached out and grabbed the warrior's spear, quickly reversing it. Before the assembled people were aware of what he was doing, he thrust it straight through Cellach's body, transfixing the young man to his chair.

PETER TREMAYNE

BLOODMIST

This is a work of fiction. All the characters and events portrayed in this book are fictional, and any resemblance to real people or incidents is purely coincidental.

A Baen Books Original

Baen Publishing Enterprises
260 Fifth Avenue
New York, N.Y. 10001

First printing, August 1988

ISBN: 0-671-65425-X

Cover art by Larry Schwinger

Printed in the United States of America

Distributed by
SIMON & SCHUSTER
1230 Avenue of the Americas
New York, N.Y. 10020

For Ise, a special friend.

AUTHOR'S NOTE

This is the story of "The Expulsion of the Dési," a tale from Irish mythology which has never been fully translated or retold in English and which is generally unknown outside of academic circles. It is set in the legendary Ireland of swirling mists and powerful magic; in the land of heroes and gods, of heroines and goddesses and frightful creatures from the Otherworld.

I have taken as my basic inspiration text the version Inndarba inna nDési, which appeared in the famous Annála Ríoghachta Éireann, a 17th-century copy of an earlier manuscript book. According to Professor Kuno Meyer, who edited the text in the late 19th century, the story of the Dési was first committed to writing about the 8th century A.D. but seems, stylistically, to date back to the 3rd century A.D.

But this novel, I hasten to say, is no mere translation from the Irish text. It is a fantasy freely inspired by the original story.

Ravenmoon, aloof and heaven hanging,
Crimson stains the disc,
Sending champions doom rushing,
Bloodmist before their eyes.
   Cionaith Ó hArtagáin
   (b. circa 910 A.D.—d. 975 A.D.)

Chapter One

Dusk was descending with rapidity as the war chariot of Orba Mac Doélta approached the dark, brooding oak forest of An Dhoire Leathan, which skirted the sacred hill of Srón Bilé. The sun was already below the distant western peaks and the sharp, long shadows had fled into a dusky greyness. The atmosphere was chill. Another moment or two and night would cast its dark mantle over the broad stretch of woods through which he had to pass in order to ascend the larger, hook-shaped hill beyond.

Orba Mac Doélta shivered in spite of the beaver-fur cloak he wore to keep out the late winter cold. He was a thick-set man whose short, solid figure seemed to blend and be one with the chariot he drove. He held the reins with a single hand—a firm hand that controlled the two sleek black mares which were yoked to the car. That it was the chariot of a chieftain of consequence was obvious by the way the wickerwork was encrusted with plates of bronze, silver and copper, beaten into mystic whorls and circles. Orba Mac Doélta of Dún Gorm was, indeed, a chieftain, chieftain of Hy-Nia in the clan lands of the Dési. Yet even with his war chariot under him, his sword strapped to his side, his shield slung on his back and his winged bronzed war helmet on his head—yes, even as fierce a figure as he made, Orba was agitated.

At the edge of the darkening oak forest he drew the chariot to a halt and peered nervously forward. The road had narrowed into a small path, too narrow for his chariot to pass along it. He would have to dismount and walk through the woods to the foot of the hill that towered beyond.

He jumped down and hitched the reins to a nearby bush, running his firm hand reassuringly over the sweaty, nervous mares and gently encouraging them with his soft, coaxing voice. The mares shared Orba's fear; they started nervously but allowed themselves to be petted and coaxed into stillness. Orba returned to the car and bent down, picking up a small bundle wrapped in furs. He held it gently against his chest with one well-muscled arm; the other hand rested lightly on the pommel of his sword. He glanced around as if to reassure himself that he was unobserved before beginning to walk swiftly into the gloomy wood.

The air was cold and damp. The vegetation produced a dull, bittersweet stench of decay. He had not gone more than a few yards along the path before he was in a gloom so dense that his visibility was narrowed to only a few yards in either direction. He peered forward to ensure that he kept to the trodden pathway, his eyes nervously flickering alternately from the path to the surrounding forest.

It was strikingly silent in the forest—no birds sang, no animals scuttled through the underbrush. It was as if Nature, life itself, had ceased. The stillness was oppressive.

Now and again Orba's hand whitened on his sword pommel in reaction to imaginary threats, but nothing materialized. The silence continued and the darkness increased.

He found himself leaving the forest almost abruptly, ascending the ground at the point where the trees ended, moving swiftly toward the high summit of Srón Bilé. Orba did not pause but, his hand still holding the bundle of furs against his chest, he bent against the hill, his mouth opening slightly to aid in the added exertion. He moved swiftly upwards with firm tread, following the narrow pathway which now and again twisted to follow the contour more easily to the summit.

As he moved upwards in the gloom, a soft, yellowing mist seemed to drift across the summit, hiding it from his view. He paused a moment, squinting upwards. The mist seemed to increase with the onset of evening. Orba bit his lip, his nervousness increasing. For a moment he wondered if his courage was deserting him. He felt a sudden anger at his faintheartedness. Was he an old woman? Who, at feasting time, would dare challenge him for the hero's portion? He was Orba Mac Doélta of Dún Gorm in Hy-Nia. His anger grew stronger than his fear and he moved determinedly onwards.

Soon he had passed an outer ring of standing stones— cold, dark sentinels, standing in their silent circle around the hilltop, taller than a tall man. He ascended a little way farther until he came to the summit of the hill itself, to a smaller circle of menhirs at the very peak of the hill. In the center of this circle stood a large slab of granite, lying altar-like. Two burning braziers stood on either side of the granite, sparks flying, twigs crackling in the gentle whispering wind that moved across the hill.

The strange thing Orba noticed was that the wind did not disturb the thick, yellow mist that seemed to hang shroud-like around the center circle of stones. It was odd, very odd that the mist left a clear vortex in its center, whose borders seemed to be the inner stones. He shuddered. A druid's mist—that's what it was. A magical mist.

Orba Mac Doélta came to a halt before the altar slab and peered around apprehensively, his free hand clenching at the hilt of his sword.

The stillness was broken by a dry, rasping cough.

Orba Mac Doélta swung around but could see nothing.

"Show yourself!" he called, his voice cracking halfway between fear and anger. "In the name of the Dagda and his children, show yourself!"

"In the name of the Dagda, I shall answer you, Orba Mac Doélta of Dún Gorm," rang out a mocking, hollow voice. The voice sounded just behind him, and he swung back to the altar stone. His eyes widened and he took an involuntary pace backwards.

A tall figure in a dark mantle stood behind the altar. It was the figure of an elderly man. His hair and beard were long, almost the color of steel. Below the beard shone the golden chains of office. He stood with arms folded, his bright eyes reflecting the light of the burning braziers. They seemed possessed of some inner life as they watched the face of the chieftain of Dún Gorm.

"How . . .?" began Orba. His lips were dry, so he paused to flick a tongue over them.

The druid smiled thinly.

"A question already? The sun warms and lights our existence, and yet I have never heard a man ask the question 'how' or 'why.' Yet when the sun is gone, when it is dark and we are fearful, then questions are always on our lips." The sparkling-bright eyes dropped to the bundle Orba carried at his chest. "Have you fulfilled your obligation?"

Orba hesitated and then nodded. He moved forward and lowered the bundle to the grey granite altar, gently unwrapping the outer layer of soft beaver skins.

A baby lay revealed in the bundle, its eyes shut in natural sleep.

"I have brought my son, even as you commanded me, Eolas."

The druid's lips thinned again.

"Then I bid you welcome to the Stone of Naming, Orba Mac Doélta. Is it still your wish that I enact the rituals whereby your son may receive his name according to the ancient ways, and whereby we may read his destiny before he is cast forth on the road of life?"

Orba bowed his head.

"It is the tradition that the son of a chieftain of Dún Gorm in Hy-Nia be named in the sacred fashion," he agreed.

"So be it."

The druid bent down to the sleeping baby and reached forth his right hand, placing the palm gently across the tiny forehead. The baby turned his head a little and moaned softly in his sleep but did not waken.

For several long minutes the druid bent to the infant, his eyes closed, the palm resting on the baby's forehead. Then, he heaved a shuddering sigh and stood up. From a fold of his robe he took out a small bundle of hazel wands. There were seventeen such wands, each cut with strange words in Ogham script. He held the bundle of wands in his right hand, the hand that had touched the baby's forehead, stood a moment, muttering inaudibly, and then cast the wands down so that they fell in curious patterns on the altar slab.

Orba stood watching with a slight frown as Eolas, the druid, bent to the wands, examining the way they had fallen. The man's face was impassive. Then, without speaking, he gathered the wands together again, laid them in a bundle on the altar and reached forward, this time placing his left hand on the sleeping baby's forehead. After a while he took up the wands with his left hand and cast them down in the same manner as before. The druid's face was a mask as he examined the fallen wands.

"What is it, Eolas?" muttered Orba, sensing disquiet about the graven face of the druid.

Eolas drew back his shoulders, rising to his full height.

"I cannot keep the truth from you," he said, lips pursing slightly. "The augury is far from good."

Orba tensed himself.

"I came to hear the truth, Eolas. A truth is a truth whether it be good or evil."

"Then hear the truth, chieftain of Dún Gorm in Hy-Nia. You have in mind to call this child, your first-born son, Aonghus, after the god of love. It is the wish of the boy's mother. Let him be called Aonghus . . . but Aonghus Gae-Adúath—Aonghus of the Terrible Spear. For it is written in the wands that he will drive his people out of the pleasant land of Éireann by a single cast of a spear. The blood of High Kings will be on his hands, and his clan of Dési will never more be heard of in the land of Bregia, wherein they now dwell. That is the prophecy of naming."

Orba's face was pale.

"Can there be a mistake?" he whispered

Eolas, the druid, shot him an angry look.

"Do you think my skill is nothing? I have read the wands. There is no mistake."

"Is there nothing good in the prophecy?"

"He will be a leader of men and sire leaders of men," the druid said indifferently. "He will have no fear, yet this much is obvious, for he was born when the sun was in the sky, and a child of the day will never see the demons of the Otherworld. But that will make him vulnerable to the tricks of unscrupulous men."

"Yet you say he will make a spear cast that will cause not only my sept of the people of Hy-Nia to be driven from their country but the entire clan of Dési as well?"

"It is as I have said," affirmed the druid.

"Then we must prevent its likelihood," Orba cried, his voice suddenly decisive. "Let this prophecy remain between us, Eolas. Let me return to my wife at Dún Gorm without the curse of this prophecy on my lips."

Eolas shrugged.

"What I have to say, I say to you at this Stone of Naming. What you recount of what I say is your own affair."

"I say this, Eolas: My son must be prevented from ever carrying a spear."

Eolas smiled. "Yet he is the son of a chieftain. Will it not be strange that he is refused instruction in the art of spear casting? A strange warrior and future chieftain will he be."

Orba was earnest. "Perhaps the prophecy can be prevented if he is forbidden the use of a spear."

"What the gods ordain cannot be changed," observed the druid firmly. "It is written in the hazel wands."

Orba bent forward suddenly across the altar and scattered the wands with a thrust of his hand.

"Now tell me what they read!" he demanded hotly.

Eolas, the druid, smiled sadly and shook his head.

"Life is not so easily changed, Orba Mac Doélta. What is written is written for all time."

"Then let me demand one thing further of you, Eolas. Pronounce upon my son a *geis*—pronounce a sacred taboo that will compel him never to touch a spear, never to go hunting with one or use it in combat, never to learn the art of a warrior's spear cast."

The druid's eyes narrowed dangerously.

"Why should I do this thing, Orba Mac Doélta?"

"Four months ago you were travelling the road to the Hill of Usna for the lighting of the Samhain fires. You were attacked by a thief and nearly slain. I chanced to come upon you and slew your attacker."

Eolas pressed his lips together a moment.

"I do not deny this."

"In reparation now, I ask you to pronounce this *geis*."

Eolas stared at the chieftain a moment, his face twitching with irritation.

"I accept that you may demand this of me in reparation. But I tell you, Orba Mac Doélta of Dún Gorm in Hy-Nia, that little good will come of it. No man can change the will of the gods."

"Pronounce the *geis*!" cried Orba.

The druid sighed impatiently.

"The *geis* cannot be pronounced until the boy has attained the age of fosterage."

Orba frowned. "Will anything happen before that age? What if the augury should come to pass before the age of fosterage?"

The druid shook his head.

"Who knows the ways of the gods? I can but tell you the ways of the laws of men, and accordingly do the Brehon Laws state that a *geis* can only be pronounced on a child of understanding. Bring the boy to me here, at the time of the Feast of the Fires of Bilé, when he enters his seventh year, before he goes to fosterage to receive his education. On that day I will pronounce the *geis*, should you still demand it. On that day and not before."

Orba hesitated a moment, then bowed his head in agreement.

"So be it."

Bending down, he wrapped the beaver fur around the still sleeping baby and picked it up gently and firmly in his arm again.

Eolas the druid was collecting the hazel wands and bundling them together. As Orba began to retrace his footsteps from the stone circle he straightened and called: "Remember that his name shall henceforth be Aonghus Gae-Adúath—Aonghus of the Terrible Spear. Man and all his works cannot alter the will of the gods."

"Man has defied the gods before now," retorted Orba across his shoulder.

"And did so at their peril," replied the druid tonelessly. "Go in peace, Orba Mac Doélta of Dún Gorm in Hy-Nia. Go in peace. For that which the gods decide will be, must be."

Chapter Two

The setting sun was gleaming on the ramparts of Dún Gorm in Hy-Nia when Orba Mac Doélta climbed up the steps to make his ritual circle of the ráth before the pale golden orb of spring finally settled below the western hills. Orba inhaled deeply as he ascended the steps. He was not as young as he once was, he reflected. Age was a process which only the Ever-Living Ones could forestall, and he was but a man. Still, it had been a good life and he had no complaints as to its quality. But, as he eased his aching limbs onto the ramparts, he paused to reflect, leaning slightly against the walls that overlooked the earthworks below. His watery eyes gazed out across the green, fertile plain of Hy-Nia which, in turn, dominated the western borders of the luxuriant lands of Bregia, the clan lands of the Dési, the most powerful tribe in all Éireann. Orba heaved a long, low sigh.

He was too old to continue as chieftain of the sept of Hy-Nia. Tomorrow, when his son Aonghus returned from Dún Mór, the capital of the Dési, he would discuss the process whereby Aonghus must take over the responsibilities of chieftainship. Aonghus was in his twenty-fifth year, and there was enough sense in his head for him to assume the heavy mantle Orba had worn these past forty years. Already Aonghus had been confirmed by the tribal council of Hy-Nia as the *tánaiste*—the second in authority to the chieftain. It was an old custom. With the objective of avoiding the evils of disputed succession, the person to succeed a king or ruling chieftain was elected by the clansmen in formal meeting during the lifetime of the king or chieftain himself. When elected, he or she—for women were eligible for election to all offices within the clans of the people of Éireann—was called the *tánaiste*, which meant, literally, the second. Often, when the king or chieftain felt too old or sick to fulfill the functions of office adequately, he would simply resign office and the *tánaiste* would be confirmed in his stead. This was the law throughout the clans of Éireann, even to its High Kings.

It was even now, in his capacity as *tánaiste*, that Aonghus Mac Orba was away from Hy-Nia attending the clan assembly of the Dési convened by Eochaidh Allmuir, chieftain of the clan and answerable to no one but the High King, Cormac Mac Art himself. For a year now Aonghus had acted as his father's *tánaiste*. The time had come when Orba must stand down and allow his son to become chieftain over Hy-Nia.

The old man pursued his lips and half nodded to himself as he leaned against the ramparts, gazing across the fecund valley below. The people of Hy-Nia had prospered over the years; indeed, as had all the people of the Dési. There had been no lean years as he recalled; each year, the crops came in with abundance. There was not a razor-back pig, not a thin, slab-sided cow, to be seen throughout the land. All were fat and healthy. No wars had spread the curse of burning thatch among the villages and the Dési ships, famous throughout Éireann, sailed in peaceful trade from their safe harbor within the mouth of the great river Boann. The wealthy ports of Britain and Gaul knew the cut of the Dési ships' sails well enough. As he recalled, only three times had the *Crois-tara*, the fiery cross, been lit to summon the clan to the muster of the High King to march with him against the rebellious clans of Ulaidh. And what harm in that? Each war simply ended in traditional fashion when the champions of both sides fought in single-handed combat in front of the armies to prove their honor.

A frown suddenly passed Orba's face.

It was true that there had been talk of trouble at the court of the High King recently. It was some years now since the great champion Fionn Mac Cumhail had been slain. The great, indestructible Fionn, leader of the Fianna, the bodyguard of the High King! And Fionn's son Oisín had disappeared, the gods knew where. Some said that he had been out in the forests one day when a beautiful goddess had ridden up on a magic horse and enticed Oisín to mount with her; that together they had vanished in the clouds, riding away to Tir na nÓg, the Land of Youth, from which no traveller ever returned. Well, that was just a story told by the bards around the evening fire. Oisín's son, Oscar, the handsome young giant, had become captain of the Fianna. Yet, if the rumors were to be trusted, there was dissension at the court of the High King at Temuir.

There were whispers of plot and counterplot, or attempts to destroy Oscar's authority over the Fianna so that the country could return to the petty wars of former days, the days before Fionn Mac Cumhail had made Cormac Mac Art the most powerful king in the western world. Ah, Cormac Mac Art! He was old now; older even than Orba. Yet he clung to power limpetlike with an old man's peevishness, growing ever more intolerant and fearful that those around him would usurp it. Perhaps there was a darkening cloud spreading across the land of Éireann?

Well, Orba's role was almost over. It would be up to Aonghus to guide his people through the storms that might lie ahead. Orba pursued his lips in thought. It had been many years since he had last meditated about the events that had occurred at the Stone of Naming on Srón Bilé, when he had taken Aonghus to the druid Eolas for the customary prophecy. Orba shivered slightly and wondered why it had crossed his mind. Perhaps the thought of the storm clouds gathering at the court of the High King, the inevitable storms through which Aonghus would have to lead the people of Hy-Nia, had caused Eolas' augury to come to his memory. By a single cast of a spear Aonghus would drive not only the sept of Hy-Nia but all the clan of the Dési from this pleasant land.

Well, the prophecy had not been fulfilled yet, and there was little chance that it would be. When Aonghus had entered the age of fosterage, on his seventh birthday, Eolas the druid had pronounced the sacred taboo, the *geis*, so that he would never learn skill in the use of spear or javelin, never touch the weapon in the hunt or in war. Soon after, Aonghus had been sent south to begin his fosterage with a chieftain whose clan dwelt in the mountains of Comeraigh. He had learned the skills for his future life, he had studied laws natural and man-made with the druids; had learned poetry, literature, art and music; had learned the honor code, the art of warfare and single combat, the use of the sword, the bow and the sling-shot. But never did he touch spear nor javelin. In spite of this he was accounted as good a warrior as any and his skill with other weapons was more deadly than any other warrior of his contemporaries. He never returned hungry from the hunt; his quick eye made the bow an extension of himself and rarely was he known to miss a quarry with his slingshot. And when his fosterage was over, when he reached the *aimsir togu*—the age of choice—at seventeen years, he had returned to Dún Gorm in Hy-Nia, a dutiful son, a handsome youth, one slow to temper and wise in council.

Orba smiled softly. Yes, it was fitting that Aonghus should take on the mantle of chieftain now.

"Father, I thought I would find you on the ramparts. I came to walk with you."

Orba started at the soft, musical voice and his gaze softened as he looked upon the gentle features of his daughter. Áine she had been named, after the love goddess. It had been Orba's wife who had decided that both son and daughter should take the names of Aonghus and Áine, god and goddess of love and beauty. "Better to give them the blessings of love than to name them from war and destruction," she had said. "Isn't there need for more love in this sorry world?"

Áine was eighteen years old now, fair of skin, with a tinge of rose red on her pale cheeks. Her eyes were wide and as blue as a summer's sky, while her hair was spun gold like corn at harvesting. She had a comely shape and Áine was a name that befitted her.

Orba hid a passing pain when he gazed on the features of his daughter. She was so like his own wife, so like . . . Ah, but she was dead these seven winters now. He felt old and tired.

"Are you unwell, father?" Áine reached forward, her pale hand on his arm, a look of concern in her eyes.

Orba shook his head and patted his daughter on the hand.

"No. Perhaps a little sad, just remembering . . . remembering the golden days, that's all."

Áine gave a soft laugh.

"Time remembered is grief forgotten," she admonished.

"You do well to rebuke me," her father smiled sheepishly. "What right have I to sadness when I remember the pleasant days that are gone?"

"And happy times to come, father."

"Ah, no. My times are done. I am old. Time for Aonghus to take up the shield of chieftainship now. My ears are too many."

"Nonsense!" retorted the girl firmly. "Do not the druids say that a man should not count his years until he has nothing else to count?"

"You are strongheaded, Áine," smiled her father. "Time enough to get you married before I depart from office."

Áine flushed.

"Plenty of time for that," she muttered.

"Is it so? You came to the age of choice four years ago. You should be wed now."

Orba smiled at the way his daughter raised her chin defiantly. He knew that she was often to be seen in the company of Cairell Mac Fios, the druid's son who was charioteer to Aonghus, and he knew it was more than friendship between them. Cairell was a suitable match in Orba's eyes, even though it was unusual for the daughter of the Dési chieftain to wed within the sept. Perhaps that was what was worrying Áine. Orba felt a desire to pull her leg.

"Indeed, Áine. I have been meaning to discuss the subject with you for some time. There is a suitable young man. . . ."

Áine pressed her lips together stubbornly, a frown on her features.

"I do not want to get married, father," she interrupted.

"I am still chieftain and your father," Orba rebuked. "The good of the tribe must come before your personal preferences."

Áine's face grew sullen. It was an expression which ill-fitted her naturally attractive features. Orba ignored it.

"As I was saying, there is a young man. He is of good family. I think you will be well suited with each other."

Áine made no reply.

"Tomorrow I shall call on the young man and his father to discuss matters. I believe he has been wanting to speak to me of marriage for some time now."

Áine sniffed. "I have encouraged no one. Who would dare press for marriage with me without indicating his intentions to me first?"

Orba raised an eyebrow mockingly.

"Encouraged no one? This young man seems encouraged enough."

"What tribe does this person come from?" demanded Áine.

Orba saw the apprehension in the girl's eyes and he suddenly softened. He could not make fun any longer.

"He is of our sept of Hy-Nia."

Áine's brow creased in bewilderment.

"I know of no one . . ." she began. Then she saw her father's grin. "Name the man," she demanded.

"Why, he is the son of the druid Fios."

"Oh!" Her face was crimson now, torn between relief and mortification at her father's joke. "How could you, father? How could you lead me on so?" Then hesitantly: "Do you mean it? Are you going to speak to Cairell . . .?"

"You know me enough to know that I mean what I say," replied Orba. "When Cairell returns with Aonghus tomorrow . . ."

"Riders approaching!"

Orba glanced up quickly toward the watchtower at the southerly gate of Dún Gorm. A warrior was leaning forward, pointing down the valley. Orba, followed by his daughter, moved as hurriedly as he could toward the south rampart and squinted down the valley floor where the long, dark shadows of a score or more riders could be seen making their way leisurely along the river banks.

"Who are they?" asked Áine.

"Can you make them out?" Orba called to the sentinel.

"Not at this distance," replied the man. "Yet one of their number is riding forward and galloping this way."

They watched silently as the rider approached, swiftly in advance of the main body. As he drew nearer to the fortress they could see he was a lean warrior dressed entirely in black and silver. His shield and weapons shone almost white, and his black mare was similarly decorated with silver accoutrements. Black hair spilled from beneath a silver war helmet, from which rose raven's wings on either side. The warrior carried himself at ease, perfectly relaxed as he reined the horse to a halt before the closed gates of Dún Gorm.

"What place is this?" he demanded, shouting up to the sentinel.

"You are at the gates of Dún Gorm in Hy-Nia, ráth of Orba Mac Doélta, chieftain of Hy-Nia."

The mounted warrior sat back in his saddle, hand on hip.

"Then tell Orba Mac Doélta that Gorta Mac Goll of the Clan Morna wishes to speak with him."

Orba moved forward.

"It is Orba Mac Doélta who speaks."

The young warrior gazed up a moment.

"Know, Orba Mac Doélta, that my lord Cellach Mac Cormac, son of the High King, is approaching with his retinue and needs shelter for the night. By the law of hospitality . . ."

"There is no need to recite law to me, Gorta Mac Goll," admonished Orba. "I bid Cellach Mac Cormac welcome. A feast shall be prepared to honor his safe arrival."

"I will ride back and tell my lord."

The young warrior turned his horse in a tight circle and trotted away. Orba watched his going with troubled eyes.

"Father?" Áine was tugging at his sleeve.

He turned and forced a reassuring smile.

"You are troubled, father," Áine pressed.

"I have heard of Cellach, the son of Cormac Mac Art. He has an evil reputation. They say he is cunning and ill-tempered and all the things his father, as a young man, was not. I have no happiness at complying with the law of hospitality this night."

Áine frowned. "Yet the law has to be obeyed. We must welcome him, provide him with feasting and entertainment and beds for him and his retinue to rest in this night."

"We?" Orba shook his head firmly. "No, my child. You will go to your room now and remain there until Cellach departs tomorrow. His reputation is bad and I shall not put his honor to the test."

"But, father . . ." protested Áine.

"Obey me in this, Áine, if you never obey me again."

Áine saw the anguish in her father's eyes and submitted.

"Very well. I shall go to my room," she said quietly.

Orba glanced back across the ramparts. The column of riders was near now. He turned and watched anxiously as his daughter went down the steps into the courtyard of the fortress and away toward her quarters. Then he turned to the sentinel.

"Open the gates for the son of the High King," he said, before turning and hurrying as fast as he could down the steps to seek out his druid, Fios, and his cup-bearers, to order preparations for the feasting. Ah, but this would be a worrisome night. He would be glad when the night gave way to morning and Aonghus, his son, returned home.

Chapter Three

Cellach Mac Cormac, the son of the High King, carried himself with an obvious awareness of his handsome looks and the privilege of his birth. But his finely chiselled features held a certain indolence, and his eyes were too narrowly spaced, giving them a mean, shifty look. He sprawled on the seat Orba had offered him with all the expectancy of the status enjoyed by his father, and yet Cellach had none of the grace or regal command of Cormac Mac Art.

Orba watched his guest nervously, for the rumors had it that Cellach was a young man of uncertain temper whose veneer of lazy self-satisfaction disguised a vicious streak. He had gathered around him a band of the sons of the richest chieftains of Éireann—those who haunted the royal court at Temuir; young men spoiled by their fathers' offices and wealth, who had nothing more important to do in life but go drinking, wenching, hunting, and sought nothing more as ambition than a fulfillment of their vanities. The adventures of Cellach and the young lords who trailed in his wake had become a scandal throughout the royal province of Midhe. Indeed, the rumors had spread from Midhe to all the provinces of Éireann—from Ulaidh in the north, to Connachta in the west, and from Laighn in the east to Mumhan in the south. Yet few dared to speak with Cormac Mac Art in order to protest the behavior of his son, for the old king had a blindness about the boy. He had spoiled him for love of the boy's mother, who had died giving him birth.

Cellach had the same willfulness for which his elder sister Gráinne had become renowned. Orba recalled Gráinne well, for he had been serving as a member of the Fianna—the High King's bodyguard—under Fionn Mac Cumhail, during those tragic days. Gráinne, Cormac's daughter, had been willful, ruthless, and passionate, but withal a shallow person. Cormac had betrothed her to Fionn, but rather than marry the greatest warrior in Éireann, she had forced an elopement with Diarmuid Ua Duibhne, a handsome and much loved warrior of the Fianna. In rage, Fionn and Cormac pursued the couple—a pursuit which had ended in Diarmuid's death. Then, fickle as Gráinne was, she was happy to live with Fionn until his own death. Now she dwelt alone at Ráth Gráinne, in the shadow of her father's palace at Temuir, the most powerful woman in Ireland, still, willful, ruthless, and vengeful. And in the cold blue eyes of her brother, Cellach, Orba could see those same aggressive features.

The feasting hall of Dún Gorm was crowded with Orba's retainers, waiting on Cellach and his twenty followers as they stretched languidly around the tables and sampled every delicacy the people of Hy-Nia could provide. Orba nodded approvingly. Let it not get back to the High King that when his son had come to Dún Gorm he had not been properly welcomed. There would be no cause for the High King's bard to compose a satire on the meanness of the feasting table of Orba, or on the lack of imported wines that graced the table.

The feasting was drawing to a close when Orba signalled his bard, Milistenga, to come forward.

"An entertainment, Cellach," he said, turning to the young man. "Let the bard of Hy-Nia sing to soothe your weariness, for he has the sweetest compositions of any in Bregia."

Cellach made a face.

"I grow weary of the squawking of bards."

Orba blinked. To refuse to listen to his host's bard was rudeness to the point of breaking the traditional ritual of hospitality.

Cellach had a crafty look on his face as he turned to Orba.

"I have been told that you have a daughter whose voice is sweeter than all the birds of the pleasant plain of Magh Mell."

Orba blinked and shifted uncomfortably.

"Come now." Cellach's eyes narrowed and a thin smile spread across his dark features. "Do you deny that you have such a daughter? Why, I hear that her singing and beauty is talked about in the halls of every chieftain of the clan Dési."

"You flatter both my daughter and my house," replied Orba, his nervousness increasing.

"The proof of flattery will be in the beholding," Gorta Mac Goll said from the other side of Cellach.

"Indeed." Cellach grinned at the old chieftain's discomfort. "Send for your daughter."

Again Orba hesitated, and a scowl darkened the brow of the son of the High King.

"It is just that my daughter has been unwell of late," Orba said hastily. "I would not wish to expose her before her sickness has ended."

"An honorable sentiment, as befits an anxious father," Gorta said dryly. "Nevertheless, it is an attitude that speaks much of a father's protection. Your daughter was well enough to stand by your side on the ramparts viewing our approach. Surely, then, she is well enough to come to pay her respects to the son of the High King?"

Orba colored furiously at the insulting tone of Gorta's voice. He had not thought that Gorta had seen Áine.

Cellach was staring at him mockingly. If Orba refused to send for Áine, his lack of gracious hospitality would come to the ears of the High King . . . at best. At worst, Cellach was of an ill-defined temper . . .

Orba turned to his cup-bearer and gave the order for Áine to attend them.

Cellach smiled broadly and returned to his wine.

"That is good. We would not wish to criticize the hospitality and entertainment we have received," Gorta said softly.

"Nor the good wine we have received!" cried one of Cellach's followers, waving his goblet. "This is the best wine that has yet sailed out of a Gaulish port. Long may the merchant ships of the Dési bring such riches to the land of Éireann."

There was a general roar of approval, the young men beating the table with the bases of their goblets or the hilts of their daggers. The wine had certainly circled well, and Cellach's followers were getting the worse for it. Orba cast a glance at his bard, Milistenga, who stood watchful in a corner of the feasting hall. Behind him stood the graven-faced druid, Fios. Ah, if only Aonghus were home!

The hall suddenly fell silent as Orba's cup-bearer returned, preceding the slim figure of Áine. She stepped forward dutifully, head held high, looking neither right nor left as she moved along the aisle between the tables to her father's chair. Here she inclined her shapely young neck.

"You sent for me, father?" she spoke softly.

Cellach's mouth had slackened slightly as he examined the girl. A lascivious grin had spread over the dark face of Gorta while even the drunken young men of the retinue had fallen silent at the girl's beauty.

Orba raised a shoulder and let it fall, expressing nervousness and an inability to control the situation.

"I did. Knowing you to be with a sickness, it was not my wish to send for you." His voice held anxiety as he tried to communicate his wishes to her. "It is the wish of our guest that you are here. Cellach, this is my daughter, Áine."

The introduction was done with the minimum of courtesy, but Cellach did not appear to notice. Nor did he rise, but simply grinned in what he thought admiration at the girl.

"You are well named, for you have the beauty that a goddess of love should have. The talk among the halls of the Dési was true, Orba."

"I do not heed the talk among the halls of the Dési," Orba replied, his lips white as they compressed. His annoyance gave rein to his tongue. "Idle chatter only occupies the minds of the idle."

Cellach chuckled broadly, although his companion Gorta frowned and slipped a hand to his side, forgetting for a moment that no weapon was ever worn in the feasting hall, only daggers for eating.

"Nevertheless, we have proof of your daughter's beauty. Now let us have proof of her gift of singing."

Áine turned her haughty features toward him.

"I beg to be excused, son of Cormac. As my father explained, I have but recently recovered from a sickness."

"Excuse you, I cannot," insisted Cellach. "Not before you have sung one song to our company so that I may boast of hearing a voice that is acclaimed more pleasant than all the songbirds who gather on the Pleasant Plain."

Áine hesitated and glanced to her father for guidance.

"One song?" she asked.

Cellach nodded eagerly.

"One song, Áine, and we will let you go."

Áine said nothing but walked slowly around the feasting tables, watched by the lecherous, drunken eyes of the followers of Cellach, and went up to the bard Milistenga, taking the stringed *cruit* from his hands. Then she returned to stand at her father's side and, with a frown of concentration, ran her slender fingers over the strings, producing a tinkling rhythm of pleasing sounds, like the gurgling of a mountain stream. Her voice was a lilting soprano and it echoed clearly around the hall, causing a silence so complete that people tried to stop their breathing for fear the sound would disturb the melody.

> Pulse of my heart, I sicken to be with you,
> Pulse of my heart, my only love and care;
> Little I'd fret if ill or well you used me,
> Pulse of my heart, if I were only there.
>
> Pulse of my heart, I pine to see you.
> My soul! I hate this lonely sea and shore!
> Gladly this night I'd sell my soul to see you,
> Pulse of my heart, whom I shall see no more.

The throbbing strings of the *cruit* silenced and there came a roar of approval from the gathering, the young men whistling and stamping and calling for more. Oblivious, Áine turned and walked back to Milistenga, handing the instrument to him.

"Another song," cried Cellach. "You cannot go with just one song."

Áine turned and raised her chin defiantly.

"I bid you a safe journey back to Temuir, son of Cormac," she said.

"Wait!"cried Cellach, an angry note creeping into his voice. "I said, I would hear another song."

Áine's eyes began to smolder with fire.

"I have sung one song, Cellach Mac Cormac. One song was asked for and one song was agreed to. I believe that the son of a High King binds his honor with his word?"

Cellach flushed, and before he could think of a reply, the girl had left the feasting hall.

Orba signalled Milistenga to step forward and the bard, judging the tension in the company, started off with a bawdy drinking song in which several of the young men relaxed and joined. The refrain was taken up by others, and so the moment passed. Yet Orba once more had a cold feeling as he observed the blank mask on the features of Cellach.

The guests went late to their beds in the hostel of Dún Gorm. Orba was last to go, heaving a sigh of relief. He laid his own weary frame on his couch and closed his eyes. Soon it would be morning and the company would depart along the road to Temuir. He felt a little ashamed with himself. Had old age brought a timidity that had been denied him during his youth and middle years? Why should he—he who had fought at the side of the famed Fionn Mac Cumhail—suddenly be fearful of a young whelp like Cellach and his cronies? Was he not Orba Mac Doélta of Dún Gorm? He sniffed angrily and, turning, composed himself for sleep.

The scream brought him from the edge of sleep, jerking him upright, his heart beating fast. Then he was reaching for his sword and running swiftly down the corridor, blood pumping in his veins.

The scream had come from Áine's chambers.

Without pausing, he burst directly into his daughter's bedchamber.

The sight that met his eyes caused him to freeze momentarily. Áine lay across her couch, her robe torn almost from her slender body, while a red-faced Cellach thrust on top of her, trying to hold her writhing hands

with one hand as the other sought to stifle her screams
by pressing hard against her mouth.

Orba gave a low, animal growl.

"By the Dadga! This night Cormac shall lament a
son!"

Cellach twisted around, his face a mask of fury. He
thrust himself away from the bruised and bleeding body
of the girl with a brutality that caused the girl to scream
in pain and fear.

Orba rushed forward, his warrior training and strength
belying his advanced years. He whirled his sword around
his head. Cellach dodged, screaming inarticulately for
help and grabbing for his own discarded weapon.

There were faint cries and sounds of running feet
within the fortress now.

The High King's son parried Orba's first blow. His
screaming words began to have meaning.

"She enticed me! She lured me here with her body! I
swear it, by the gods!"

Áine had tried to wrap her torn robe around her
convulsed and shaking body and backed in a corner of
the couch, huddled and weeping.

Orba's mouth was a thin slit, his eyes cold, and he
continued to hack remorselessly at the younger man.
There was no emotion save hate in his eyes.

Cellach's mouth was slack with fear now. He was no
match for a warrior, even an old man such as Orba.

Then, abruptly, Orba felt a sharp pain in his back.
He started for a moment, his eyes wide, and blood
began to trickle from his mouth. Cellach's expression
had changed to a malicious grin of triumph. He stepped
forward and stabbed twice with his full weight behind
his sword until Orba Mac Doélta collapsed in death on
the floor of his daughter's bedchamber.

Áine screamed and threw herself forward, grabbing
her father's head in her arms.

Cellach smiled brutally across the dead body to where

Gorta Mac Goll stood impassively wiping his bloody sword on the tapestries that hung in the room.

"Not before time," Cellach observed. "The old buzzard was strong."

Gorta shrugged as he resheathed his weapon.

Cellach now tossed his sword aside distastefully and reached down to grab Áine's wrist, dragging her upwards, struggling and screaming again, beating futilely at him with her fists. He sneered at her.

"Now we will finish what we started."

He swung her viciously onto the couch while Gorta began to drag the dead body of Orba to the chamber door.

It burst open and Fios the druid stood there; behind him, the horrified features of Milistenga the bard.

Fios took in the scene in one astonished glance.

"The gods will curse you for this, Cellach Mac Cormac," he said slowly. "You are cursed in this world and the next. There will be no safe haven in Éireann for you when the High King, your father, knows of this atrocity."

Gorta smiled tightly and pushed at the old druid so that he stumbled back into the corridor against Milistenga. Then he dragged the body of Orba through the door and shut it behind him, smothering the sobbing cries of Áine.

"You cannot hope to get away with such infamy," Fios was shaking with rage. "You have killed Orba, you may kill me, but there are many in Dún Gorm who will bear witness for their slain chieftain. You cannot kill us all."

Gorta chuckled hollowly.

He ceased only when several of his followers came running along the corridor, rubbing the sleep and the effects of their wassail from their eyes.

"What is the disturbance?" demanded one.

"Orba tried to kill Cellach," Gorta lied easily. "This heinous crime shall not go unpunished."

"Is Cellach safe?" cried another.

"Safe enough," Gorta assured him. "He will join us soon. But he orders that everyone in Dún Gorm is guilty of complicity in Orba's crime. They must all perish before we leave. See to it!"

For a moment, the followers of Cellach hesitated; then, they met the black gaze of Gorta Mac Goll.

"Death to Dún Gorm!" cried Gorta, raising his sword high.

The cry was taken up and Cellach's men rushed to secure their weapons.

Fios stood shaking his head.

"There will be no peace for you in this world or the next. May you be reborn even as a lowly earthworm." His voice was cold and sharp as steel.

From beyond the closed door to Áine's bedchamber there came a shrill, horrible scream which ended abruptly in a choking gurgle.

Even Gorta's face whitened a little. Then the door opened and Cellach stood framed a moment in the doorway. There was a wild animal look on his features, and his eyes burned darkly. In his hand was a blood-stained sword.

"Give the word, Gorta," he whispered hoarsely. "Put Dún Gorm to the torch."

"You cannot!" cried Fios. "Have you no thought about your soul?"

Cellach's maniacal eyes focused on the druid.

"Nail him to the gates when we ride out!"

Chapter Four

The chariot swayed dangerously along the well-laid highway that ran through the valleys between the rounded hills of Bregia. It was drawn by two grey horses, heads thrusting forward, their great shoulder muscles rippling as the flicking reins urged them to greater speed. Their hooves pounded on the wood of the roadway, for it was a well-constructed road, as were all the highways of Bregia—a road of oak beams laid on thin rails of oak, ash and alder. The roads of Bregia reflected the prosperity and wealth of the clan Dési.

The chariot itself belonged to a person of rank. The car was made of wickerwork, supported by another frame of strong wooden bars made from the wood of the holly tree, as was the wood of the single shaft. The car was covered with eaten panels of white silver and high-lighted here and there by a copper roundal. The large wheels were iron shod.

A young man balanced in the car, his long red hair streaming behind him although he wore a golden circlet on his head—the *gripni*, or special mark, of a charioteer. He was clean-shaven, sharp featured, but with a face that smiled easily. His eyes were light, almost a brilliant blue. He wore a jacket and kilt of deerskin, the jacket close-fitting so as not to impede the free action of his arms. He held the reins loose, standing legs apart, well balanced and totally at one with his horses and vehicle.

To his left and just behind him stood a darker man. He was tall, well muscled beneath the loose jacket and kilt of white wool he wore. Around him he clutched a multi-colored cloak, of a plaid denoting his rank, which was fixed with a large silver brooch containing semi-precious stones, sparkling in the early morning sun. A sword hung on his left hip. He wore no helmet but his fair, almost golden hair danced in the wind. He, too, was a young man with a broad forehead and handsome features. His eyes were grey, moody like the seas, and as changeable. His skin was tanned and he carried himself as one at ease with combating the elements. He clung easily to the side of the chariot as it thundered along the highway. As the car lurched over an obstruction in the road, he bared his teeth in a grin.

"Steady, Cairell. Why do you hurry so?"

The charioteer did not glance back. His face was drawn tight in a frown of concentration.

"I feel uneasy, Aonghus. Since dawn I have experienced an odd disquiet. Something tells me that we must hurry our return to Dún Gorm."

Aonghus Mac Orba pursed his lips.

"When we left Dún Mór last night you did not feel uneasy," he said.

"Only after we passed the river into Hy-Nia did some feeling seize me—a feeling that all is not well at Dún Gorm," replied the other.

Aonghus did not laugh at his charioteer. He knew better than that. Cairell was the son of the druid Fios,

and while the youth had decided not to follow his father
into the long years of training by which he, too, would
become a druid, Aonghus knew that Cairell shared
many of the mysteries of the druid fraternity. Aonghus
knew enough to realize that second sight was not something to be dismissed. As he gazed at his companion he
also began to feel uneasy. Something wrong at Dún
Gorm? Why?

He had been away for three days, attending the clan
assembly of Eochaidh Allmuir, chieftain of the Dési and
all its septs. There was nothing out of the ordinary to be
discussed—simply the price of corn, cattle and the prof-
its earned by the merchant ships of the Dési, which
could be spent on the welfare of the tribe. A peace lay
on the land of Bregia. There was nothing to cause
concern. No strangers had landed on the coast, no
raiding parties had come sailing out of the north in
search of plunder, and no clans had broken the peace of
the High King. What could be wrong then?

Aonghus gripped the side of the chariot, mouth tight
and frowning. His mind was full of thoughts of concern
for his father and his young sister.

Cairell slowed the chariot as the road led up through
the hills, winding slightly as it crossed the shoulder of a
large hill that marked the boundary of a lush green
plain, at the end of which stood Dún Gorm, the fortress
of his father, Orba. As they came within sight of it,
perched on a hill at the far end of the valley, Cairell
pulled the horses to a halt with an exclamation.

Aonghus stared forward, mouth open

Across the valley a pall of black smoke hung in the
windless sky. It rose from Dún Gorm.

Cairell recovered his power of motion and was franti-
cally urging the horses forward with hoarse cries. The
chariot went plunging down the hill, thundering across
the plain toward the smoking ramparts.

Aonghus' eyes narrowed as he saw the blackened

walls. A flock of crows ominously wheeled and circled in the heavens far above the black pall of smoke. But apart from their threatening black shapes there was no sign of life anywhere.

Cairell had scarcely drawn the chariot to a halt outside the fortress when Aonghus was down and drawing his sword.

The great oak gates of Dún Gorm stood open. Although they were scorched, the fire had not destroyed them. For a moment Aonghus thought that a man was standing by the gates, waiting to receive them. He formed a question on his lips but the words choked in his mouth as he neared the figure. Fios, the druid, was slumped in a bloodstained huddle of rags. His arms were outstretched, held against the wood of the gates by iron nails.

"Father!"

With a choking cry, Cairell pushed by and began to lever the cruel iron from the old man's hands. Aonghus paused only a moment before he fell to and helped his companion. The old druid groaned in agony.

"He's still alive!" cried Cairell.

As gently as they could they dragged forth the nails that transfixed him and carefully laid him down. Aonghus went to the nearby stream to get water, trying not to rush headlong into the charred buildings of the fortress in search of his own father and sister. He knew well, from the silence, what he was likely to find.

The cold water trickled into Fios' mouth. The old druid grunted and his eyes flickered open. There was no recognition in them, just clouds of pain and anguish.

"Father, what happened?" urged Cairell. "Who did this?"

Fios made an inarticulate sound. They eased more water into the old man's mouth.

"Who did this?" whispered Cairell again.

"Cellach . . ." the word came as a sigh. "Cellach, son of the High King."

Cairell exchanged a glance of astonishment with Aonghus.

"Cellach Mac Cormac? Are you sure?" demanded Aonghus, astounded.

Fios nodded but was seized with a spasm of pain.

Aonghus was on his feet now and moving into the charred and still smoking fortress. His father's clansmen lay here and there. Most of the bodies spoke of a slaughter that had come as a surprise, for only one or two had their weapons by them. Aonghus' mouth tightened as he saw the bodies of women and children among the slaughtered. He moved with deliberation through the great hall, where the remains of a feast still showed in spite of the eager tongues of the fire.

Face white and pinched, he forced himself into his father's living quarters. He found no body and so strode quickly on down the corridor toward his sister's chambers. The flames had barely touched the area, for it was well built of granite blocks. He had no difficulty in recognizing the sprawled body of Orba, his father, in the corridor. It was no use giving way to grief. It was plain that his father was dead. The blood was already congealed on the wounds

Steeling himself, he thrust open the remains of the smoldering door and gazed into his sister's bedchamber. A body lay on the bed. Only by the flowing spun gold of her hair did he realize it was Áine. An inarticulate cry of rage and grief broke from his lips before he stifled it, biting hard on his lip and drawing blood. He stood trying to control his feeling and then, unable, found himself stumbling away, pushing back into the courtyard and gasping for air. The smell of burning, the nauseating stench of roast meat, clung to his nostrils.

Someone was barring his way. It was Cairell, face white and hard.

"My father is dead," cracked the young charioteer's voice.

Aonghus stared at him for a moment.

"They are all dead," he said harshly.

Cairell blinked.

"Áine? Where is Áine?"

"Dead." He jerked his head.

Cairell was gone for quite a while. When he returned, his face was drawn and grim.

"Cellach Mac Cormac will pay for this," he said between clenched teeth.

"Did your father tell you how it happened?" asked Aonghus quietly.

"Cellach and a band of his lackeys came demanding hospitality last night. They became drunk. Cellach slew Orba and . . . and raped Áine. He then ordered his men to slaughter everyone and burn Dún Gorm. He had my father nailed to the gates to die."

Aonghus groaned softly.

"Why?" he demanded. "Why?"

Cairell gave a harsh bark of laughter.

"For no other reason than it was his humor."

Aonghus clenched his hands.

"By the dead bodies of Dún Gorm, I want justice! But there can be no compensation adequate to the crime Cellach has committed here. Only the law of retaliation is a just one. Blood must pay for blood."

Aonghus turned and strode from the smoldering ruins of Dún Gorm to where the chariot stood.

"Come, Cairell," he called across his shoulder. "We go to Temuir to demand justice at the court of the High King."

Cairell took a step and hesitated, the voice of reason trying to prevail in a world gone insane.

"Is it not right that our dead should be buried first?"

They heard a shout and turned to see a group of horsemen riding across the valley. Aonghus slid his hand to his sword hilt, eyes narrowing. Then he rested easy. A broad-shouldered warrior with flecked grey hair and long moustaches, riding in advance of the main body, came galloping up. Aonghus recognized him as Biobal, chieftain of Hy-Macalla, a neighboring Dési sept.

"We saw the smoke rising," he called, swinging from his horse and turning to stare at the ruins of Dún Gorm. Then he took in the graven faces of Aonghus and Cairell and knew not to ask if there were survivors. "Who did this deed?"

It was Cairell who told him.

Biobal shook his head in bewilderment. The rest of the warriors came crowding up, demanding information.

Cairell seized the opportunity to enlist Biobal and his men in removing the dead from the ruins and digging a shallow grave by the walls of the fortress. Aonghus stood a little apart, the flush of blood on his face showing his controlled anger.

"Will you come back to Hy-Macalla, Aonghus?" asked Biobal when the dead had been given a proper burial. "I will send word to our chieftain, Eochaidh Allmuir, to tell him what has happened."

Aonghus shook his head.

"Cairell and I will go on to Temuir," he said shortly. "We have delayed long enough, and blood calls for blood."

Cairell hesitated. His first flush of anger had swept over him and softened. Now he could think more clearly.

"Perhaps . . ."

Aonghus cut him short with an angry gesture.

"By the Mórrígán, whose creatures wheel and swoop above, Cairell, we go to Temiur. Blood must wash out blood!"

The young man nodded, almost reluctantly, and took his place in the chariot, gathering up the reins. He glanced at the flushed, graven face of his companion and then urged the horses forward.

Biobal and his men followed the chariot with their eyes until it disappeared across the hills. Then the chieftain stirred himself.

"I want a man to ride to Eochaidh Allmuir at Dún Mór."

A young man stepped forward and asked instruction.

"Tell our chieftain what has transpired here, and that Aonghus Mac Orba and Cairell Mac Fios are riding to Temuir. Tell Eochaidh . . . tell him that I fear the bloodmist clouds Aonghus' eyes and there is no telling what may come of it."

The young warrior sprang for his horse and was soon out of sight while the others mounted more slowly and rode from the valley of Hy-Nia with the smoking ruins of Dún Gorm to their backs.

Chapter Five

They came to Temuir by Slige Dála, the Way of
Encounters, which was the southwestern highway, one
of the five great roads that united the provinces of
Éireann with the ancient seat of the High Kings. It was
acrawl with people, with horses, carts, chariots and
pedestrians moving to and from the royal capital. Those
moving toward Temuir generally had the flushed faces
of expectation. Those moving away were either exultant
or downcast, as their respective business at the court
had variably transpired.

Temuir rose above the verdant plains of Midhe, the
royal provinces of the High Kings, breathtaking and
dominant on its central hill. Where the five great highways converged there stood a number of ráths, or circular fortresses, which housed the family and retinue of
the High King. No other part of the country was so rich
in dwellings and monuments, for was this not the very
navel of the world, the center from which all things
were governed? Even to Aonghus and Cairell the sight

of Temuir was impressive, rising three hundred feet above the surrounding, luxuriant countryside, the green, grassy plain of Midhe. And despite the numerous fortresses that rose there, one was left in no doubt which was the royal fortress. For on the great hill that towered to the west and sloped gently to the east, there stood Ráth na Ríogh, the Fortress of the High Kings of Éireann.

Cairell turned the chariot from the highway, which ran to the eastern side of the large stone fortress, and guided it up the gentle incline toward the shadow of its forbidding ramparts. Its hugeness dwarfed everything around it. Moving through the entrance between the towering walls, they came to a wooden bridge stretching across a large, dry moat before a second high wall. The ráth of the High King was protected by a double set of walls with a moat in between. Only the wooden bridge provided an entrance or exit to the fortress, and this was well guarded. A group of tall warriors, in superb physical condition, wearing the royal insignia of the Fianna, the bodyguard of the High King, stood guarding the way. Their leader moved forward and motioned them to stop.

"What is your business here?"

"I am Aonghus Mac Orba of Dún Gorm in Hy-Nia," replied Aonghus. "I seek justice in the Hall of my High King."

The leader of the guard looked duly impressed.

"May the gods grant you that justice, Aonghus Mac Orba. You may proceed to the Forradh and report to the gatekeeper there."

He motioned them to proceed. Once inside the ramparts, their eyes grew round with wonder. Inside were countless small timber buildings and then a cleared space around the crown of the hill on which rose two circular stone fortresses—fortresses within the giant fortress. One sheltered behind another dry moat, in which were planted numerous sharpened stakes, presenting a formidable obstacle to any who might seek unlawful entrance. Then, almost adjoining this ráth, was another one, but slightly smaller, presenting an almost figure eight shape.

Cairell halted the chariot uncertainly and called to a passing woman: "Where is the Great Hall of the High King?"

The woman halted with a frown of surprise.

"You are strangers in Temuir not to know that."

"We are strangers, indeed," agreed Cairell.

The woman gestured toward the larger ráth. "That is the Forradh. Teach Cormac, the residence of the High King, is next to it."

Cairell saluted her and guided the chariot around the walls of the ráth, following the trackway to the wooden bridge that led across the double ditches and two more sets of ramparts. Surely the dwelling of the High King of Éireann was the most impregnable fortress ever built. At the gates there were even more warriors of the royal guard than at the main gates of Temuir.

"Halt, strangers!" A dark-haired warrior came forward. He carried the insignia of the Fianna, but next to it he wore a clan badge of black feathers of the *snagbreac* or magpie. Aonghus recalled that magpie feathers were the badge of Clan Morna.

"What is your business here?"

Aonghus repeated his name and business, but the warrior's response was different from that of the commander of the main gate.

"What justice?" he demanded.

"That is a matter that concerns only the High King."

"I am the *dóirseoir*—doorkeeper to the High King," snapped the warrior. "It is within my gift to grant or deny you entrance here."

Aonghus felt the blood of anger pulsing at the attitude of the man.

"I seek no gift of you, *dóirseoir*," he replied. "I demand my right of entrance to see my High King."

The warrior's frown deepened. "No man demands anything in Temuir unless he be High King."

Aonghus found his hand slipping to the hilt of his sword, but even as it did so another voice demanded: "What is this?"

A fair-haired giant of a man, with light blue eyes and a muscular body, that even the great warrior god Lugh Lamhfada might envy, emerged from the gate of the Forradh. He moved with a supple grace, easily, almost lazily, a gentle smile on his features. He seemed self-assured. He exuded the confidence of command. He was a handsome young man whose clothes denoted the wealth of his position. He carried only a ceremonial knife at his belt, but it was richly enjewelled. His cloak was multi-colored, fastened at the shoulder with a brooch of gold and semi-precious jewels.

The *dóirseoir* turned and scowled at him.

"No business of yours," he snapped

The young giant laughed pleasantly at the man's curtness.

"Am I not commander of the High King's Bodyguard?" His voice was bantering. "What is it that should not concern me at the gates of the High King's ráth?"

Aonghus exchanged a quick glance with Cairell. Was this Oscar, son of the hero Oisín and grandson of the great Fionn Mac Cumhail?

"I am Aonghus Mac Orba of Dún Gorm in Hy-Nia," Aonghus said to the fair-haired young man.

An incredibly blue pair of eyes turned and examined him, their softness disguising the hard scrutiny of the gaze.

"I have heard the name Aonghus Mac Orba mentioned among the chieftains of the Clan Dési," he said slowly. "They speak of Aonghus as being blessed of the gods of poetry, wisdom and war. Do you come in peace to this place, Aonghus?"

"I come seeking justice from my High King," replied Aonghus.

Oscar frowned slightly.

"It is your right to enter and speak in the Hall of Justice before the High King and his judges."

The dark-haired warrior of the Clan Morna drew in his breath with a sharp hiss.

"I am *dóirseoir*!" he snapped.

Oscar turned and met the man's gaze evenly.

"Then fulfill your office and let this stranger in." His voice, though quiet, held an icy sharpness to it.

The *dóirseoir* hesitated staring at the champion of the Fianna, but it was he who dropped the gaze from the piercing blue eyes of Oscar first. He shrugged and waved Cairell through. As the chariot lurched forward, Oscar grabbed the side rail of the wicker basket and swung himself up beside Aonghus.

"I'll ride with you as far as the Hall of Justice." He indicated a great, long wooden building in the center of the ráth.

"I thank you for passing us inside," Aonghus began.

Oscar smiled and shook his head.

"It is no more than your right."

"But the commander of the gate would have denied it."

Oscar sighed.

"Alas, Aonghus Mac Orba, since the passing of my grandsire, Fionn, the old enmities have begun to split the Fianna once more. We are no longer the Fianna Éireann; we have again become Clan Bascna and Clan Morna, each quarreling over petty divisions, each sid-

ing with factions. Sorrow has fallen over Temuir since
my grandsire's grave was measured."

"How is this?"

"Men grow old. The fire of youth is often quenched
in old age."

"The High King?" pressed Aonghus. "Is that whom
you speak of?"

Oscar shrugged.

"The High King is still the shield that protects the
country from civil disturbance . . . he is the rope that
unites the clans."

"It is in my mind to see what the High King's protection is worth," Aonghus said softly.

Oscar glanced at him curiously.

"There is bitterness in your voice, Aonghus Mac
Orba."

"Bitterness indeed."

When Aonghus made no further comment, Oscar
sighed.

"You have chosen the day well, for Cormac Mac Art
sits in the Hall of Justice with the Brehons, dispensing
law."

Cairell halted the chariot outside the imposing structure and a young man came forward to take the horses
and draw the chariot to a stabling area.

Oscar leapt lightly down.

"Come, Aonghus. I will take you into the presence of
Cormac Mac Art myself."

"For that I am indebted."

"No debt. May the gods send you a good judgment."

The young giant turned and led the way into the
magnificent building, through the throng of those gathered outside whose station was such that they had not
the right to enter the Hall of Justice, but clustered
around the door hoping for a glimpse of the High King,
ruler of all the provinces of Éireann. With Aonghus

and Cairell following, Oscar pushed his way through the doors into a small vestibule where attendants came forward to remove Aonghus and Cairell's weapons. By ancient law and custom, none could enter the hall of the High King bearing arms except the members of his immediate bodyguard. From the vestibule, Oscar pushed through a second pair of doors into the great hall itself.

Chapter Six

The great hall of the High King was lit with numerous burning torches that gave it an ethereal quality, heightened by the light reflecting on polished panels of red yew with their embellishments of bronze and silver. The hall was crowded with chieftains and their ladies, with bards, Brehons and other high officials of the kingdoms of Éireann, and with petitioners waiting their turn to speak before the assembly.

Oscar motioned Aonghus and Cairell to wait at the threshold of the hall. Aonghus paused, Cairell at his left shoulder, and followed Oscar's tall form with his eyes as the young man walked through the concourse to a raised platform at the farthest end. The platform was covered with rich furs, and on it was an ornate throne of bronze. An elderly man sat there. Although he was flanked by two young men who were richly dressed, it was he who commanded attention. He was handsome, of that there was no doubt, his skin smooth and unwrinkled although one could see that he was past middle age. Yet there was not an ounce of surplus fat on him. His muscles were as well-cast as any youth. Only his eyes belied his age, deep and sunken with an unfathomable sorrow in them. They restlessly roamed the faces of those before him. Aonghus did not need to see the simple gold torque about the man's neck to know that this was Cormac Mac Art—the High King.

Aonghus peered forward to appraise the man—Cormac, who had made the name of Éireann feared and respected throughout the world. He was Son of Art the Solitary, who had defeated the tyrant Fergus Dubhdedach the Blacktooth to become High King. Was it not said of Cormac that he was blessed by the gods? That the god of the oceans, Manannán Mac Lir, had taken him on a wondrous voyage to the Otherworld and had given Cormac a magic branch of silver that bore golden apples, so that when it was shaken, sweet music sounded and the wounded and sick forgot their pain and age became meaningless? Was that not said to be the secret of Cormac's seeming youthfulness? For, while others became bent and rutted with the weight of age, Cormac looked as youthful as ever. Had not the mighty Fionn Mac Cumhail grown old in Cormac's service, while the High King had hardly aged?

Oscar was speaking earnestly to the High King now, gesturing toward Aonghus. The restless grey eyes of the High King peered toward Aonghus and he raised a hand, a gesture that silenced those in the hall. So deathly still did it become that Aonghus heard his own heartbeat booming like thunder in his ears.

"Come forward, Aonghus Mac Orba of Hy-Nia."

The voice of the High King was soft yet commanding.

Aonghus strode forward toward the dais, Cairell walking one pace behind his left shoulder. The people in the hall watched in silence, wondering who this young stranger was. At the foot of the dais, Aonghus halted. Oscar had backed to one side of the platform and smiled encouragement at him. Aonghus stared boldly up at the face of the High King. Again he had the impression of a man weighed down by some sad burden. Then he glanced quickly at the two young men who sat flanking Cormac. The similarity of features betrayed them as the offspring of the High King, but their faces and postures gave the impression of indolence, of young men who never had to fend for themselves. One of them, a dark-haired, well-featured youth, was gazing at him with open hostility. The other, of similar features, looked indifferent and perhaps slightly bored. Which one was Cellach? He felt his anger rise.

"What is it that you seek here, Aonghus Mac Orba of Hy-Nia?" asked Cormac Mac Art softly.

"Justice," returned Aonghus.

"It is in my gift to dispense justice," nodded the High King, turning slightly to a white-robed druid who stood to one side. "Come forward, Indech. As my chief Brehon and adviser, you may assist me in this matter."

The druid bowed and moved to stand at the foot of the dais below the High King. The man was young and yet seemed ageless, for his face was pale, the skin tightly stretched over the bones, making it seem more a skull than a face of flesh and blood. Light, cold eyes gazed unblinkingly at Aonghus.

Behind Aonghus, Cairell stirred uneasily, for who had not heard of the chief druid of Éireann? Indech had been chief druid since his predecessor had mysteriously vanished on a pilgrimage to the Paps of Anu in the west at the time of the death of Fionn Mac Cumhail. Rumor had it that Indech had a hand in that disappearance, yet rumor was one thing, open accusation another. Few would dare to match their wits with Indech, for he was a powerful and devious man. Indeed, his very name, given him on his attainment to the druidic order, implied his craftiness, for he wove intrigue as a weaver might create an intricate tapestry, and so he was named after the threads carried by the shuttle of a weaver's loom.

"State your plaint," Indech said, his voice as crisp and cold as the ice of winter.

"Yesterday morning I returned to my father's dún—Dun Gorm in Hy-Nia, in the land of the Dési. I had been attending a council of our chieftain, Eochaidh Allmuir. When I came to the Dún I found it a blackened ruin. My father had been slain. My sister, Áine, of eighteen summers, lay ravished and slaughtered. All of my father's household—men, women and children—were dead about them . . . warriors, attendants, musicians and story tellers. All had been put to the sword."

Aonghus was aware that the dark—haired young man on the High King's right hand was flushing, his lips thin, his expression murderous.

There were murmurs of horror and sympathy throughout the hall.

"This is a terrible tale you bring to us, Aonghus," observed Cormac Mac Art. His concern seemed genuine.

"That it is," agreed Aonghus. "But there is more. My father's druid, Fios, was nailed by his hands to the gates of the dún and left to die."

Aonghus turned his gaze on the flushed face of the High King's son and fixed it there. He had identified the hostile youth on the left as Cellach. The young man blinked, his eyes dropping before Aonghus' scrutiny.

"But when we reached the dún, Fios was not dead."

He paused, watching with grim satisfaction as the face of the High King's son went ashen.

"Go on," invited Cormac.

"With your permission, I will let my charioteer, Cairell, son of Fios, speak of what his father told him."

Cairell came forward and gazed up at the High King.

"With his dying breath—calling Donn, god of death and guide to the souls on their journey to the Other-world, to verify his words—my father told me what had happened at Dún Gorm. The night before, a party of young men had come to Dún Gorm and, it being late, they sought hospitality with Orba's household. The hospitality was freely given. But the young men became drunk. They forced Áine, daughter of Orba, to entertain them with her beauty and her songs. Then the leader of these men raped Áine. Her screams brought Orba to her aid and he was slain for his pains. In frenzy the leader ordered his men to slaughter those at Dún Gorm and destroy it by fire. My father, Fios, was nailed to the gates, but the gods allowed him to live long enough to tell the story."

The dark-haired young man on the High King's right was white now and trembling slightly. He sat back, gripping the arms of his chair, his eyes locked with those of Aonghus.

Cormac Mac Art seemed deeply disturbed, but oblivious of the side-play between Aonghus and his son.

"This is a thrice terrible tale. Such a crime is unthinkable in this land. The perpetrators must be caught and punished. Did Fios give you any method of identifying the young men who did this deed?"

There was a hush in the hall.

Aonghus turned his gaze to the High King.

"Yes, Cormac Mac Art."

Cormac frowned as Aonghus paused.

"Who was it, then? Speak."

"Fios the druid, before his death, named your son Cellach as the leader of the band."

Cormac came upright as if he had received a slap in the face. There was a gasp of incredulity in the hall, only dulled by the sound of a chair being thrown back as the dark-haired young man leapt to his feet.

"He lies! It's all lies!" he screamed.

Cormac looked at his eldest son in shocked silence.

Indech, his features blank, held up his hand.

"This is a grave charge, Aonghus Mac Orba. One who makes a false charge is also open to punishment."

Aonghus scowled: "I make no false charges. The blood of my kinsmen is still freshly staining the scorched grass at Dún Gorm."

The druid shrugged.

"That is one thing, but to make an accusation against the eldest son of our High King is another."

"It is the dying testimony of Fios the Druid that accuses him," snapped Aonghus.

Indech's lips thinned.

"Justice cannot question a dead man." He turned to the white-faced Cellach. "What do you say to this accusation, Cellach Mac Cormac?"

The young man thrust out his chin, defiant in spite of the fear in his eyes.

"I say it is false. The man lies."

"You deny it?" interposed Cormac, almost eagerly.

Cellach seemed to have regained his composure a little. He motioned to an attendant to replace his chair and seated himself again.

"Of course." He smiled mockingly at Aonghus. "Bring forth your witnesses, Aonghus of Hy-Nia, and I will call them all liars, even as I call you a liar."

Aonghus' teeth ground. "I have no doubt you will lie to save yourself."

Indech was peering into the assembly.

"Let Gorta Mac Goll stand forward."

A dark warrior stood forward.

"You were commanding the bodyguard of Cellach during his time away from Temuir," prompted Indech. "What do you say to this charge?"

Gorta smiled insolently at Aonghus.

"It is false."

"You swear it by the gods?" asked Indech.

"By any god," replied Gorta.

Indech turned to Cormac Mac Art. "We could produce all of the warriors who accompanied Cellach. But first we should ask Aonghus Mac Orba to produce his witnesses in support of such a grievous charge."

"You know that they are all dead by these swords of Cellach and his men," cried Aonghus in frustration.

"Then you must withdraw your charge and make reparation to the son of the High King for such outrageous claims," replied Indech calmly.

Aonghus stared hard at Cellach. Now that he had seen him, watched his face, he had no doubt of his guilt. A red anger was pouring through his veins which he could scarcely control and he turned to Cormac.

"No, I will not withdraw my accusation, for I have the right of justice. Since you will not listen to the truth, it is my right to challenge Cellach to the *Fir eómlainn*—the truth of single combat!"

There was a gasp from the assembly.

Cellach's head snapped back. "I . . . I refuse!" he gasped.

Cormac's face was graven now.

"The challenge has been made," he said, turning to his son. "You cannot refuse unless you accept that Aonghus of Dún Gorm has made true accusations."

Indech bit his lip. In spite of his partisan support for Cellach, even he had to admit the law.

"So it is written from the days of the Ollamh Fodhla, the fortieth High King to sit at Temuir, who gave the law to our land. Truth may be found in single combat, for the gods of justice will ever aid the truth against deceit."

Cellach looked trapped.

"But I am not skilled enough to fight him . . . he is a warrior."

Cormac was frowning in anger now.

"Do you shame me before all Éireann? If you refuse, you incur disgrace and admit your guilt."

"I cannot."

"Do you admit the truth then, of what happened at Dún Gorm?" pressed Aonghus.

Indech suddenly intervened, a cynical smile on his thin features.

"Cellach admits only that he is no warrior and no blessings of the gods can transform him into one. Instead, Cellach invokes his right to make his choice of a substitute. According to the law of the Ollamh Fodhla, he can appoint a warrior to represent him in single combat."

There was a new tension in the hall now. Cormac, his face a mask of relief, turned anxiously to Aonghus.

"Do you accept the law, Aonghus of Hy-Nia?"

Aonghus scowled as he realized that Indech was outwitting him.

"I accept," he said bitterly. "Since your son is too cowardly to accept the truth of single combat, I must accept that another will suffer in his place."

Cormac nodded reluctantly.

"Cellach, you have to make a choice. Which warrior do you choose to represent you in this combat? Gorta of Clan Morna?"

Cellach gazed thoughtfully at Aonghus a moment and then a smile formed on his lips.

"No, father. I choose . . . Oscar, son of Oisín, to fight for me."

Aonghus blinked.

Oscar was the greatest warrior of the Fianna, blessed of the gods, and no one had ever defeated him in battle or in single combat. Did not the bards tell that Oscar's father, Oisín, the son of Fionn by the goddess Sadb, daughter of the ocean god, dwelt in the Land of the Ever Living? No mortal could hope to overcome Oscar.

The blond giant took a step forward. His face was troubled and his eyes met those of the High King. Before he could speak, Cormac Mac Art said quickly: "You must take up this challenge, Oscar," as if reading his thoughts. "It is my flesh that asks this of you. Your father and your grandfathers pledged their lives and loyalty to me. You also have pledged loyalty to me as commander of the Fianna. You must champion my son."

Aonghus felt a terrible passion as he saw how cunning Cellach was. The young man was now sprawling back in his chair, openly smiling at him with mocking self-assurance. A vision of his violated and slain sister swam before his eyes, of the scorched ruins of Dún Gorm and the bodies of his brutally murdered father and his retinue. A red mist began to form in front of his eyes, and his blood seemed to boil around his brain, his temples throbbing. He had no control over the wave of anger that swept through him.

"Gods of justice!" he found himself crying. "This evil will not go unpunished!"

One of the Fianna moved forward, spear across his chest, as if to protect Cellach. The throbbing in Aonghus' temples became unbearable. A terrible bloodmist of anger enwrapped his mind. He reached out and, pushing the warrior of the Fianna backwards, grabbed the spear from the man's hands, quickly reversing it and, before the assembled people were aware of what he was doing, thrust it straight through the body of the son of the High King, transfixing the young man to his chair.

Cellach gave a single scream of fear before he slumped back with blood trickling from his mouth.

With an inarticulate cry of animal fury, Cormac Mac Art leapt forward from his throne. Aonghus, still in the throes of the bloodmist, his mind working automatically, wrenched the spear from Cellach's body, pulling it back with such force that the butt flew straight into Cormac's right eye.

The High King gave a curious grunt of pain and fell back to the ground with blood spurting from his injured eye.

Aonghus whirled around in a fighting crouch, face contorted with his battle frenzy, but he and Cairell were already surrounded by Gorta Mac Goll and half a dozen men of the Fianna with spears pointed at their throats.

It was the silence that caused Aonghus to sober; a silence more shattering than any tumult or din. The bloodmist receded as rapidly as it had come, and the threatening quiet swept over him like a wave of ice cold water. He looked down at the bloody spear in his hands, shuddered and dropped it. Time seemed to be standing still, and his heart seemed to stop beating. As if he had been abruptly transported out of the Great Hall of Temuir, he found himself a boy again.

It was his seventh birthday and he stood in the cold gloom before the sacred Stone of Naming while before him loomed the tall figure of Eolas, the druid of Srón Bilé. In the misty gloom, the druid stared down at him with bright, gleaming eyes and a stern face that made the young child clutch his father's hand fiercely.

"Do you understand, child?" came the stentorian tones.

Aonghus was too fearful of the place and the seemingly threatening figure before him to understand the words.

"A *geis* is a prohibition," went on Eolas, "a sacred prohibition. The power of this bond is above human jurisdiction."

The druid's eyes seemed to burn into his.

"Never are you to lay hands upon a spear with intent to use it, Aonghus Mac Orba. Never are you to learn the art of casting a spear, either in the hunt or in battle. This is your *geis*. You must never violate it."

Aonghus swallowed nervously. Then, almost to his surprise, he found himself asking: "Why?"

A cloud of anger drew Eolas' brow into a deep furrow. Then, oddly, the old man's eyes softened.

"May the gods keep you from that knowledge, for when you have achieved that understanding, your *geis* will no longer safeguard your path through life."

Aonghus stared back with incomprehension.

His mind returned to the Great Hall of Temuir and

his eyes focused on the bloody spear that lay discarded on the floor before him. And now he knew. Fate? For a brief moment, he accepted the fulfillment of his destiny; then his mind rebelled. No! He was the master of this fate. No man's fate was preordained! If he had to fight the world and the gods themselves, he would show that man's course in life was not chartered by the careless whim of the gods. Man was his own master.

He stared about him.

The chilling silence in the Great Hall of Temuir, which, in reality, had lasted for the pause of a heartbeat, shattered into a wild cacophony. People began crying: "Murder! Murder! He has slain the High King!"

Around the prostrate form of Cormac Mac Art, several white-robed druids and courtiers were bent.

"He is not dead!" cried one of the druids. "Cormac is gravely wounded. We must take him to his private chamber."

Oscar was standing by with bewilderment written on his handsome features, as if he could not believe what had taken place

Cormac's second son, who had been sitting on the left-hand side of his father's throne, had risen and was calling for silence, apparently quite calm in all the turmoil in the Great Hall.

"Take my father to his chambers and send physicians to him."

Indech the druid now rose from the High King's side, his eyes glinting wickedly.

"And these murderers, Cairbre?" he demanded of the High King's son, gesturing toward Aonghus and Cairell. "We should take them out and put them to death immediately. This is a crime for which no one may tolerate delay in punishment. It is a crime that strikes at the soul of Éireann."

Cairbre seemed about to nod agreement when Oscar took a pace forward.

"That is not the way of the law, Indech. You are Brehon and must know this. If we ignore the law, then we are guilty of a greater crime."

Cairbre hesitated, caught Indech's glance, and said: "I act in my father's place until the gods decide whether he lives or dies or until the assembly chooses a new High King. Take these two to the Duma na nGall—the Mound of Hostages. Have them slain!"

Hands reached eagerly forward to grab Aonghus and Cairell, but there was a stirring from those around the High King. Cormac himself was sitting up, supported by his druids. He held one hand over his right eye, from which blood was being pumped, oozing between his fingers. His face was contorted in pain.

"I still give orders at Temuir!" he grunted. Through the pain that made his speech difficult there came a sibilant venom which cast a fearful silence over the assembly. Cormac's single bright eye glared with burning hatred at Aonghus. "Do not kill them . . . yet. Take them to the dungeons to await the punishment that is prescribed by law. Let Aonghus Mac Orba dwell on the crime he has perpetrated this day. When the time comes for his death he will pray that it is quick, but a quick death is no punishment for this day's deed. Aonghus Mac Orba will die a thousand times before his death finally comes. By that time he will welcome it joyously as a friend."

Chapter Seven

Cairell sat with bowed head upon a low stone bench that ran alongside one of the dark, musty walls of the dungeon that lay below the royal court of Temuir. The dungeons were constructed under the Mound of Hostages, within the great enclosure where the cells were scarcely ten feet high and of similar proportion in width and length. They were just large enough for those incarcerated to take a few paces in. The guards had thrown both Cairell and Aonghus inside one without ceremony.

Cairell had been particularly shaken by events and had enveloped himself in gloomy introspection, while Aonghus strode the prison like a wild beast, eyes flickering from side to side in the gloom, watching and waiting some opportunity. Only a burning brand torch set in the corridor outside, which light infiltrated the tiny cell through a small aperture was latticed with bars, gave any light.

An eternity seemed to have passed since the death of

Cellach and the injury to the High King. Cairell finally raised his head to glance at Aonghus' nervous pacing.

"It will profit you nothing to waste energy," he muttered. "Even if we get out of here, we cannot avoid the consequences of our actions."

Aonghus halted abruptly and made a sardonic noise.

"*Our* actions?" he queried.

"I am as guilty as you," shrugged Cairell.

"I own to no guilt," replied Aonghus sharply. "I apologize for nothing."

"Man cannot set himself above the law, even in extremity."

"I am the arbiter of my own fate, Cairell," Aonghus said. "And if my memory is not false, I recall you demanded reparation when we found your father at Dún Gorm."

"That is true. In a moment of anguish, a man often makes wrong judgments."

"I suggest we quarrel no more about things past," Aonghus replied. "It is my intention to escape as soon as an opportunity presents itself. There will be no justice at the court of Cormac."

"If not at the court of the High King, where, then?" Cairell responded.

"I intend to present my case before Eochaidh Allmuir, chieftain of the Dési."

Cairell smiled.

"You make it sound easy. Yet we are here, imprisoned, and there is no way of knowing for how long."

"There is no pleasure in doing an easy thing," grinned Aonghus, uttering an old druidic saying. He shrugged and sunk down to the hardstone floor of the cell. "We must think a while. We have not slept in two days and nights, so it is best to take sleep while we can get it."

Cairell sighed. He stretched himself on the stone bench, but had little hope that sleep would come. His mind was too full of the terrible events of the last two days. Yet sleep did snatch him unaware—a sleep of strange and terrifying dreams, a sleep in which Cairell was never sure whether he was awake or dreaming. When he did awaken and realized that he had slept, he felt curiously refreshed.

A guard was putting a plate of unappetizing scraps just inside the door of the cell as Cairell stirred. Aonghus was already standing in the far corner, his eyes watchful. But two other guards stood outside the cell door with drawn swords.

"Eat," instructed the guard. "Soon you will be taken before the Brehons for judgment."

"They say that Cormac is devising a spectacular punishment," chuckled one of his companions.

"Then we are condemned already?" yawned Cairell, feigning disinterest.

The guards laughed.

"Do you doubt it? With all the witnesses that were in the great hall when you slew Cellach and injured Cormac, there is little need for an appeal to the Brehons." The guard nodded to the food. "Eat. It may be your last meal in this world."

The door slammed and they heard the rattle of bolts.

Cairell rose and picked up the plate of scraps with a wry grimace. He set them down on the bench but made no effort to eat.

Aonghus, however, squatted down and selected a few morsels.

"Best eat, Cairell," he suggested. "We will need our strength if we are to obtain freedom."

"Freedom? The only freedom we will obtain from this place is the freedom of death," said the charioteer.

The bolts rattled again and the door swung open. A tall man in druid's robes stood there. Aonghus stiffened as he recognized Cormac's chief druid, whose oily craft and guile had made him look foolish in the hall of assembly.

The man came forward into the cell. He was an unprepossessing person. Even in the semi-gloom he had an unhealthy pallor and skeletal features. He had a large beak of a nose and his eyes, an unfathomable pale color, glinted unnaturally close to it. So pale were those eyes that one had to look closely to find out where the irises ended and the whites began . . . only then did one notice that the whites showed all around the irises. He stood still, arms folded across his chest but upwards, so that the palms rested on his breast, displaying long, thin fingers—corpse-like, with tapering dirty fingernails that caused Aonghus to shudder slightly

The slit of his mouth was twisted as if in a perpetual grin.

"I am Indech," he spoke, his voice squeaky in its normal pitch

"That much I know," replied Aonghus.

"Then know this, Aonghus Mac Orba of Hy-Nia. Your crime is great and only death is a fit reparation. It behoves me as chief druid and Brehon to the High King to examine you and recommend judgment."

Aonghus' features curled into a sneer, but he said nothing.

"There is no argument with the judgment of death," went on Indech. "But death may come easy, or death may come hard. You have a choice to make. Death will come easier if you confess your guilt before the tribunal of the Brehons, the chief judges of Éireann. If you insist in your lies about Cellach—may Donn grant him an easy passage into the Otherworld—then your death will be hard."

Aonghus said nothing, but Cairell stood up.

"Terrible and evil was the crime done at Dún Gorm. By the dying oath of my father, Fios, Cellach stood accused. The only wrong Aonghus did was pre-empting the judgment of the Brehons."

"Who had, in my person, already absolved Cellach

from the charge," rasped Indech. "However, rumor is like fire in Temuir, and already your unjustified charges are on everyone's lips. If you retract them publicly, confess that you acted in a fit of madness, then your deaths will be easy. Refuse . . ."

Indech raised an eloquent shoulder.

"I fear not my crossing to the Otherworld, Indech," interposed Aonghus in an angry voice. "There is only one thing I fear—the loss of truth—for truth is the shield of my soul."

Indech chuckled cynically. "Whatever satisfies the soul is truth."

"There is a saying, Indech," intervened Cairell. "Truth and oil always come to the surface."

The druid grimaced.

"Truth and falsehood are but twins, and duration is a gauge of neither. A man will believe or reject according to his prejudice."

"If you are certain that truth or falsehood will not matter, why are you so concerned that I make a confession of guilt before the Brehons?" demanded Aonghus.

Indech hesitated.

"It is best to leave no doubts in the minds of people."

"You mean it will stop the rumors," rejoined Cairell. "It will save the reputation of the High King and his son and our deaths will be called just."

The druid shrugged.

"An easy or a hard death?" he asked, staring at Aonghus.

"Death is death in any form."

It seemed to Aonghus that the druid's pale eyes had suddenly taken on a curious opaqueness, a milky creaminess flecked with little golden sparklets. The irises seemed to twist and circle, pulsating with some strange light that, after a moment or two, became a natural rhythm. He felt an elation, a sense of well-being. The face before him seemed to offer him comfort and hope.

Of course he should trust the face before him; why had
he been fighting it? He frowned. Had he fought it? It
was right that he should confess his crimes to the
Brehons. It was right.

He had acted in a moment of madness. He had been
wrong.

He was aware of some tugging at his arm. A voice
was shouting in his ear. A hand pulled his head to one
side and he blinked into the anxious face of Cairell.

"Don't gaze into his eyes!" cried the charioteer.

Aonghus stared at him in bewilderment, shaking his
head. It was like coming out of a deep sleep.

"His eyes, avoid his eyes!" Cairell said urgently. "He
has all the tricks of his profession."

Aonghus suddenly realized what had happened and a
deep growl arose in his throat. He turned toward the
druid.

"You tried to bewitch me!"

He took a threatening step forward, but Indech held
out a langurous hand

"Stop!" Indech's voice was soft.

Aonghus found himself unable to move his muscles,
halting unwillingly.

"You will obey me, Aonghus Mac Orba," came the
rasping voice.

Sweat poured off Aonghus' brow as he tried to move.
He twisted his head from side to side, grunting and
shaking as he tried to break loose from the curious
unseen bonds that held him.

"You will do as I say," came Indech's voice again.

"Never!"

"You will confess to the Brehons."

Aonghus yelped a little in pain as some hidden force
thrust him forward to his knees.

"Never!" he grunted.

The force became unbearable but he refused to give
in, even though some gentle, lilting voice was softly

telling him that he had but to obey the druid and the pain would be gone, gone forever.

"Never!" he screamed again.

The pain became so great that he suddenly sank into a dark, velvety pit that seemed without bottom.

When he recovered consciousness he was lying on the floor of the cell with Cairell kneeling by his side, anxiously dabbing at his forehead with a damp cloth. He groaned and sat up.

"What happened?"

"Druid's magic," replied Cairell. "Beware of Indech— he is a powerful wizard."

Aonghus stared at Cairell.

"He tried to take over my mind and force me to confess."

Cairell nodded. "Indech would not go to such lengths unless he was afraid."

"Afraid?" Aonghus did not understand.

"It is obvious that many people must feel that his judgment of Cellach was unjust, that he deliberately tried to save the High King's son. Even though you placed yourself in the wrong, nevertheless, if Cormac kills us without proper inquiry into the rights and wrongs of Cellach's crime, there will be stirrings against him and his justice. Indech wants to parcel things neatly, prevent a hearing of Cellach's crime by getting you to admit total guilt. That was why he came, and that was why he tried to use his druidic arts against all moral law to force you into a confession. If you admitted guilt, then Cormac's Brehons could simply condemn you out of hand and no man in the five provinces would be able to cry out 'injustice'!"

Aonghus gazed in wonder at the wisdom of his charioteer.

"In that case, we must escape as soon as possible, for I have tasted Indech's power and do not feel I will be able to withstand it again."

Cairell raised his arms hopelessly.

"The intervention of Indech alters nothing. It is still hopeless."

Aonghus rose, ignoring him, and went to the door. The smoking torch in the corridor outside the chamber still faintly illuminated it. Aonghus tested the bars, but without much conviction as to any weakness there.

"Hopeless," Cairell muttered.

"For one whose father was a druid, you are too much a fatalist," replied Aonghus with some display of spirit.

He craned his head against the narrow embrasure in the door, peering out into the corridor.

"Warrior!" he called softly. Then again, more distinctly: "Warrior!"

There was a muttering and then one of the guards appeared.

"What is it?"

"We lack a candle."

The man guffawed.

"There is plenty of light, unless you wish a candle to show you the way to the Otherworld. Candles are too precious to waste on spirits."

"Would you deny the wish of a dead man?" demanded Aonghus.

The warrior was puzzled.

"Tomorrow we are to be taken to be judged by the Brehons, and by sundown we shall be dead," pressed Aonghus.

"That much is known throughout Temuir."

"Then we are already dead. Would your refuse the wish of the dead?"

The guard tugged at his lower lip, trying to follow Aonghus' reasoning.

"Soon it will be the festival of Samhain, my friend," Aonghus went on, with emphasis. "The night when the Otherworld becomes visible to this one. Then is the time when the spirits of the Otherworld are let loose upon the living—when the dead come to seek retribution from those who have wronged them in this world."

The warrior shifted his weight uneasily

Aonghus gave an evil chuckle. Only Cairell could tell that it was contrived.

"A candle is important to me on my last night in this world. If I am deprived of it, I shall bide my time to Samhain and cross back to this world to punish him who would deny it to me."

The warrior's face whitened, and with a smothered exclamation he hurried away.

Cairell was frowning at Aonghus.

"I have never heard you being cynical about the gods before."

"No cynicism, in it," smiled Aonghus softly. "I do need a candle."

A moment later the door was opened and the guard came, thrusting a lighted candle inside.

"Now haunt me never!" he snapped as he slammed the door to after he had deposited the candle in the cell.

Cairell watched as Aonghus took the lighted candle and set it on the stone bench.

"What has this availed you?"

"A means."

"A means of escape? Do you think a candle will help you escape from Temuir?"

"I know it will," Aonghus grinned.

He gathered all the loose straw that covered the stone-flagged floor and set it in a heap at the foot of the door. Cairell continued to watch him in perplexity. Then Aonghus placed the lighted candle at the bottom of the door and began to build the straw around it. Soon, with a snap and crackle, the straw caught alight, and wisping smoke began to rise, followed by the eager tongues of the flames.

Aonghus turned to a jug of water, which the guards

refilled twice daily to meet the prisoners' drinking requirements, and, tearing off a piece from his cloak, soaked it. Then he thrust the jug at Cairell.

"Do the same," he ordered.

Cairell obeyed.

Flames were roaring at the wooden door now. Although it was thick and strong, it was also old and dry. Before long it had caught alight in one great, sheeting mass. Aonghus motioned Cairell back into a corner. The smoke was thick now and causing them to cough and splutter. Aonghus wrapped the wet cloth around his mouth and indicated Cairell should follow his example.

They heard shouting.

Clutching at Cairell's arm, Aonghus pointed to the door, making a motion with his arm that he had used a hundred times before when they were hunting together. It was the signal to make ready.

There was a banging outside the door, then the hiss of water being thrown over it. But the flames were too strong to be doused by a mere bucket of water. The door burst in. One warrior came running into the smoked-filled cell, sword in hand, coughing and blinded momentarily.

Aonghus sprang forward, his body uncoiling like a spring set loose. A fist smashed against the warrior's jaw and the sword dropped. Even as the warrior slipped to the ground, Aonghus had scooped up the sword and motioned Cairell to move forward with him.

He plunged through the fiery frame of the door, into the corridor.

Outside stood a guard, a bucket in one hand, surprised and undecided. He dropped the bucket and attempted to draw his weapon, but Aonghus' newly acquired sword stabbed straight to his heart. The man groaned and crumpled up.

Trying to wave aside the swirling smoke, Aonghus

saw that there were several cells along the corridor. Shouts and screams for help echoed from all of them.

He turned and felt along the wall to where a great ring of iron was hung on a hook. On the ring were several keys. He had noticed it before. He seized the ring and spent several precious seconds trying to fit one into the lock of the door at the end of the corridor. One did fit. It turned and the door was open. It gave into an enclosure that was the Mount of Hostages. Darkness enveloped the area and, blinking in the gloom, he could see no signs of other guards. He ran back into the corridor to where Cairell was picking up the weapon of the fallen second guard and tossed the keys into the nearest cell.

"Unlock yourself and the others," he called to its inmate. "Here is an opportunity for escape."

Then, without pausing, he beckoned Cairell to follow and together they hurried from the Mount of Hostages.

They could hear cries of alarm as smoke began to billow upwards into the dark night. They had to press back into the shadows as two guards, who had obviously been on duty at the gate of the Mount of Hostages, came running to investigate. It was as if the gods were smiling on them, for it left the way clear to move from the circular ráth of the prison into the walled area that surrounded Teach Cormac.

"This way," called Aonghus, as he ran toward the dark shelter of the great ramparts.

It was no use trying to find their chariot and, indeed, war horses would be swifter than such a vehicle. Aonghus hurried through the gloom, closely followed by Cairell, around the dark and shadowy walls, until they came to an area of wooden rails where a dozen or more horses stood patiently tethered. Each was bridled and saddled and obviously belonged to the guards.

Aonghus seized the nearest one and, a moment later, Cairell was mounted on another.

"Straight through the gates!" hissed Aonghus.

"Lead the way!" Cairell replied.

Aonghus wheeled the horse and urged it into a gallop toward the main gates of the fortress.

As he approached he saw the gates shut and guards running nervously forward.

"Aside for the High King's envoys!" Aonghus yelled in an authorative tone. "Aside, I say!"

There was only a split second of hesitation and then, incredibly, the gate was swung open and the guards leapt out of the path of their galloping horses.

Scarcely believing his luck, Aonghus threw himself alongside his horse's neck and urged it onwards.

Across the main area of Temuir, toward the central gates they rode. The gates stood open but warriors barred the way. Aonghus repeated his cry but this time none would move and he had to haul on the reins of his steed.

"Aside, I say, or we'll ride you down!" he cried.

Behind him he could hear a great outcry. It was obvious that their escape had been realized.

The guard at the gate was suspicious.

"We must check with the inner guard." He turned to signal one of his men to move forward and take Aonghus' bridle. Aonghus suddenly slapped his beast across the withers with the flat of the sword, which he still carried in his hand.

"Ride!" he cried.

The guard went down, striking valiantly at Aonghus with his sword, trying to catch at the belly of the horse as it passed. Then Aonghus was through the gates and heading south along the road, away from Temuir toward the rolling hills of Bregia. Cairell was only a hand's-breadth behind him. They plunged into the darkness of the night, for not even the moon shone through the cloudy sky to light the way. But the darkened night was a boon to them. They rode on in silence, along the winding trail that left the highway, and began to climb swiftly across the hills that bordered the clan lands of the Dési. The horses were sure-footed over the precipitous pathway, through the heavy brush and across small streams.

"Ride!" called Aonghus to Cairell in fierce exhultation at the easiness of the escape. "We will escape their pursuit yet, for they will think that we have taken the easy path along the Slige Dála to Bregia."

"Where are we heading?" demanded Cairell from behind.

"To Dún Mór, to the fortress of Eochaidh Allmuir. We will place ourselves at the mercy of the chieftain of the Dési. Let him and his Brehons be our judges."

Chapter Eight

Eochaidh Allmuir sat on his carved chair of office in the great hall of Dún Mór and gazed with a troubled expression at Aonghus and Cairell, who stood before him. There was no one else in the hall except for his chief druid, Iolar. Eochaidh Allmuir was a broad-shouldered man who had obtained the chieftainship of the Dési when he had been a young warrior of twenty-one years. Now he had iron-grey hair and his face carried the creases of age and responsibility. His body was still firm, his eyes alert, and his mouth set with determination yet, withal, the light of compassion and understanding in his glance. Eochaidh had been born of a Dési father and yet the name "Allmuir" denoted one from over the seas. It was applied to him for it was recalled that his mother, a beautiful woman, had come to Éireann from the mist-swept island of Inis Manannán, which lay halfway between Éireann and Britain.

"Are you prepared to hear judgment?" Eochaidh asked.

Aonghus drew himself up and nodded. It had been

seven days since he and Cairell had escaped from Temuir and ridden through the hostile territory of Midhe to reach the borders of Bregia and the land of the Dési. They had pressed straight to the court of Eochaidh and thrown themselves on his judgment. The druids of the Dési had been in debate for several days, and it was known that messengers had arrived from Temuir already with demands that Aonghus and Cairell be given up to the justice of the High King.

"I am prepared, my chieftain," said Aonghus softly.

Eochaidh turned to the young charioteer at Aonghus' side.

"And you, Cairell Mac Fios? Will you hear judgment?"

"I am prepared," echoed Cairell.

"Then hear the judgment." Eochaidh motioned to his druid.

Iolar, Eochaidh's druid, stepped forward. He was a stern-faced but kindly man of Eochaidh's own age and had served him ever since Eochaidh had assumed office. Iolar looked first at Aonghus and then at Cairell.

"Great the crime that Cellach did. Yet crime should not be answered with crime. Aonghus and Cairell, you should have appealed to the Brehons to right this terrible wrong done by Cellach. You should not have gone to Temuir without consulting the druids of the Dési first, for harm done to one sept of our clan is a harm done to everyone. We have, however, weighed the matter carefully. It is written that if the cause is taken away, then the effect ceases. First cause governs the world. It is also written, therefore, that in taking retribution by himself, a man becomes even with his enemy. In giving up his revenge, he is superior, for revenge proves its own executioner."

Aonghus and Cairell waited, frowning, trying to understand the judgment.

"In taking revenge, you have made yourselves even

with those who have wronged you. No more, no less. That is our judgment."

Aonghus was bewildered.

"Then what is to be our fate?"

Eochaidh Allmuir smiled.

"You have made your own fate. You may return to Hy-Nia."

"But what of Cormac . . .?" began Cairell.

"Cormac is High King. Judge of judges. He will be told that justice has been carried out. He will see reason, for now the heat of anger will have left him. It is a terrible thing to know that one's flesh and blood can commit such crimes as Cellach has."

But Cormac did not see reason. It was late on the following afternoon, while Aonghus and Cairell were still enjoying Eochaidh's hospitality, that a warrior came riding hard up to Dún Mór. The man was covered with the dust of travel and something else . . . congealed blood stained a terrible wound in his shoulder. He was shown into the great hall of Dún Mór, saluted Eochaidh weakly, and collapsed on his knees.

Concern on his face, the chieftain of the Dési moved forward to raise the man.

"It is Gabur of Dún Glas!" exclaimed Eochaidh, recognizing the chieftain who was accepted as *tánaiste* of the Dési. "What has happened?"

Iolar the druid had brought a goblet of water for the man to drink, and when his lips had been moistened, the man replied.

"It was at midday," Gabur groaned, blinking from the pain of his wounds. "Our people were working in the fields around Dún Glas when a great host appeared, armed and accoutred for war. Without warning, without notice, they fell upon us—men, women and children— and great was the slaughter. They set fire to the fortress and spared no man."

"Who were they?" cried Eochaidh in horror.

"The men of Clan Morna. I could tell by the magpie feathers they wear. And, the gods defend me, the High King rode at their head!"

Eochaidh's face whitened.

"Cormac Mac Art led them, you say?"

"Never have I seen such evil mirrored in a human face. And he lacked his right eye."

Aonghus bit his lip and glanced anxiously at Cairell.

"Tell me all," Eochaidh said slowly.

"My warriors and I, those who survived the first onslaught, fell back into the feasting hall of Dún Glas. Seeing ourselves hopelessly outnumbered, I called for terms. Cormac would give us none but told us to lay down our weapons if we so wished. We did so. By the Mórrígán's curse! Cormac then ordered those who were with me to be put to the sword at once. Then he had his men scourge me, and finally ordered me to ride to you with a message."

"A message." Eochaidh pursed his lips.

Gabur licked his lips and his brow puckered as he strained to recall the exact words: "This is the message of Cormac, High King. As Dún Glas has been destroyed, so all the fortresses, the towns and settlements, the harbors and the great fleet of the Dési shall be destroyed unless Aonghus Mac Orba of Hy-Nia and his charioteer, Cairell Mac Fios, be handed over to vengeance immediately. He will wait three days upon the border by Dún Glas for a reply."

Iolar's face was crimson with anger. Yet for a moment, no one spoke. Then Aonghus pushed his way to Eochaidh's side.

"Shame and sorrow on me that I should be the cause of this tragedy," he said slowly. "I was wrong to seek sanctuary here."

Eochaidh's face was a mixture of emotions: he was both appalled by the news and angered. "There is already a judgment in this matter, Aonghus."

"It seems that the High King knows nothing of that judgment. In his anger he plans to destroy the Dési for what he deems my crime. That cannot be. I must surrender to him or leave Bregia."

"No!" Iolar the druid spoke sharply. "The Brehons stand above the High King. Great is the crime that Cormac has performed this day, and when it is known then Cormac, too, shall be judged."

"No Brehon can argue with an army," observed Aonghus dryly.

Eochaidh had signalled for Gabur to be taken to the house of the warrior's sorrow, where his wounds could be tended and dressed. He now turned to Iolar, his anger unconcealed.

"Aonghus is right, Iolar," he observed. "What can we do?"

"There is only one thing," pressed Aonghus. "I am willing to surrender to prevent this blood madness of Cormac's."

"If we let you do that, Aonghus, we should be guilty of a crime," replied Iolar. "No, let me, representing the Brehons of the Dési, go to meet Cormac and appeal to him. He was a great and good king who ruled this land for years in justice. He will listen."

"Did he listen to Gabur?" demanded Aonghus. "Even in battle madness I have never heard the like of the crime Cormac has done this day."

Eochaidh nodded slowly.

"Crime indeed," he said. "But Iolar is right. We must plead with his reason. But while we do so, I will send the *crois-tara* to raise the septs of the clan so that no other fortress may be surprised and destroyed in the manner of Dún Glas."

By evening the messengers of Eochaidh Allmuir had traversed the land of Bregia bearing the grim news and issuing their call to arms. All the dúns, or fortresses, of the Dési were fortified and their gates closed against attack. Those who lived outside, in small farms and settlements, took their valuables and withdrew into the shelter of the hill forts of Bregia. At the same time, each dún and each sept mustered a force prescribed under law and sent these warriors to Dún Mór, the fortress of their chieftain.

Aonghus and Cairell had placed themselves at Eochaidh's disposal, Aonghus still arguing that he be allowed to present himself to Cormac to prevent further misfortune to the Dési. Eochaidh, however, was firm in maintaining the judgment of the tribal Brehons.

Iolar and two of the Brehons had ridden to Dún Glas to act as envoys to negotiate with Cormac. The sun had descended and Eochaidh's fortress was lit with numerous torches when Iolar returned. The nervous sentinels heard the sound of a single horse approaching and then Iolar's voice cried out. The gates of Dún Mór were opened for him.

Eochaidh, surrounded by his chieftains, Aonghus, Biobal of Hy-Macalla, Each-Tiarna, his personal champion, and Gabur, now recovering from his wounds, went forward as Iolar slid from his horse. The druid was shaking with barely controlled anger.

"Where are the Brehons who went with you?" demanded Eochaidh, for it was clear that Iolar was alone.

In answer the druid took a sack from the saddle of his horse and threw the contents to the ground before the Dési chieftain's feet.

"Cormac sends them back to you," he said hollowly.

There was no sound from anyone as they gazed at the severed heads of the Dési Brehons.

"I was spared only to bring you this message, Eochaidh," went on Iolar. "It is the same message that Gabur brought to you. Cormac is possessed of some strange madness—a madness that passed into him at the death of his son, Cellach, and the loss of his right eye. He is intent on vengeance. He says that you have until sun-up to answer him. Yet because you have defied him thus far, you must pay him an annual tribute, a *boramha* of five hundred cattle, three hundred of which must be milch cows."

"Is the High King gone insane?" breathed Eochaidh in amazement.

"I fear so," sighed Iolar, his voice heavy. "He lacks the eye that Aonghus took out and his one eye blazes with a terror that I never wish to behold again in any man. Both loss of his son and his eye have turned him into a creature that even Fionn Mac Cumhail, if he came back to this world, would not recognize."

"But surely his druid, Indech, remonstrated with him and told him that his acts cannot be supported by any law made by the gods or men?"

Iolar shook his head.

"His druid Indech is a vainglorious man, full of schemes for power and wealth. He uses his knowledge in ways that shame the true brotherhood and that bring down discredit on the druidic order."

"So there is no check to Cormac's rage?"

"None, I fear. I did not see Oscar of the Fianna or Clan Bascna with Cormac. The men that fawn around him are members of the Clan Morna."

Eochaidh bit his lip. He gazed long and thoughtfully at the severed heads at his feet, then signalled for them to be removed.

"Well, if Cormac is bent on death and destruction, we must meet him."

Aonghus made to intervene but Eochaidh waved him to silence.

"This is no simple affair of justice or retribution. Cormac has gone mad with bloodlust and there are none to check him. The name of justice can scarce be applied to what he proposes. No. We will have to meet his fire with fire and his steel with steel."

He turned angrily away, then paused and glanced back at his chieftains. His eyes flashed with passion.

"Tomorrow, at sun-up, we will march to face the armies of the High King. If he wants blood, then we will give it to him. We will attack him and draw so much blood that Cormac will regret crossing into the land of Bregia."

Yet it was Cormac Mac Art who attacked first.

That night he sent warriors to destroy the great hazel tree that stood in the center of the clan lands of Bregia. Each clan of Éireann, or confederation of clans, was possessed of its own sacred tree, for the druids venerated the tree as the oldest living object on the face of the earth. The *crann bethadh*, or tree of life, was the symbol of the clan's virility and health. Sometimes in wars between the clans the object of hostile attack was to invade the territory of the enemy and cut down the sacred tree as a dramatic gesture that would shame and demoralize the clan.

To destroy the sacred tree of life was the greatest insult of all.

When the news was brought on the next morning that Cormac had cut down and destroyed the scared tree of the Dési, all knew that there could be no backing away from the ugly abyss of war. Under the Brehons either the Dési must go under before Cormac's onslaught or Cormac Mac Art must be forced to admit his fault and make reparation.

Eochaidh Allmuir knew that whatever the outcome, only death and destruction would stalk the Dési in the land of Bregia for the days to come.

Chapter Nine

For ten days the armies of Cormac Mac Art marched and countermarched across the land of Bregia, leaving slaughter and burnings in their wake. Every time Eochaidh Allmuir tried to come to blows with him, army against army, Cormac would disengage, preferring to strike at an individual Dési fortress or village and leave it as a funeral pyre to its inhabitants. By the end of this period most of the fortresses and settlements of Bregia had been destroyed or abandoned and each petty chieftain and his septs had withdrawn for protection to Eochaidh's great fortress at Dún Mór.

As Cormac ravaged the lands of the Dési, driving off the great cattle herds, the prized boars and pigs, plundering the grain crops, and destroying the famed merchant ships of the Dési whenever he found them in harbor, Eochaidh made a desperate appeal to the Brehons of Éireann at the court of Temuir. He sent envoys to the courts of the provincial kings, pleading with them to intervene. But no one would go against the High

King. Perhaps they saw the madness that possessed him and feared for their own safety. No messages were received in answer to Eochaidh's pleas.

The only chieftain in all Éireann who openly criticized Cormac was the chieftain of Clan Bascna, Oscar Mac Oisín, commander of the Fianna. It became significant that the Clan Bascna, which comprised half of the Fianna, the High King's bodyguard, refused, in the person of Oscar, to participate in the campaign against the Dési. Yet the Clan Morna, which comprised the second half of the Fianna, under their chieftain, Gorta Mac Goll, who had participated in the attack on Dún Gorm, were foremost in the plundering and burning. Eochaidh Allmuir sent a message to Oscar asking for help. But Oscar pointed out that while he refused to lift his weapon to aid Cormac in his terrible vengeance, he could not lift his weapon against him for, as commander of the Fianna, he had taken an oath at the sacred stones of Temuir to protect Cormac from his enemies. He had withdrawn to his own fortress on the Hill of Allen.

Fire and destruction therefore spread like a plague across the land of the Dési. During this time a great depression descended on Aonghus Mac Orba as he saw the fruits of his actions. Not once but several times did he plead with Eochaidh Allmuir that he be allowed to surrender himself to Cormac's encampment in order to save the Dési from further slaughter. Both Eochaidh and Iolar, his druid, were adamant that such an action would be useless in the face of Cormac's blood madness. If Aonghus had committed a wrong, the wrong had been wiped out sevenfold by the deeds of Cormac.

Yet Aonghus keenly felt the responsibility for what he had done and he nurtured a brooding anger. He took risks in battle, flinging himself into any skirmish with scant regard for his own life.

Eochaidh Allmuir had divided his clansmen into three divisions. To Biobal of Hy-Macalla he had given command of the foot warriors. Each-Tiarna, whose very name meant "horse lord," for his prowess with the beasts, commanded the cavalry, while Gabur of Dún Glas and Aonghus had command of the charioteers. But Cormac was cunning enough never to try his strength against Eochaidh Allmuir, perferring to wear down the Dési in skirmishes and raids. Aonghus roamed the plains of Bregia trying to entrap Cormac's army. Whenever he found scouting parties of Cormac's men, he gave them no quarter. His brooding anger made him a merciless enemy.

It was, however, on the tenth day of the fighting that scouts reported that Cormac and his army had encamped in battle array in a nearby glen, and not long after their report an envoy arrived from the High King, taunting the Dési to try their mettle against Cormac with a warning of a terrible retribution when they were defeated.

"Know, Eochaidh, that Cormac has decreed that there will be, thereafter, no more Dési in any of the five provinces of Éireann," jeered the envoy. "You will be as chaff before the wind!"

Eochaidh's answer was to call his men to muster.

"Be circumspect," warned Iolar. "Do you not see that this is what Cormac wants you to do? He has worn down our people, burnt and killed and harried and avoided confrontation until this time. He thinks to strike now while our people are weary and demoralized. Many of our men think that Cormac is invincible and have lost heart. See how they march before you; see their bent shoulders and tired faces? See the slope of their arms carried carelessly across their shoulders? They have lost the battle ere it has begun."

But Eochaidh would have none of it. He gathered his army and marched to the valley where Cormac waited with the confident expectation of an easy victory.

Dawn came slowly that morning. The eastern light

was sullen, scarcely breaking through the cloud banks.
Finally the valley was bathed in a grey light and Cormac's
army was seen on the far side, deploying with cavalry
and chariots on the wings and his foot soldiers, supported by bowmen and slingers in the center. Eochaidh
decided to make a similar deployment with Biobal in
the center, Aonghus and Gabur on his right, and Each-
Tiarna commanding the left. The horns and trumpets
sounded as Cormac urged his commanders to advance
their standards. The lightly armed skirmishers advanced
immediately, the slingers coming forward and sending
their deadly little stones ringing like hail on the shields
of the gathered ranks of Biobal's warriors. Here and
there a warrior fell as the tiny missiles, screaming like
angry hornets, passed armor and shield and struck home.
Having discharged their weapons, the slingers retired.

Down came Cormac's chariots, charging over the
plain and cutting into Eochaidh's foot soldiers, driving
them mercilessly backwards against the rear ranks. Soon
the ground was soaked in blood. Eochaidh made the
signal to his own charioteers, but before they could
move, the chariots of Cormac were withdrawn. The
field lay confused now, here and there groups of warriors engaged each other, screaming and howling. Somewhere in the distance a horn blew.

Aonghus, keeping his charioteers in check, saw the
charge of Cormac's cavalry commence. The cold dawn
cut into his bones and he longed to be in the fray. He
watched as the horses surged forward, racing down to
make a solid wall of animals, a surging mass of death
and destruction. Then he saw Eochaidh's signal and he
waved his chariots forward. Across the far side of the
valley he could see Each-Tiarna's horsemen thundering
down toward the seething mass.

The once-green glen was mud, churned by the horses,
chariots, and warriors. The heather and grass lay bruised
and broken, stamped into the ground by countless feet.

Over everything lay a red hue, the sticky stain of blood. Around came the strange sounds of men in battle— shrieks, curses, moans, the noise of pain and anguish and fear.

Arrows bounced off Aonghus' shield and off the chariot itself as Cairell guided it expertly through the confusion. Aonghus slashed and hewed at the fighting mass around them. As in all battles involving large numbers, Aonghus and Cairell knew nothing of what was happening more than a few yards beyond them. Each man fought with desperation until he could wield his sword no more. Only Eochaidh could see the overall picture of the battle from his position high on the side of the hill. He saw Cormac's warriors pressing strongly onto the Dési and heard the sounds of piercing horns as more of the High King's men came remorselessly forward. Cormac's men were too numerous; they were pushing steadily forward while the Dési were being forced back.

The High King had chosen his time well and was tightening the vice easily, tighter and tighter, around the doomed forces of the Dési. Mounds of men, slain and wounded, horses and shattered chariots, lay scattered over the red sward. The noise and smell were ugly. Eochaidh turned to his trumpeter. The horn sounded the disengaged and recall of the chariots and a further signal told the foot soldiers to fall back. Most of them could not. Cormac's men were closing in on them, cutting down the outer ranks and jamming the rest in a tight mass around their standards like cattle in a pen. The Dési were just as helpless. They fought desperately, realizing the High King would give them no quarter. They fought or died.

Eochaidh Allmuir, astride his war horse on the hillside, watched and groaned aloud as he realized his impotence.

"The battle was lost before it was begun," sighed

Iolar at his side. "There was no heart in the men. Cormac had worn them down before he faced them. We must withdraw back to Dún Mór."

Eochaidh clenched his hand, his body tense, as if he would ride forward into the mêlée himself. Then he nodded. The order was given to flee from the field.

Slowly, painfully, the survivors of the Dési began to withdraw from the bloody valley. Soon the withdrawal became a flood of panic-stricken men, a route streaming back toward the protection of Dún Mór.

Cormac was all for following and destroying the Dési there and then, but wiser counsel in his army prevailed pointing out they had their own wounded to nurse and dead to bury. They were exhausted and needed rest before pressing on to the storming of Dún Mór. And Dú Mór was one of the most impregnable fortresses in the country, standing close by the banks of the great river Boann, named after the water goddess and mother of the love god Aonghus Óg. Cormac's army would need its strength to carry out a siege against Eochaidh's fortress. And so the army of the High King remained in its encampment and rested from battlefield exertions. And it was while they were encamped that Oscar Mac Oisín, chieftain of the Clan Bascna and commander of the Fianna, came to his High King.

The remnants of the Dési streamed into the great earthworks of Dún Mór, exhausted and dispirited. The huge wooden gates were slammed shut, and those warriors unwounded and with sufficient strength in them clambered to the walls fearing an immediate onslaught. It did not come. The afternoon sped by and dusk descended and still there was no sign of Cormac's pursuing army. Puzzled, yet thankful, the warriors of the Dési slumped into a fretful sleep, mostly dozing where they stood.

In the smoky light of the feasting hall, Eochaidh

Allmuir, bleary eyed and exhausted, gazed sadly at his chieftains and advisors.

"A third of the clan was butchered today," Iolar said heavily. "So far, half of our people have perished in Cormac's attacks."

"This is a war of madness!" Biobal's voice was full of suppressed emotion.

"Cormac offers us only one choice—extermination," Eochaidh said. "We have to make him pay heavily for our destruction. Better to die like men than merely be slaughtered like sheep."

"Is there no alternative?" asked Aonghus.

"No provincial king or chieftain, nor even the Brehons of Temuir, will intervene and help us come to accommodation with Cormac."

There was a shouting without the hall. They heard the sound of the gates swinging open. Cairell came bursting in the chamber.

"A messenger has arrived from Oscar Mac Oisín."

Eochaidh half rose in a spasm of hope. Was Oscar offering help?

"Bring him in, bring him in."

A tall warrior was ushered in.

"I am Brocaire of Clan Bascna," he said, addressing the Dési chieftain. "I speak for Oscar Mac Oisín and Oscar now speaks for the assembly of the High King."

Eochaidh nodded slightly, trying to restrain his sudden optimism. "Well?"

"Too much blood has been shed already. Now is an end to stop it."

"We did not invade the clan lands of other tribes," Eochaidh rebuked. "Nor did we demand unjustifiable reparation. Neither have we avoided attempts to negotiate an honorable settlement. We never sought slaughter."

Brocaire shrugged. "My message from Oscar is that the bloodshed must end."

"Why doesn't he tell Cormac Mac Art?" demanded Aonghus, edging forward. "We are not the ones with bloodlust."

"Oscar has had council with Cormac," replied Brocaire dispassionately. "Oscar is the High King's champion and commander of his bodyguard. He has grown sick of watching the terrible destruction in the land of Bregia and has offered to intercede in this war to stop further bloodshed and conciliate between the High King and the people of the Dési."

Eochaidh smiled wanly

"How is Oscar able to do that when Cormac listens to no reason?"

"Cormac has listened to Oscar and has agreed that this matter may be settled by the ancient law of the *cáirde chlaidib* . . . the agreement of the sword."

Eochaidh raised his eyebrows in surprise.

"Cormac has agreed to that?"

"He has."

"And the terms of the challenge?"

"Champion against champion . . . until the death."

Each-Tiarna stepped forward proudly. He was Eochaidh Allmuir's champion and therefore it was his place to accept any challenge affecting the Dési.

"I am ready."

Brocaire looked at him in amusement and shook his head.

"Cormac has agreed to this settlement only if the Dési are represented by Aonghus Mac Orba. Oscar therefore challenges Aonghus Mac Orba to meet him five days hence, as laid down by law, at the Ford of Visions that marks the border of Bregia and Midhe. As prescribed by law, each champion may be accompanied by his charioteer and by a witness. If Oscar wins, then the war is over, but a heavy tribute in cattle will be demanded by the High King. If Aonghus wins, then the Dési may be entirely free."

Aonghus stared back at Brocaire. He had not fought
Oscar at Temuir when Cellach had tricked him into the
contest not only because he saw the High King's son
escaping from justice but because Oscar was more than
mortal, beloved of the gods, grandson of the daughter
of Manannán Mac Lir, god of the seas and oceans. No
warrior had withstood combat with Oscar. He hesitated, but realized there was no choice to be made. Not
now. He was tired; tired of the continual bloodshed and
killing. The Dési were being destroyed because of his
action, because he had allowed the "bloodmist" to get
the better of him. Only he could now end the death
and destruction he had unleashed upon his people.

Eochaidh was frowning a warning at him. "Oscar is
the mightiest warrior in Éireann. No one can withstand
him."

"I agree to meet Oscar in single combat," Aonghus
said softly. "Truth may withstand him. If I have of-
fended the gods, then so be it. The gods know what
happened at Dún Gorm. I place myself in their hands."

Brocaire smiled approval and nodded.

"Then five days hence, as prescribed by law, you
shall meet with Oscar at the Ford of Visions."

"Five days. Then our blood will put an end to this
greater shedding of blood," agreed Aonghus.

Chapter Ten

Cairell eased the war chariot to a halt on top of a grassy bank overlooking a point where a stream wove through an avenue of tall silver birch trees and more lowly weeping willows, softly green in the late spring sunshine. The ford, where the stream shallowed and frothed over a pebbled path, marked the boundary of the lands of Bregia and the High King's territory of Midhe. The Ford of Visions was a tranquil spot where birds sang, where the sun mellowed the verdure into a bright assortment of pastel shades and gave an impression of everlasting peace.

The witnesses had already gathered on the banks of the stream. Iolar, on the Bregia side, stood stiffly erect, his profile almost eagle-like as he stared to where a second druid stood on the Midhe side of the stream. Aonghus' eyes widened a little as he recognized the evil features of Cormac's druid, Indech. Near him, on the same bank, stood Oscar's chariot, the charioteer making adjustments to the harness while Oscar stood a little way apart, arms folded across his massive chest.

Cairell glanced at Aonghus anxiously.

"Would you could ask me to drive on, Aonghus, that you may avoid this slaughter. What man can slay one born of the gods?"

Aonghus smiled wearily.

"Would I find a place to rest my head in this world or the next if I refused to meet Oscar?" he asked. "Oscar's father may have been the son of the goddess Sadb, but Oscar is no god. He is a great warrior, but only a warrior, who can bleed and die like any other."

Aonghus spoke the words with conviction, but it was a conviction he did not feel. Nevertheless, he had to work up some enthusiasm for the fight or else present himself to Oscar's sword immediately.

"Better to live without honor than die with it."

"Shame on you, Cairell," rebuked Aonghus. "It is best to be a victim to the sharp metal of valor, skill and bravery than to be withered by abuse, mockery and reproach. I will face Oscar."

He glanced across the ford and saw Oscar walking down to the stream. Aonghus descended from the chariot and made his way to meet him. They met each other at the ford and stood two sword arms' length from each other.

"Little joy in this meeting, Aonghus Mac Orba," Oscar greeted.

"Little joy indeed," affirmed Aonghus.

"Comac is seized with a vengeance against you and all the Dési. He wishes to expunge the Dési from the land of Éireann. Only I managed to persuade him to accept a resolution of the conflict by judgment of the sword. Yet my heart is heavy, for I know the death of Cellach was just and that you were provoked. But that you struck out the eye of the High King and thus caused him physical blemish is another matter. There has to be retribution."

"As my soul lives, Oscar, has there not been retribution given in the death and destruction he has since wrought on the Dési?" demanded Aonghus.

Oscar sighed deeply. "We are each the prisoners of our deeds, Aonghus. Our fight here will cause peace, though I admit my heart is not in this fight."

"Mine either. But if it is to be, so be it. What weapon shall we use?"

"The challenge is mine," Oscar said indifferently. "You must take first choice."

"Then let the decision be by the sword."

Oscar nodded and moved back to his chariot. Aonghus did the same. Each man divested himself of cloaks, surplus armor and weapons. They took their shields, round and thick with bronze bosses, and their long, double-bladed swords. Thus equipped they returned to the ford. Both men halted and looked toward Iolar and Indech, their witnesses.

"Bear witness to this combat," called Oscar.

"Our mouths shall relate what our eyes see and our ears hear," affirmed Iolar.

Indech smiled thinly. "So be it," he echoed dryly.

Oscar turned and fell into a fighting crouch.

From the moment their blades met, reverberating, clanging steel on steel, it was obvious that neither contestant truly had his heart in the conflict. Indech watched with disapproving, narrowed eyes as the two warriors waded back and forth across the ford.

"Come, Oscar, the Dési needs no lessons in swordplay," called the High King's druid. "Cease playing with him."

Oscar grimaced at the insulting tone.

"Defend yourself, Aonghus," he grunted almost apologetically.

Suddenly Oscar's gleaming sword point was everywhere, quick and sharp. Aonghus was hard put to raise his weapon in self-defense, and several painful little jabs touched his unprotected body.

Still Indech was not satisfied.

"Be true to your oath to the High King, Oscar," called the druid. "If you do not want to kill the Dési, let him kill you."

Aonghus grew bitter as he heard the insults levelled against the champion of the Fianna. Oscar was a brave man, but it was obvious that he knew that Cormac was in the wrong.

Yet the combat must be resolved. Aonghus began to move forward, using all his strength, but he realized that he would need all the power of the gods behind him to keep from getting killed, for there was no doubt that Oscar Mac Oisín was the greatest warrior in all Ireland.

Indech's insults had subsided and he stood with a grim smile on his skull-like features as he watched the two warriors sweating and grunting in the shallow waters of the gushing ford.

There was no doubt that Oscar was superior, but he was fighting as a cat might play with a mouse. There was little sign of exertion, his confident smile telling louder than words that he was restraining himself, letting Aonghus wear himself out. Around and around they circled, alternately retreating and advancing. The din of their clashing swords and heavy breathing were the only sounds that echoed in the small ford above the rushing of the stream.

Again Aonghus redoubled his efforts and sent his blade moving so swiftly that it appeared as a sheet of gleaming light. But as swift as Aonghus was, Oscar was swifter and held him easily at bay. They had spent the best part of an hour in the fight when Oscar suddenly drew back a pace and held his left hand palm upward.

"We will settle nothing this way," he said. "Let us break off from this."

Aonghus nodded and dropped his sword point.

At once Indech's angry voice snapped across the stream.

"What is this? Do you quit the combat, Oscar?"

"No!" snapped the leader of the Fianna. "But it is fitting, as the rules of combat decree, that we rest an equal time to that which we have fought. We will then renew the combat."

"Agreed," said Aonghus. "But let us renew it with slings and missiles."

The two warriors walked back to their respective sides of the ford and their charioteer came to them, wiped their brows and gave them refreshment.

Indech looked impatient, moaning and grumbling to Oscar that he was too soft and should finish the combat immediately. But Iolar, conscious of the duties of a witness, removed himself alone and rested against a tree until the time drew near when the contest should begin again.

Equipped now with slings, the two warriors approached each other again across the ford.

There was a shout in the distance and they both turned, uncertainly.

It was the warrior Brocaire of the Fianna, riding hard, head down against his horse's neck, heading toward them.

Oscar glanced at Aonghus.

"The truce continues?" he asked.

Aonghus nodded.

Oscar turned and waded back to the bank to greet Brocaire as he sprung from his horse. For a moment he whispered breathlessly to Oscar. The Fianna leader's face whitened as he bent listening. Then he snapped one or two questions at the man and bit his tongue at the final answer. Abruptly he turned back to Aonghus, his face a mask of anger.

"This contest is ended, Aonghus. I will fight with you no longer."

The statement brought forth a cry of protest from Indech.

"The contest is not resolved! Are you submitting to this Dési murderer?"

Oscar scowled.

"If that is what it takes to end the contest, then I submit. I shall shed no more blood in the service of the High King."

Oscar threw down his weapons.

Aonghus stared at him in bewilderment.

"Dishonor will be your lot!" screamed Indech.

"No!" replied Oscar. "Dishonor is already the lot of Cormac Mac Art!"

"What does this mean, Oscar?" demanded Aonghus. "What news did Brocaire bring?"

The young giant looked troubled.

"Aonghus, I wish you to know that my actions were honorable."

"I know it," agreed Aonghus.

"Then hear this. Contrary to the laws of justice and truth, Cormac Mac Art and his son Cairbre have, while we have been contesting here, started to move their armies against Dún Mór in the hope of catching Eochaidh Allmuir unprepared."

Aonghus stared at Oscar in bewilderment.

"But that is a violation of the code of single combat!" cried Iolar, speaking for the first time.

"I know it," Oscar replied grimly. "It seems that whatever the outcome of this combat, Cormac is resolved to destroy the Dési."

Aonghus bit his lip. "Then he was using our combat here as a subterfuge, luring Eochaidh and the Dési into a false sense of security and then striking at them when they were unprepared."

Oscar nodded agreement.

There came the whinny of a mare and the thunder of hooves. Indech, Cormac's druid, was spurring away from the ford.

"Shall I chase after him and slay him?" called Brocaire from the far bank.

"No, let him go," Oscar said quickly. "He is only a jackal gone to report to Cormac." The leader of the Fianna turned back to Aonghus. "I can promise you only this, Aonghus of Hy-Nia—that Clan Bascna will have no part in the destruction of the Dési."

"You are a man of honor, Oscar," replied Aonghus.

"Honor sometimes is a rope by which men hang themselves," Oscar sighed. "I foresee the end of the Fianna in this. Cormac has brought the High Kingship into disrepute. Maybe even the High Kingship itself will be destroyed and Temuir itself will wither and decay."

Iolar smiled without humor.

"If Cormac has fallen so low as to perform these deeds, then truly has the High Kingship fallen. There is no honor in the sovereignty Éireann."

Oscar thrust out his hand to Aonghus and the young warrior took it without hesitation.

"There is nothing left that I can do, Aonghus. Cormac is set upon his path. The Dési must either destroy him or he will destroy you. There is no middle course."

"Is there no help for the Dési among the other clans of Éireann?" pressed Aonghus.

"None that I can see. Each clan wishes to protect itself from the fury of the High King."

"The Fianna fought for justice and truth—surely they will fight for the Dési?"

Oscar smiled sadly and shook his head.

"Already the Fianna are divided again into the clans

of Bascna and Morna, and warring against each other.
But there is one thing above their petty loyalties: the
Fianna are the bodyguard of the High King, and Cormac
is still High King until the assembly of Temuir decides
otherwise. The Fianna cannot go against the code of
honor and betray their oath to the High King."

"Then there is no hope for the Dési?"

Oscar shrugged.

"Only death renders hope futile, Aonghus. The gods
go with you."

Aonghus stood silently as Oscar waded back across
the stream to his war chariot and, with Brocaire riding
ahead, the fair-haired giant was gone, his chariot thundering across the plain.

Slowly Aonghus picked up his weapons and, with Iolar,
returned to his chariot, where Cairell stood with an
anxious expression.

"Where shall we go, Aonghus?" he asked.

Aonghus glanced at him with a cynical smile.

"Need you ask?"

Cairell waited until Aonghus and Iolar were aboard
and then turned the grey mares toward the hills on
which Dún Mór rose, toward which the army of the
High King was marching in its final attempt to extermi-
nate the Dési.

Chapter Eleven

Forewarned of Cormac's sneak attack, Eochaidh
Allmuir was able to gather the surviving members of
the Dési behind the grey granite walls of Dún Mór while
Each-Tiarna rode out with mounted warriors to lure
Cormac away by raiding his flanks. He showed such
tenacity that the High King's generals believed there
were greater numbers preparing to attack and demanded
that the army halt and regroup. It was like two men
wrestling. One was tall and heavy, the other small and
light. The heavy one ever sought to come to grips with
the lighter one, while the lighter combatant skipped
hither and thither out of range, thrusting suddenly and
stinging, as might a wasp in summer. But nimble dodg-
ing is a wearisome exercise, and Each-Tiarna's horsemen
were soon worn out.

Eochaidh Allmuir had gathered the remnants of his
army, depleted as it was, and marched them out to face
Cormac Mac Art in the valley that stretched in front of
Dún Mór. For a whole day the two armies remained

encamped on opposite sides of the valley. The Dési were resigned to their fate. All they could do was sell their lives as dearly as they were able.

Toward midday on the second day there was a stir within the camp of the High King and his battle standards were moved forward. The noise of his horns and trumpets came echoing to the Dési warriors. With silent determination they began to make their way with painful slowness to their battle positions.

The chariots of the High King were spreading along the valley floor now. The warriors of Clan Morna stood ready with their javelins behind the charioteers as the vehicles thundered remorselessly onwards. Even as the Dési warriors ran forward to form their lines, the scythe—wheeled chariots were upon them, rushing in, delivering their attack and wheeling in tight circles to return out of range of the spears of the enemy. Eochaidh watched in helpless despair as Cormac's chariots cut his foot soldiers like wheat before the scythe.

He signalled toward Gabur and his mounted men, who swarmed down on the left flank with considerable noise, heads down, well forward against their horses' necks. But before they had even reached the High King's chariots, Cormac had withdrawn them, ending the skirmish. Gabur halted the charge and turned his cavalry back. This was the moment Cormac had anticipated. There came a wild shouting and cheering, mingling with the sounds of hooves, as Cormac's cavalry moved fast toward Eochaidh's defenses. Gabur's cavalry, spent by their initial charge, stood in confusion as the enemy horses smashed into their rear lines. A tide of Clan Morna warriors broke against the Dési. Aonghus, waiting impatiently, and impetuously too close to his enemy, glanced anxiously at Eochaidh. But Eochaidh was cautious. He realized that Cormac, having stung the Dési twice, would expect him to send his chariots down in vengeance.

A second wave of chariots broke against the forward lines, the warriors twisting and turning, hurling their javelins, their swords cutting a swathe in the lines of men while the chariots wheeled in complex and bewildering maneuvers, returning again and again against the depleted lines. Javelins and spears fell like rain, taking many of the Dési to the ground.

Finally, as Gabur and Each-Tiarna managed to disengage their cavalry, Eochaidh gave the signal for Aonghus to move. Aonghus waved to his chariots to close up behind him and urged them to charge forward on the men of the High King.

A crash from the heavens gave the armies but a moment's warning of the storm that had been brewing in the heavens. In the tension before the battle, no one had noticed the mounting clouds or the whistling of the wind about the hilltops. Now the storm had broken, and soon the warriors were soaked and weary, clambering across the mud and fast-flowing streams and over the sodden grass. The swiftly sodden ground made the use of chariots impossible. The Dési counter-attack faltered and halted as the chariots became bogged down.

Cormac, in spite of his madness, had lost none of the craft that had made his name renowned for battle throughout the western world. He ordered his foot soldiers forward, using slingshots and bows. They moved slowly but remorselessly, pressing on the Dési and forcing them backwards. For a time that seemed without end the lines of men struggled desperately, hand to hand, foot to foot, slipping, sliding and struggling over the soft, muddy ground as the grey curtain of rain pattered ceaselessly on friend and foe alike. Then more men, freshly conjured by Cormac, came rushing forward in a compact mass to fall savagely on the Dési.

The Dési lines quivered and then began to break. Eochaidh, looking down from the hillside, slumped his shoulders in resignation. This was the last battle. He knew it. Exhaustion finally overwhelmed his spirit. He signaled his trumpeter and the mournful notes calling for disengagement echoed over the valley. What a moment before had been a resolute line of fighting men, suddenly became a mob of fugitives whose only remaining strength was in their legs as they turned and began to run before Cormac's victorious warriors. Many were cut down, Gabur of Dún Glas among them. Others, such as Aonghus and Biobal and Each-Tiarna, refused to loose their fighting formations and so were able to move back in good order.

Once again, the remnants of the defeated Dési streamed back into the protection of Dún Mór. Only nightfall prevented Cormac from storming the walls. Tired as he was, Eochaidh Allmuir called a meeting of his chieftains and advisors in the great hall.

"How many survived?" he asked Iolar.

"Of the warriors?" asked his druid. "Not more than two hundred."

Eochaidh lowered his head to hide the pain. It had once been his boast that the Dési could put an army of five thousand warriors into the field.

"And of our people—the women, old men, children?"

"Not much above four hundred are sheltered in the fortress."

Each-Tiarna gave a low moan.

"Are the Dési to be no more? Has it come to this?"

"We shall perish when Cormac strikes tomorrow," Biobal said in resignation. "Let us make our end glorious and sell our lives as dearly as we can."

Iolar shook his head. "There is another path we can tread," he said softly.

There was something in the druid's voice that made Aonghus turn to him.

"You have a plan?"

Iolar smiled. "Once the Dési fleets were spoken of

with awe, not only in Éireann but in the ports of Alba, in Britain and in Gaul . We will use them to escape."

"But Cormac has destroyed our ships," Each-Tiarna pointed out.

"Not all," replied Iolar. "Three have escaped destruction and are sheltering at anchor in the river not far away. I have given orders for their captains to bring them up river under the shadows of the ramparts as soon as it is dark."

"What then?" demanded Aonghus. "Cormac will see them when it is light."

"We won't be here when it is light," Iolar said heavily, as if speaking to a simple child. "The captains and the crews have good Dési hearts. Every man, woman and child who survives in this fortress will be aboard them before dawn so that we can drop down river to the sea before the morning tide."

"You mean . . ." Biobal spoke slowly, "that we must flee the land of Bregia?"

Iolar nodded calmly. They were quiet as they realized the implications of what he was saying.

"We must flee the land of Éireann," Iolar confirmed. "There is no hope for our survival here. We must set sail in search of a new homeland where we can live in peace."

Eochaidh stood decisively.

"There is no time to lose." He glanced solemnly at each of them in turn. "Our people must be divided into three. I, with Each-Tiarna and Iolar, will go aboard the first vessel. Biobal will go aboard the second. Aonghus, you will go aboard the third vessel. Go now into the fortress and gather our people. They are to take only what they can carry and nothing else."

Under cover of the night the remnants of the Dési were gathered into three groups of equal numbers and, as instructed, as quietly as they could, taking only what personal possessions and weapons that could be carried,

they moved out of the side gate of Dún Mór. Through
the darkness they went to the moonlit waters of the
great river Boann, which passed at the back of the
fortress. Here, in a sheltered pool of the river, the dark
shadows of three ships were anchored. Large vessels
were these—ships that had once traded with the western ports of Alba, with Britain and Gaul. They were
large, flat-bottomed ships with timbers a foot thick
and iron rivets. They had oars in case of calm seas, and
a large central sail, plus two small guide sails. There
was room below decks for storage and for many people.

Once the Dési could boast of several dozen such
ships, but Cormac had managed to destroy most of
them in the harbors along the coast of Bregia. Now only
these three remained, and these had been gathered together by the far-sighted Iolar. They were named after
birds of prey, the *Cúr*, after the goshawk; the *Méirliún*,
named for the merlin; and the *Spioróg*, or sparrow
hawk.

The evacuation of Dún Mór was carried out with
stealth and expertise. Eochaidh ensured that all the
lights of the fortress burned brightly so that the scouts
from the army of the High King, encamped across the
glen, waiting for dawn to attack, would think that those
in the fortress were huddled awake, lights burning in
case of a sudden night attack. Indeed, it was Iolar's
knowledge that demanded that Eochaidh's men raise a
noise now and then to reassure the scouts of Cormac's
army. A group of a dozen men, under Aonghus, were
left behind until the last minute to cause this diversion.

By first light, however, everyone had been safely
evacuated—old, young, infirm—with the warriors going
last as protection. The ships were filled, with Eochaidh,
Each-Tiarna, and Iolar in the *Cúr*; with Biobal in the
Méirliún, and with Aonghus and Cairell going on board
the *Spioróg*. The captains of each ship were to have
full control over their vessels, but the ultimate deci-

sions affecting the welfare of the people were to be left to the chieftains of the Dési.

Eochaidh's general plan, conceived with Iolar, was to leave the mouth of the Boann and run northward, beyond the island of the ocean god, Inis Manannán, through the Straits of Alba, and seek landfall there, beyond the jurisdiction of the High King of Éireann.

Like three grey shadows in the pre-light of dawn, the ships moved slowly out of the sheltered pool behind the dark ramparts of Dún Mór and on to the waters of the great river. Timbers creaked as the large canvas sails filled out before the western breeze, which came off the mountains toward the sea. Slowly, the ships began to drop down the river.

It was as if the gods were finally helping the Dési at last, for behind them, as they moved downriver, they could hear a great shouting and clamor. The final attack was beginning, and soon Cormac's men would be in Dún Mór. They could see flames leaping from the outer walls of the fortress. Too late! The Dési were safely departed. Now they heard the furious blare of war horns and cries along the embankment. Cormac's scouts must have seen the ships and realized that the Dési were escaping.

On the quarter deck of the *Spioróg*, Aonghus stood at the taffrail, Cairell at his side, gazing anxiously behind. Maraí, the captain, stood at the tiller. He was a short man, thick and muscular, with berry-brown skin and twinkling blue eyes that moved watchfully as he steered the vessel downriver. Now and then his voice would whisper orders to his crew as sails needed adjustment. The waters ran smoothly under their keel.

"Cormac's men must have spotted us," whispered Cairell, as the horns blared again.

"If we get to sea, we will be fine," replied Maraí. "There's not a vessel can catch the *Spioróg* running before the wind."

Aonghus turned to the river mouth and observed, in the grey light, a sea mist lying close to the coast and enveloping everything in its dirty white hue.

"Can we go through that?" he asked dubiously.

Maraí chuckled.

"The sea mist can be our friend," he replied.

A series of shouts sounded nearby from the direction of the bank, and suddenly they heard the hiss of arrows, and thuds as some of them landed on the deck or hit the wooden superstructure. They were fired haphazardly and did no great harm. The flow of the river beneath their keel was increasing and the ship was moving rapidly now.

"Better time going downriver than coming up last night," observed Maraí. "We had to row the *Spioróg* up to Dún Mór. If we were rowing now, we would not have a chance against Cormac's bowmen."

Soon the river widened, so much so that all three ships could have sailed abreast with plenty of room to spare. Aonghus suddenly caught the salt smell of the sea and the freshening wind on his face. He could hear the thunder of breakers as the grey seas rolled into the shore, hear the gurgle of waters where the river pushed into the sea, where fresh and salt waters met and joined in uneasy alliance.

The *Spioróg* began to rock a little as the waters roughened but Maraí, the mariner, did not seem to mind at all. He looked like a man entirely in his element and he grasped the tiller with a gleam in his eye.

It was then that Aonghus realized they were leaving the land of Éireann, perhaps forever. He turned, straining to peer through the encompassing mist for a last look at the rolling hills of Bregia—at the land of his birth, the land of his ancestors. He could see nothing as the rolling mist swept over the headlands and hills and engulfed the ship.

Ahead of them a horn sounded. Aonghus glanced in query at Maraí.

"The horns will keep our three ships together until the mist clears," explained the seaman. He signalled one of his men to give an answering blast.

"Is there no fear of being thrown back on the coast and wrecked?" asked Cairell nervously.

Maraí gave a bark of annoyance.

"For three decades I have sailed these waters, fair weather and bad. I know them blindfolded. Fear not, charioteer, as I would not fear were I a passenger in your chariot and you racing your team over the land."

Cairell peered anxiously into the mist.

"Even so, I would not drive my chariot headlong into a mist."

"Can it be that Cormac could follow us?" interposed Aonghus quickly, seeing Maraí's shoulders hunch in anger at the implied criticism of his ability.

"First Cormac would have to find ships," replied the seaman. "He destroyed all the ships of the Dési except these, so he will have a job to find some quickly enough to be able to follow. His ships are in the north."

Cairell nodded. "We have seen the last of the High King. May the gods curse him! I hope he rests happy now that he has driven the Dési from their ancestral lands."

Cormac Mac Art was in an evil temper as he stood in the smoldering ruins of Dún Mór and stared at Indech.

"Escaped in ships?" His tone was incredulous and his one eye glinted dangerously.

Indech nodded impassively.

"They have fled to sea, Cormac," he said again. "Escaped."

Cormac raised a hand and clenched it into a fist, sending it smacking against the open palm of his other hand.

"They will not escape me! No man that wrongs me shall escape my vengeance, nor his kith nor his kin."

"What do you propose, son of Art?" asked Gorta Mac Goll, one of a group of warriors standing near him.

"I intend to pursue them, even though they seek sanctuary in the Otherworld. Find me the best ships that ever sailed from our eastern ports and gather me the most valiant warriors in Éireann. I will have my vengeance!"

Oscar Mac Oisín moved forward from the small group of men from Clan Bascna. He had come to plead with Cormac, having heard that Dún Mór was about to fall to him, and had been surprised on learning of the escape of the survivors of the Dési. Nor was he unhappy at their escape. But now Cormac's bloodthirst was taking matters too far.

"The Dési are destroyed, Cormac Mac Art," he said slowly. "They are killed. Only a remnant are left, and these have been driven from our shores. Is that not vengeance enough for you?"

The one bright eye glinted in anger at the young giant.

"I wonder you dare come near me, son of Oisín. Only for your father and your grandfather's sakes do I hold my temper at your treachery."

Oscar's eyes hardened, but he kept his face expressionless.

"You have done a great wrong, Cormac," he replied, his voice soft and even. "Wrong has answered wrong, and so the cycle of events has come full circle. Yet you were High King and you could have broken that circle. Wrong answers wrong again."

"He who plants thorns must never expect to gather roses," sneered Cormac.

Oscar's mouth twitched a little.

"There was once a High King of Éireann who was wise and learned. He once spoke at a council that ended the feud between my clan of Bascna and the clan of Morna. These words he spoke: In the taking of retribution a man is but even with his enemy, but in foregoing retribution, a man makes himself superior. Blood cannot be washed out with blood."

Cormac's angry eye narrowed.

"That is the judgment of a fool, Oscar Mac Oisín."

"A judgment of a wise High King. The High King was yourself, and you made that judgment when my grandsire Fionn Mac Cumhail won your heart and a place at your right hand as leader of the Fianna."

Cormac turned away with an angry flush.

Indech stepped forward to his rescue.

"It is known that you consider yourself a great warrior, Oscar Mac Oisín," he sneered. "Do you now say that you may not hurt your enemy when he has struck the first blow?"

Oscar jerked his head around and stared into the skull-like face of the druid.

"Would you were a warrior, Indech," he said softly. "Then I might have the pleasure of testing my steel against you."

"You refuse to reply to my question," pressed the druid.

"I said that wrong answered wrong. Aonghus Mac Orba came to exact vengeance on Cellach for a heinous crime. In taking vengeance he did wrong. Cormac taking vengeance on Aonghus and the whole clan of the Dési did even more wrong. When will the cycle of wrongs end?"

Cormac had recovered himself.

"When the last whelp of the Dési perishes from the face of this earth. I will set sail in my ship, the *Dioltas*, as soon as it is made ready."

"The Fianna will follow you, Cormac," cried Gorta Mac Goll.

"No man of Clan Bascna will, that is for sure, so do not speak for the Fianna, Gorta," Oscar imposed.

The dark young warrior grimaced.

"Then I speak for the men of Clan Morna!" he retorted. "The honor and heroism of Clan Bascna, which has been observed already in the war against the Dési, is not needed now."

"The Fianna will never take part in a dishonorable war while I command it," Oscar said firmly.

"But Clan Morna stands loyal to the High King," replied Gorta. "Let Cormac order and we will follow to the Otherworld itself."

There came a muttering of approval from the members of Clan Morna who had gathered.

The young leader of the Fianna drew himself up. Slowly, with his left hand, he drew out his sword and, holding it in the traditional way to indicate no threat or injury was intended to anyone, he took a pace to a nearby wall. A silence descended on the group within the courtyard of Dún Mór as they watched him.

"This sword served Cormac, High King of Éireann." Oscar's voice was low, yet full of authority. "It is the tradition that when a High King is no more, the captain of his bodyguard destroys the sword that has been sworn in his service."

With a quick movement that made those assembled gasp, Oscar turned and smashed the blade against the granite rock so that it broke cleanly in two.

Cormac's one eye narrowed.

"You disavow your allegiance to me, Oscar, son of Oisín?"

Oscar turned and met his gaze evenly.

"You are no longer qualified to be High King, Cormac Mac Art."

There came an astonished gasp from the assembly, a cry of outrage from Cormac's supporters.

"You tell me so?" Cormac's voice was dangerous.

"If your druids and Brehons do not possess the courage, I tell you so," replied Oscar. "Is it not stated in the laws of the Brehons that a king must have no blemish either on his soul or on his body?"

Cormac blinked.

"Is this law denied?" pressed Oscar.

Indech shifted his weight uncomfortably and said nothing.

Oscar picked up a piece of his broken sword, showing the brightly polished silver, mirror-like, to Cormac.

"Look at your face, Cormac, and tell me you have no blemish."

Brocaire nodded emphatically in support of his chieftain.

"The law is the law. No one shall be High King if he have a blemish. The moment Oscar lost his eye he became unfit for the office of High Kingship."

There was a silence. The sheepish looks of the Brehons and druids in the High King's retinue showed that the subject had been discussed amongst them, but no one had had the courage to speak to Cormac of it.

"The law is the law," echoed Indech, "but before a decision is reached it has to be discussed in the High King's assembly."

Cormac opened his mouth and then snapped it shut. He glanced angrily from Oscar to Indech.

"Such matters take time," he said savagely. "The Dési will escape me if I delay. I mean to pursue them now."

Cairbre, Cormac's second son, as sly and indolent as his brother had been, was an interested spectator. Now he moved forward with a smile.

"Then leave me here in Éireann as your *tánaiste*, father. You continue your pursuit of the Dési and I will watch over the kingdom and ensure that you are properly represented in argument against the Brehons and the assembly when they debate their decision."

Cormac glanced at his son. Had he not been so besotted with his thoughts of vengeance, he would have seen the cunning that was mirrored on the young man's face.

"You will ensure the Brehons come to a just decision?" he asked.

"I will keep the kingdom safe," Cairbre replied, his eyes hooded.

Oscar frowned as he glanced at the slothful features of Cormac's son. He had heard whispers of Cairbre's ambitions and knew those ambitions boded ill for the future of Clan Bascna and all the people of Éireann.

"Then that is taken care of," smiled Cormac. "Who will come with me to finish this pursuit of the Dési?"

Gorta Mac Goll and a dozen others of Clan Morna moved forward at once, apparently unaware of the new dissensions that had been sown within the kingdom.

Cormac turned to his druid.

"And will you join me on the *Díoltas*? It is not right that I should go without my man of wisdom."

Indech was frowning at the slyly smiling Cairbre, sensing the greed and ambition in the youth. Yet there was time to deal with him later. His own star was firmly linked to Cormac, for it had been prophesied that Cormac and he would greet Donn, lord of death and conveyor of souls to the Otherworld, together.

"I am always in the service of the rightful High King," he said. "My skills are yours to command."

Chapter Twelve

The *Spioróg* was lost in a grey world. Since it had entered into the sea mist with the *Cúr* and *Méirliún*, forty-eight hours before, it had drifted slowly northward in the enveloping wispy strands of grey that enclosed and sealed it in a world where only visibility was denied but all sounds were dulled. Even the slapping of the waves under the keel was distant, muted, as if it came from another world. Maraí, the captain, complained from time to time that he had seen nothing like this continuing mist in all his years of sailing the seas between Éireann and Gaul. He cursed the weather and even the gods.

Everything was draped in a thin film of moisture left by the grey tentacles of the mist. It covered the decks, the wooden rails, even the clothes of the crew and the weapons of the warriors. Every now and then a man at the stern of the ship and another at the bow blew their horns and paused, waiting for an answer from the *Cúr* or *Méirliún*. But the last time they had heard an answer-

ing call had been late on the evening of the first day.
Now there was a strange chill and silence.

Maraí had sent one of his men out on the bowsprit,
hunched beyond the dipping bow wave, a javelin in his
hand with which he occasionally probed into the mist.

"Are we lost?" asked Aonghus, coming to where Maraí
stood at the tiller.

"Lost?" replied Maraí, scarcely disguising his tone of
disgust. No landsman should accuse Maraí of being lost
on his own ship. "We are two days' sail from the mouth
of the Boann. How could we be lost?"

"But where are the other ships?" pressed Aonghus.

"They are out there still. Only the blanket of fog
dulls the sounds and we cannot hear their replies to our
horn blasts."

"Will they follow the same course as we?"

"Surely. The *Cúr* is captained by my brother Mairnéalach, and the *Méirliún* by my brother Bádóir. They
know the sea as I know it. I'll wager five milch cows
with you that when we leave this cursed mist their
ships will come out within sight of us."

Aonghus grinned crookedly.

"A safe wager, as we do not possess one cow between
us."

A lantern came bobbing through the mist. Cairell
came out of the gloom, an anxious expression on his
face.

"There is a chill in the air."

"It's the mist," replied Maraí.

Cairell suppressed a shiver.

"I feel something else. For the last hour I have had
pains in my head that I cannot dispel. I have a feeling
of nausea."

Aonghus glanced at Maraí, knowing how supersti-
tious seafaring folk were. He turned, tucking his arm
under Cairell's and leading him aside.

"You are feeling seasick," he said firmly.

The young charioteer shook his head vehemently.

"This is another sickness—one I do not understand."

"What ails you?"

"There is a cold fear on me and yet I do not know why—I have no fear of fogs. The gods know there are plenty that cover the land of Éireann, so why should I be fearful here, on the sea?"

Suddenly Aonghus strained an ear.

"Did you hear a horn?" he asked quickly. "Maybe it was the *Cúr* or *Méirliún*?"

Cairell shook his head.

"But there it is again," Aonghus insisted.

Sure enough, there came a strange sound from out of the shifting wisps of fog—a choking cry like the sound of a creature in pain. Aonghus moved quickly across the deck to where Maraí stood in a listening attitude at the tiller.

"I hear it," he said before Aonghus spoke.

"What is it, then?"

The sea captain shrugged.

"Your guess would be as good as mine. In these seas be many creatures."

Now the cry was sharp and clear and very, very close. The timbre vibrated their eardrums so that they gasped in pain. There came a muffled scream from the bow and the sound of a splash, as if someone had fallen in the water, then something scraped the side of the ship. There arose in the air a terrible odor, a bitter stench that caused Cairell to turn aside, a hand to his mouth.

Aonghus, on instinct, rushed to the stern mast, seized his shield and sword, and stood peering into the streaky mist. Something was slithering coldly across the rail of the ship—a long, brown tentacle. Out of the gloom a single baleful eye of yellow stared unblinkingly.

"By the gods!" breathed Aonghus.

"The gods between us and all evil!" cried Maraí, seeing the terrible vision in the gloom.

A huge head reared up through the mist, towering above them. People were screaming down in the well of the ship. Aonghus gazed upwards, his eyes mesmerized by the single, baleful eye that caught and compelled his gaze until the sweat stood out on his forehead. He fought to avert his eyes, aware that he had become stiff and immobile. He was aware of Cairell shouting, but his limbs were like lead. It seemed that the thing had singled him out and was sucking, vampire-like, on his strength of mind, his manhood, devouring the innermost recesses of his subconscious—eating his mind, consuming his essence. Aonghus tried to fight, but it was hopeless.

He heard Cairell again, and felt the young charioteer at his side, snatching the sword out of his frozen limb. Dimly he saw him hurling it, javelin-like, toward the eye of the creature.

There was a great scream and the eye seemed to erupt. A thick yellow liquid gushed out like a geyser, splashing through the grey mist.

Then Aonghus was suddenly free of its spell. He collapsed on the deck, once more breathing the overpowering stench.

The creature screamed again, then it was was gone—as if it had never existed. The air smelled salty and fresh again, and the mist began to dispel with such abruptness that within a moment they were in the cold but clear light of day, with nothing but miles of blue sea in every direction, save to the north, where the distant black hump of an island could just be observed. As they emerged from the mist, they stared backwards, but there was no sign of anything in the shifting grey mass behind them.

A voice cried: "Sail to starboard!"

Within a mile of them two other ships were sailing

out of the mist, wind thrusting their canvas sheets
forward. The *Cúr* and *Méirliún* began signalling and
turning in their direction.

Aonghus gazed around him like a man in a dream.
For a moment, he wondered if he were losing his mind.

Maraí was shaking his head.

"Never in all my time at sea . . ." he began.

A crewman hastened forward to report.

"It seems we have lost the man I sent into the bows,"
Maraí said quietly.

"Well, that much was no dream," Aonghus said.

"If any of it was a dream, then we all dreamed it,"
Cairell said. His face was pale. "I knew something was
wrong. I felt it just before . . ."

Aonghus turned to his charioteer, his gaze curious.

"You think there was a connection between what you
felt and what happened?"

Cairell bit his lip and nodded.

"Indech," he said. "Indech's responsible."

"Cormac's druid? What has he to do with this?"

"I think I underestimated Indech's power. To be
chief druid of Éireann is not a position anyone can
fulfill. Indech is a powerful magician. He has the knowledge of centuries and corrupts the practices of the
druids with evil usage. I believe it was he who sent the
mist . . . he who sent the creature."

Aonghus chuckled in disbelief.

"No man could do that, not even a druid."

Cairell was not reassured.

"My father was a druid. I know some of the ways of a
druid. It can be done. The old knowledge is not to be
dismissed lightly. Indech worked on your mind before.
You must beware of him, Aonghus. He is quite able to
reach out across the sea and use your mind to create in
reality that which you fear most. He can use you as an
instrument to project images through."

Aonghus shook his head in disbelief.

"Nonsense. Indech is a vain and evil man. A druid, I grant you, but no man, druid or not, can work such magic."

"Be warned," urged Cairell. "Be warned. Until you realize what power Indech is capable of possessing, you will not know him, and not knowing him, you will be powerless against him."

Aonghus patted the pale-faced young man on the shoulder.

"Go and lie down, Cairell. We will talk more of this when you are better."

Cairell started to say something, then hesitated and strode away. Aonghus watched his going with less self-confidence than he affected. He shivered slightly. Could such a thing be possible? The idea was surely ridiculous.

The *Cúr* and *Méirliún* had closed upon the *Spioróg*, and Eochaidh signalled a council on his ship. A boat was lowered and Aonghus was rowed across to the *Cúr*. A second boat brought Biobal from the *Méirliún*. They bobbed and danced across the gentle swell of the sea until they reached the shelter of the side of Eochaidh's ship. The immediate talk was of the mist, but only those on the *Spioróg* had actually seen the creature.

"It was a strange mist," Iolar the druid agreed. "Thanks be to Manannán Mac Lir, who protects and guards the oceans, that we did not founder in it."

Eochaidh nodded. "The sea god was good to us, for he ensured that our ships kept together."

When Aonghus pressed them about the sea creature, they shook their heads.

"We saw nor heard nothing in the blanket of mist," Eochaidh assured him.

"What manner of beast was it?" asked Iolar.

"We could not be sure in the mist," replied Aonghus.

Biobal cast an apprehensive glance around, as if to assure himself of the emptiness of the seascape.

"Well, no sign of it now," he said thankfully.

Eochaidh turned to the point of the meeting then.

"Now that we can navigate these seas, I thought it best to discuss our destination."

"I thought it was decided that we would make land-fall in Alba!" asked Aonghus.

Biobal nodded. "Alba has much to commend it. It is said that the people of Alba are of the same race as the children of Éireann—that they share the same language and customs, worship the same gods, and hold the Brehons in regard above all men."

"Then we are decided?" asked Eochaidh.

"Alba. So be it," they affirmed.

"In that case, we have only one problem. We lack water for the voyage across the northern seas. Our casks are almost empty."

"The same is true on the *Méirliún*," Biobal said.

Aonghus felt chastened that he had not checked the situation with the casks of the *Spioróg*. He made a guess: "Neither do we have sufficient."

Eochaidh gestured toward the distant black hummock.

"That seems a fair-sized island. Before we set off to cross the wild northern sea, we shall put in there. There's bound to be fresh water for our casks."

Chapter Thirteen

The ships of the Dési found safe anchorage in a small cove where a shallow, shelving sandy strand provided an excellent landing spot. Around this, great granite thrusts of rock rose forbiddingly on all sides. The sea grumbled angrily as it washed against the base of the fortress island. Its persistent, deep-throated roar acted as counterpoint to the wild, screaming cry of the sea birds—the gannets, with their elongated necks, and the black-tailed herring gulls—that whirled, circled and darted over the cliffs.

Eochaidh Allmuir ordered Aonghus to take a boat from each ship and go ashore in search of fresh water. Each-Tiarna and Iolar decided to accompany him and, with Cairell, the expedition numbered some twenty men in all. They drew their boats up the sandy shore, above the waterline, and stood examining the terrain, hoping for a sign of some small stream emptying itself into the sea. But while the shady cove offered a splendid and comfortable shelter, it provided no fresh water

or green vegetation among the bare granite that might
indicate the presence of a stream or rivulet.

"We will have to go inland," Aonghus announced.
He ordered three of the men to stand guard over the
boats and led the rest of them across the shore toward a
passage in the rocks that marked the only possible path
away from the cove.

It was a tough climb up the rocky height. The path, if
such it could be called, was twisting and perilous. It
was some time before they paused on the rocky cliff and
looked down at the ships riding at ease below them in
the protection of the cove. From this point the island
looked as forbidding as it had seemed when they had
approached it from the sea. There seemed nothing but
the almost blue-grey color of granite everywhere, rising
in a series of serrations that formed a mountain group
toward its center. There was no hint of heather or trees
or grassland to relieve the somberness of the landscape.

"Can there be water in such a place?" wondered
Cairell as he gazed around him.

"One thing is certain," replied Aonghus firmly, "we
cannot sail without water."

Iolar gestured toward the bald mountains in the distance. "There is bound to be water in the vicinity of the
mountains, unless this island be at war with nature."

The druid turned and began to lead the way forward,
picking a path over the smooth rocks away from the sea.

They had not gone far when a cry echoed on the air;
it was a high-pitched female cry—a cry of fear.

The Dési warriors halted, then Aonghus drew his
sword and motioned his men to be silent. He moved
with the stealthiness of a warrior born, in the direction
of the cry. They came to a granite mound and, turning
around its shoulder, came upon the vista of a small
plateau, that had hitherto been hidden from them. In its
center was a gushing spring of water, apparently rising
from the rocks, and forming a small pool and stream.

But it was not the finding of water that caused them to halt in astonishment. About a hundred yards from them, near the side of the pool, were two tall warriors clad from heel to poll in black, raven-colored cloaks over black leather harnesses. Even their gaunt faces were dark, surmounted by hair as black as pitch. Between them they held a young woman, bound at her wrists, arms behind her. One of the warriors was trying to insert a gag in her mouth, while she made a futile attempt to evade them.

"Stop!" yelled Aonghus.

The two warriors wheeled around in astonishment, staring in disbelief at the group of Dési as they emerged from the shelter of the rocks.

One of the warriors thrust the woman aside so roughly that she fell to the ground with a smothered cry. In one swift movement the warrior was reaching for a missile in a pouch at his waist, a sling already in his hand. He apparently was undeterred by the number of Dési crowding behind Aonghus. Even as he was fitting the shot in his sling there came a buzz like an angry hornet and a small stone struck him squarely on the forehead, dropping him with a grunt to the ground. Cairell stood ready with a second shot. The other warrior stared for a moment and, with amazing agility, bent forward, lifted the inert body of his companion over his shoulder and vanished between some rocks.

The Dési advanced cautiously, fearing some ambuscade, for surely the fact that neither of the two warriors had shown fear at their numbers meant there were more of them in the vicinity.

Iolar was frowning.

"Curious," he muttered, as the Dési quickly searched the area, "it seems the very ground has swallowed them."

Aonghus was perplexed at the rapidity with which they had vanished.

Cairell was bending over the woman and untying her bonds while she watched the strangers fearfully. She was very attractive; more a girl than a woman. Like the warriors who had been mistreating her, her hair was a tumble of raven blackness, falling to her shoulders. Her eyes were as dark as her hair yet her skin was pale, almost a translucent white. Her long limbs were well shaped. She seemed no more than eighteen summers. She trembled a little as Cairell removed the cords that bit deeply into her slender wrists and gazed about her with frightened eyes.

"Have no fear." Cairell bent forward with a smile of reassurance. "Do you understand the language of the children of the Gael?"

The girl glanced up at him, frowning a moment before responding to the smile on his boyish features.

"Who are you?" Her voice was soft and musical.

"We mean you no harm," Aonghus said, replying for them all. "We are of the clan Dési from the land of Éireann. Who are you, and why were those warriors ill-treating you?"

Cairell helped the girl rise to her feet. She stood rubbing her wrists to restore the circulation.

"I am Aige," she replied. "The men were warriors of my lord Balor. He is the ruler of this land."

"Which is?" prompted Aonghus.

"This is the Island of Towers, the land of the Fomorii."

Aonghus took an involuntary step backwards while several of the Dési gasped aloud.

Fomorii! Had they not heard of the terrible people, the Fomorii, who once contested the sovereignty of Ireland with the gods of the Dé Dana? Didn't the gods drive them from the land back to the Island of Towers from whence they came? They were the personification of all that was evil in the world, a misshapen and violent people. Yet, according to the stories told by the bards in the feasting halls, they were not immortal.

Aonghus pursed his lips. No, they were not immortal, for Cairell's slingshot had demonstrated that.

"And you?" pressed Cairell. "Where do you come from? What do the Fomorii want with you?"

The girl frowned at him.

"I, too, am Fomorii. I am handmaiden to the lady Eithne, daughter of Balor at the Evil Eye, ruler of the Island of Towers."

Cairell gazed at her in surprise. All Fomorii women were surely witches, so the stories of the bards said. This young girl looked like no witch that he had ever seen. Could the legends and stories about the Fomorii be wrong? Were they just human after all?

"Then why were they ill-treating you?" asked Iolar.

"I ran away. My lady begged me to leave her and seek help."

"Help?" Aonghus was puzzled. "What help would the daughter of your ruler need?"

The girl sighed deeply.

"It is a story that may be long in the telling. Noble warriors," she suddenly spread her hands, appealing to them all, "I do not know what fate made you chance upon this island, but you must have been sent by the gods for a purpose. Help me, I beg you! Help me rescue my lady from her plight."

Aonghus raised his eyebrows at the appeal.

"If your lady, Eithne, is the daughter of Balor, your king, what plight could she be in that she needs the assistance of strangers?"

Aige's face was troubled as she turned to him.

"Alas, she needed succor from the moment she was born." She paused and then continued. "When Eithne was born, her father, Balor of the Evil Eye, received a prophecy that he would one day die by the hand of his grandson. Eithne was his only daughter and child. It was obvious to Balor that a son of Eithne's would be responsible for the deed. To forestall the fulfillment of the prophecy, Balor had Eithne locked up in a tower, isolated from his fortress, on the edge of the sea. There Eithne grew up, guarded by twelve female warriors who have orders not to allow man or boy near her so that she will remain a maiden forever.

"I was sent to serve her when I was sixteen, the year when she had been eighteen long summers in the tower. From that time on, my lady Eithne and I talked of nothing but how, one day, we might effect her escape. For years she had begged and pleaded with her father, Balor, to release her, but always he turned a deaf ear. I had to share her imprisonment as punishment for my mother's crime of refusing to sleep with Balor.

"Eithne and I made several plans but none were of use. Then, this very morning, a chance presented itself to me . . . an open window, a ladder left by a careless mason. I fled . . . but not to save myself. Eithne is still imprisoned, and I have sworn by the gods to find help and rescue her. Warriors of Éireann, I beg you, help me in that task."

The girl's voice had risen with passion and, as she fell silent, the Dési stood awkwardly about her.

It was Cairell who broke the stillness first.

"What would you have us do, Aige?" he asked.

She turned, her dark eyes suddenly hopeful.

"I would have you storm the tower of Balor and rescue my lady from her perpetual imprisonment."

"But the guards . . . the warriors who caught you . . . what of them?" Iolar asked. "Your lady will be doubly guarded since you fled. How long before this Balor knows we are here?"

Aige shrugged as if the question were not important.

"Balor knows all things. He will know you are here already."

"Then we must leave the island at once," Each-Tiarna said, breaking his long silence.

Cairell turned with an angry scowl.

"The men of the Dési are no cowards. We will not flee like frightened children from the wrath of the Fomorii ruler. We must rescue Aige's lady, for the conduct of this Balor is an abomination in the sight of the gods of our people."

Aonghus paused, his mouth compressed. Then he said: "It would lie heavily on my conscience if we fled this island, leaving such evil and injustice."

Aige caught at his hand.

"May the gods bless you, warrior. Will you come?"

Aonghus glanced at his followers and then nodded.

"Aonghus Mac Orba of Hy-Nia is prepared to test his mettle against the warriors of Balor. Are there any who will follow him?"

Cairell stood forward immediately. One by one, the others voiced their agreement until, finally, Each-Tiarna nodded reluctantly.

The girl, to their discomfiture, fell to her knees and, seizing Aonghus and Cairell's hands, kissed them in thanks. A slow flush of painful embarrassment spread over Cairell's face. He drew the girl to her feet.

Aonghus was trying to work out a plan.

"If Balor is warned of our presence, we must act directly. Iolar, you will hasten back to Eochaidh and tell him of our situation. Get more warriors to fill the water casks from this stream but be vigilant in case of attack from the Fomorii." He turned to Aige. "How far away is this tower in which Eithne is imprisoned?"

Aige pointed toward the distant mountains. "It lies five hours' march in that direction, beyond the mountains, which can only be crossed through a secret passageway."

"Do you know the passage?"

"I can retrace the path I took," replied the girl promptly.

"And are you willing to lead us to the tower?"

"I have sworn by the gods that I will rescue my lady."

The girl's chin came up in emphasis.

Aonghus turned back to the druid. "Then, Iolar, tell Eochaidh that unless he is attacked by Balor and his ships are placed in danger, he should await our return. But if we have not returned before the sun reaches its zenith tomorrow, then he is to mourn our loss and sail on for Alba."

"May the gods of our ancestors be with you, Aonghus," Iolar said as he departed.

"Where the brave go, there are the gods," smiled Cairell. "We have challenged the might of Cormac Mac Art, mightiest High King. He could not quell us. How, then, will this ruler of a poor, bare rock in the northern seas show himself more powerful than the son of Art?"

This raised the spirits of the Dési warriors and, with Aonghus, Cairell and the girl, Aige, at their head, they turned their faces toward the distant granite mountains and began to march forward with a light tread, the excitement of the adventure making their spirits buoyant.

Chapter Fourteen

The landscape was bleak—a dusty granite tumble of rocks in which no vegetation seemed to thrive. Only now and again did some hardy plant, a tiny, flowering shrub, appear to have found an anchorage in the clefts of the rocks. The sun was high in a fairly cloudless sky, reflecting against the rocks and causing a warm discomfiture among the Dési as they made their way carefully along the track where the girl, Aige, led. Now and again, from a high point, they caught sight of the sea's broad blue expanse to their right, but mostly they were confined to rocky defiles among the granite landscape.

Once Aige stopped and pointed to the great thrusts of rock ahead.

"The Bald Mountains of Cruas," she said. "It is through those that we have to pass to get to the land of Balor."

"Balor is well protected then," Aonghus observed. "Is there no other way into his domain besides the passageway?"

"None," affirmed the girl. "The mountains encircle

his lands like the walls of a fortress. Only through the caves can one enter and leave."

The Bald Mountains of Cruas loomed a dull yellow in the sun, towering fully two or three thousand feet high. Even in their state of forbidding bareness they were imposing, with the bright rays of the sun touching their dull surface and causing a million sparks of burnished golden light to dance over their curious rock formations.

"How far is it to the entrance of these caves?" asked Cairell.

"No more than an hour or so."

Aonghus turned and raised his hand to bring his warriors to a halt.

"We will pause and rest a moment here," he said loudly.

"But we have no need for rest, Aonghus," Each-Tiarna protested.

"There is always need when one faces the unknown," Aonghus replied in the same tone. "Who knows when we may rest again?"

They halted, spreading themselves out on the stones. Then Aonghus turned to Cairell and Each-Tiarna and said in a low voice: "Do not look around. Behave as if we were resting."

They frowned at him.

"We have been followed for the last hour or so."

Aige shuddered and moved close to Cairell.

"Is it Balor?" she whispered.

"That I would not know," shrugged Aonghus. "I can tell you that it is only one man. Perhaps it is the warrior who escaped unwounded from us."

"All Balor's guards are clothed in black. It is difficult to tell them apart," said the girl.

"Are you sure it is only one man?" asked Cairell.

"One man," affirmed Aonghus.

Cairell looked thoughtful and turned to the girl.

"You say that it is no more than an hour to the cave entrance which leads into the land of Balor?"

"Yes," replied Aige.

"And this paths leads to it?"

She nodded.

"Then you will lead Each-Tiarna and the others to the cave and wait for Aonghus and me there. We can deal with one man. Perhaps we can capture him and make him useful to our purpose."

Aige looked anxiously at the charioteer.

"Can't we all stay together?"

Aonghus chuckled. "That will not coax him into the open. No, Cairell has a good plan. You and the others go on. We will deal with this Fomorii. If the path becomes tricky before you reach the cave entrance, Each-Tiarna can scratch a sign on the rocks so that we may be guided by it."

They set off a short time later with Aige leading the way down a narrow defile in the rocks. Once Aonghus and Cairell were sure that the person following could not observe them, they moved swiftly into a small side passage and hid themselves while the others moved on. They waited some time but no one passed by.

Cairell leaned forward with a frown.

"Could you have been mistaken?" he whispered.

"The man following must be a good tracker, for he is surely following on a parallel track. We must move after him, lest he gain the advantage."

Aonghus swung himself up onto the high rocks, but no sooner did he do so than he dropped back, almost colliding with Cairell.

"I was right," he hissed. "The warrior is scarcely fifty yards away."

He indicated the direction with his head.

Cairell, without waiting for an order, moved to the left in an attempt to circle their prey while Aonghus moved cautiously to the right.

Fifty yards away from the granite a broad-shouldered warrior, cloaked in black with a black shield and sword

in hand, was moving swiftly in the direction taken by
Aige and the Dési. He wore a black bonnet with its
visor pulled across his face. Aonghus was sure that it
was the Fomorii who had escaped them earlier.

Cairell suddenly appeared on the left of the man,
causing him to halt and stand hesitantly. Then Aonghus
closed up rapidly behind him.

"Who are you who follows us like a wolf in the
night?" demanded Aonghus.

At the first sound of his voice the warrior wheeled in
surprise.

"I am Morca, stranger," the man replied, recovering
swiftly from his astonishment. "This is the land of the
Fomorii, and you have chosen it as your dying ground."

Aonghus smiled.

"That remains to be seen."

The black-clad warrior chuckled, but there was no
mirth in his voice. Then he leapt forward, his sword
whirling over his head.

Aonghus saw Cairell reaching for his slingshot and
motioned him to hold back, moving forward to meet
the Fomorii's attack.

Within the first few cuts and parries Aonghus realized that the Fomorii was no great swordsman. The
man relied on brute strength rather than an ability with
his weapon. Within moments Aonghus had pricked the
man on the forearm, causing the blood to flow. The
Fomorii gave voice to an angry cry.

"Lay aside your weapon, Morca," called Aonghus,
"and you may live. That you can do in honor."

"No honor in surrender," gasped the warrior, closing
again with a series of hacking blows.

"No sense in a useless death," replied Aonghus.

"All strangers who land on the Island of Towers must
die," was all the man said. "That is the law of the
Fomorii."

He raised his sword for another blow but Aonghus
stepped swiftly forward and thrust his blade upwards.

The Fomorii dropped his blade and staggered back, his eyes full of surprise and pain.

"A useless death, Fomorii," muttered Aonghus as the warrior dropped to his knees.

"No death . . . no death is useless when . . . it offers . . . a chance of rebirth. I . . . I merely precede you . . . to the Otherworld."

With a grunt the man fell forward on his face and lay still.

Cairell hurried to Aonghus' side.

"Are you hurt?"

Aonghus shook his head, gazing down in disgust at the Fomorii's body.

"The fool refused to surrender. It was a useless death."

"Useless or not," Cairell sighed, "one should die proudly when it is no longer possible to live proudly. Would you have surrendered?"

"That would have been different," Aonghus protested.

"How so?" smiled Cairell. And when Aonghus hesitated, he observed: "A person's death, the manner of his passing to the Otherworld, seems always to be more the concern of those who remain than the one who has gone."

Aonghus expelled his breath in exasperation.

"More and more you sound like a druid, Cairell. Come, let's get after the others."

Aige must have led them at a good pace for despite the fact that Aonghus and Cairell moved swiftly, they were unable to overtake them before the black shade of the mountains loomed. Now and again, as the path twisted, they saw a scratch mark left by Each-Tiarna to show the passage of Aige and the Dési. But when they neared the base of the cliff-like mountains, and saw the black pits of caves along the walls, they could see no sign of any of them.

"Perhaps they are waiting within the mouth of the cave," suggested Aonghus.

"Look," Cairell pointed. "There is another mark left by Each-Tiarna."

"Then we must move on to the caves. They are probably waiting for us in their shelter."

Cairell was just about to fill his lungs and sing out when he paused and held his head to one side.

To the ears of both men came the distant sound of crooning—a soft, sweet-sung lullaby.

"Is that Aige?" wondered Aonghus.

Cairell shook his head.

"It is an older voice," he replied. "It comes from beyond that outcrop of rock."

As he led the way cautiously forward, a second and third female voice joined in the chorus of the lullaby.

About a hundred yards away, under the shadow of the giant, protruding mountains, stood the large black entrance of a cave. It was of immeasurable width—certainly large enough to take a tall building into its jagged maw. There was no sign of the Dési warriors or of Aige, but a small fire blazed at the entrance of the cave, with an iron spit on which a roast was turning slowly to the soft hiss and crackle of the flames. Seated around the fire on small boulders were three long-limbed women clad in dazzling white dresses hemmed with gold embroidery. Their golden tresses reached beyond their waists but were held back from their faces by bands of jewels inlaid with gold. Never had either Aonghus or Cairell beheld such beauty on the faces of mortal women before.

"Who can they be?" whispered Aonghus softly in astonishment.

One of the women strummed a small stringed instrument on her lap while all three crooned in lilting voices:

> Can we forget so soon,
> My love, oh my love,
> How we lay face to the moon,

My love, oh my love.
If you forget, then you forget
The pulse of your heart
My love, oh my love.

"Let's ask them if they have seen Aige and the others," suggested Aonghus.

He was surprised when Cairell held him back.

"What is it?"

Cairell shook his head, watching as the three beautiful women sat singing softly. Now and again one of them bent forward and basted the meat on the spit with a long copper spoon. The smell of roasting pork came to their nostrils—a sickly-sweet smell.

"I don't know," Cairell said. "I have a strange feeling of disquiet."

Aonghus knew better than to question Cairell further. He knew that the young charioteer had inherited some strange sensitivity from Fios, his druid father—something that made him feel things which no ordinary man or woman could sense. For a while Cairell continued to gaze on the scene and then he said:

"There is something wrong here, but I don't know what it can be. Wait here, Aonghus; keep out of sight. I will approach these women and ask them what has become of Aige and the others. No need for both of us to place ourselves in danger."

"I will keep a close watch, Cairell," Aonghus assured him.

The young charioteer stood up and walked toward the cave entrance. One of the women—the one playing the stringed instrument—glanced up and saw him coming. She stopped playing and a gentle smile spread across her pleasant features.

"Welcome, young stranger," she called, her voice low and musical.

The other two raised their heads and copied her smile of welcome.

Cairell found his breath catching at their pale-skinned beauty, the soft grey eyes and perfectly shaped features.

"Blessings upon you," he replied gravely. "What place is this?"

"These are the Bald Mountains of Cruas, and this is the Cave of the Cruachan Mór," replied the one with the instrument.

"And you would be a stranger not to know these things," added the second woman, holding the copper spoon to the roast.

"That is no secret," replied Cairell. "I am looking for my companions from whom I have been separated."

"Companions?" The third woman continued to smile.

"A young girl and a score of warriors."

"Indeed," replied the second woman.

"You have seen them, then?"

"We have seen them," confirmed the third woman.

"Where?"

"They passed into the Cave of Cruachan Mór not long since," said the first woman.

Cairell frowned. "They were supposed to wait outside the cave for . . ." he hesitated, nearly saying "us," but managed ". . . for me."

The smile on the face of the second woman did not alter.

"As we were here when they passed in and told of your coming, they asked us to show you the way after them. But, before you do so, perhaps you would like to sit with us a while and eat?"

She pointed with her copper spoon to the roasting joint of meat.

Cairell shook his head.

"I must hurry after them," he said, unable to shake off the feeling of threatening danger. Yet what danger could threaten from these three beguiling women?

"Perhaps you will be hungry on your return, noble youth," said the third woman.

"Perhaps," said Cairell. "Which direction did my companions take?"

The first woman laid aside her instrument, stood up with suppleness and grace in her every movement.

"I will show you, young warrior."

"And I!" "And I" echoed her two companions, rising and moving to either side of the charioteer.

"Follow me," called the first woman, going to the cave.

Cairell moved after her, his two female companions on either side.

In his hiding place, Aonghus watched the women escort Cairell into the black maw of the cave entrance. He stood up quickly, drawing his sword from its sheath. Quietly, quickly, he made his way across to the cave.

Ahead of him in the gloom, he saw the three women conducting Cairell farther into the dark recesses of the cave. It was lit with smoking torches. The huge maw narrowed rapidly into a small, dark passageway that twisted and turned into the bowels of the mountain.

"How far ahead are my companions?" Aonghus heard Cairell ask anxiously.

"Not far, not far," came a soothing voice.

Abruptly, the passageway opened into a large cave that was filled with a smoky semi-gloom. All around the place, hanging from every crevice, were dusty webs—spiders' webs—the like of which Cairell had never seen before. He stared about him in curiosity.

"What place is this?" he whispered, feeling an unwilling awe at the size of the webs.

The first woman turned to him, smiling a gentle smile. Then she opened her soft red lips and began to cackle with a hideous screech. The sound froze Cairell's blood.

Chapter Fifteen

"By the gods!" began Cairell, staring in horror at the beautiful woman who made the ghastly, hair-raising noise.

Then he stepped back in further horror as the shapely forms of the three women seemed to shimmer and dissolve before his gaze, dissolve and reform. He stared aghast. Three crones stood around him, cackling in a mirthless chorus—misshapen, grotesque, ancient creatures without a hair on their wrinkled skulls. Their backs were bent under ugly humps. Their faces were wart-covered and cracked with age. Eyes burned from the depths of horribly sunken sockets on either side of beak-like noses. Thin lips drew back from discolored, decaying gums in which only yellow fangs served as teeth. Skeleton arms reached out with thin, claw-like bony fingers and dirty, cracked nails. They gave the impression of emaciation—spindle legs attached to torsos that seemed to be distorted and bent. Never had Cairell witnessed such visions of repulsiveness.

He tried to draw his sword but one of the old women threw something toward him. He felt its icy wetness. It was a sticky substance that encased him entirely. He tried to reach up with his hands and claw it away. It was soft and clinging, a thin, sticky silkiness—like a spider's web!

Cairell struggled to free himself from its enveloping folds but it was tightening and suffocating.

The shrieks of mirth echoed in his ears as he fell, rolling over the cave floor in his efforts to free himself.

One of the crones bent forward, thrusting her neck out like an ancient gander. He could feel her hot, fetid breath on his cheek.

"My, but you are a handsome one. We will have much sport with you, my fine warrior."

Cairell closed his eyes and shivered convulsively.

Aonghus heard the shrieking laughter and his blood ran cold. Sword ready, shield on his arm, he broke into a run down the rocky floor of the passageway and did not draw breath until he burst into the large cavern.

He halted in astonishment.

In the gloomy, smoky light he saw the hanging webs, saw Cairell enmeshed in a silky sheen on the floor of the cave with the three old women dancing around him.

Then he saw what Cairell had failed to see.

Across the far side of the cave were Aige and the Dési warriors. All were bound in the revolting grey mesh of the webs. All were helpless and mute, eyes staring wide and fearful.

One of the crones bending over Cairell had turned her head to the others.

"Go, sisters, back to the fire, lest our meal spoil. We do not want to ruin our feasting."

"But what of this one?" demanded one of the others in a petulant whine.

"We will save him for a special feast. Go now. I'll attend to him."

Aonghus drew back from an immediate frontal assault. Better to deal with these witches by stealth. Let them separate . . . He stepped back into the shadows by the entrance to the cavern before they saw him. His foot slipped on something on the rocky ground. He swayed for a moment, recovered his balance and glanced down. The floor was wet and sticky. He turned to examine the red substance. It was trickling from a side cave of lesser dimensions than the cavern. He peered into and found it lit by a burning torch. It took all his strength of will to keep from crying out in disgust.

On a rocky shelf nearby, still recognizable, were the neatly butchered limbs of one of the Dési. Each limb was cut and separated—the head, severed at the neck. The torso, the arms, the legs . . . except that one leg was missing. Aonghus felt a quiver of nausea as he abruptly recalled the shape of the turning roast over the fire outside the cave. His hand spasmodically gripped his sword.

The cavern reeked with an overwhelming stench. Beyond the first shelf the smoky torchlight illuminated the scene. Oozy mud with filth carpeted the floor of the small cave, which was littered with all manner of unspeakable garbage. The odor of decomposing flesh mingled with the sickly smell of wild beasts. Aonghus blanched as he beheld the severed limbs, arms, legs, trunks of men, women and children which were strewn about. Into this was littered swords, jewels, garments and boots of every kind, forming the uncollected spoils of the harpies' booty.

Aonghus stepped back, his hand sweating on the handle of his sword, so tight did he hold it.

He turned back and found one of the crones hobbling toward the entrance where he stood, intent on fulfilling her sister's instruction to take care of the ghastly meal cooking on the pit outside.

A cold anger seized Aonghus. He waited until the crone was close to him and then stepped forward, swinging all his weight on his blade. The old woman made no sound as the blade hissed through the air, severing head from body. Maddened by what he had seen, Aonghus drove his sword twice through the headless body as it collapsed to the ground.

"What was that, sister?" he heard one of the others cry.

"What?" grumbled a voice. "I hear nothing."

"I thought I heard . . ."

The other interrupted with a sniff.

"There is nothing, I tell you."

The other was not satisfied.

"I will go and see while you attend to this."

She turned while her companion, with incredible strength, lifted the web-bound body of Cairell and threw him across her humped back as if he were but a baby.

Aonghus saw the old woman moving to the cave entrance. His heart beat rapidly. The hobbling woman saw the severed body of her sister and let out a curious, venomous hiss.

Aonghus stepped forward into the light, sword and shield ready.

She saw him immediately, her eyes wide in astonishment for a brief second before they narrowed and a look of ghastly malevolence clouded them.

She hissed again, her tongue long, red and serpent-like, darting between her thin lips. Her body started to shimmer.

For a second Aonghus paused, seeing the form of a sleek, snake-like being reforming where the old woman stood.

He moved swiftly, swinging his sword and slicing at it like a madman.

The hissing immediately turned into a shriek and before him lay the bloodied corpse of the second crone, all sign of a writhing serpent vanished.

Then he heard a cry of anguish across the cave. It was Cairell's voice.

Crouching low, Aonghus ran forward.

On the far side of the cave Cairell was lying, still wreathed in the silk of the web.

There was no sign of the third woman.

Aonghus dropped to his knees and began to hack away at the silky bonds, concentrating on freeing the area around Cairell's face.

"What manner of creatures are these?" he panted as he worked to free the charioteer's arms and legs.

"Creatures from the black depths of the Otherworld," gasped Cairell. "Have a care, for there is a third nearby. She heard her sister's dying and fled into the blackness."

"Well, there is only one left, and I can deal with her," grunted Aonghus. "Can you release the others?"

Cairell nodded.

There was a crackling sound, a soft hissing.

Cairell's eyes went wide as he stared beyond Aonghus's shoulder.

Aonghus wheeled around. He had already suffered too many shocks to be moved at the sight that met his eyes. A gigantic spider, nearly twice as big as himself, emerged into the gloom of the cavern. Large antennae waved from its terrible head and giant pincers snapped the air in front of the awesome creature. Aonghus felt its tiny, malignant eyes on him, saw its slobbering mouth and rows of tiny, sharp-pointed white teeth. Its body was a grotesque, glossy black sack that trembled as it swayed on tall, stalk-like legs.

With a clicking noise and an odd, sideways motion, the spider made a swift rush toward Aonghus.

Aonghus swung, ready to face it, sword and shield before him. His mouth was dry now but a strange, uncontrollable trembling was seizing his limbs. There was a fear chilling his veins that no self-reproach could quell.

"Aonghus!" cried Cairell. "It is only the crone."

Aonghus found himself unable to answer. His limbs were numb with fear.

He heard Cairell's voice, cracking with urgency behind him.

"It is an illusion that you see. The old crone can create illusions. They can shape change by causing you to see them as they want to be seen, not as they really are."

Still Aonghus was unable to drag his eyes from the ghastly spectacle of the spider. He heard Cairell's words but could not believe them.

"Look at the reflection on your shield!" cried the charioteer in desperation. "Look to your shield and you will see her as she is."

Aonghus blinked, forcing his eyes down to the bright silver polish of his shield. The cave's image reflected dully there. There was his own pale face and beyond . . . yes, beyond was not the spider but the hideous, misshapen form of the crone. He glanced up and immediately saw the threatening spider again. He dropped his gaze to his shield and, keeping the image in view, advanced, jabbing with his sword.

The crone tried to dodge, shrieked—and was transfixed by his sword thrust.

Aonghus turned his gaze from his shield. The spider was no more. The reality mirrored the image. The woman lay writhing on the ground, blood pouring from her heart. The gaze of malevolence that still shone from her eyes sent cold waves of terror into the Dési chieftain. The body started to shimmer and reform as a hooded snake which lunged forward. Some force thrust Aonghus aside as the snake stabbed its poisonous jaws at him and Cairell's sword cleaved its head. The illusion

shimmered back into reality again and the crone's head
went flying from her bloody body.

"Are you all right?" demanded Cairell, holding
Aonghus' arm.

Aonghus shook his head slowly.

"Never did I believe such things could exist in this
world."

"They exist only in the minds that want them to
exist," observed Cairell dryly. "Let's free the others."

He turned to where their companions and Aige were
trussed up and took some time cutting away the silky
spider webs which bound them. They were shaken
and white-faced. All were accounted for except for a
warrior called Slibire, a lanky, pleasant-mannered man.
No one talked of the terrible fate that had obviously
befallen him.

It took Aige some while before she could recover
from the shock of the experience, and she fell into a fit
of trembling from which only Cairell's attentiveness
calmed her.

When eventually she recovered in the fresh air, away
from the putrid smells and sights of the cave of the
crones, Aige was able to tell them that the passageway
through the mountains to Balor's valley, through which
she had travelled, lay half a mile away from the spot.

"The gods looked kindly upon you, Aige," Cairell
said feverently. "It is terrible to contemplate what fate
would have befallen you had your path crossed with
those witches."

The girl shivered and sought his hand.

"Then we would never have met," she said quietly.
"And you would never have been able to mourn me."

When they had rested a short while, Aige led the
Dési along the base of the towering mountains and
eventually halted outside a cave that was much smaller
than the broad entrance of the Cave of Crauchan Mór,
which the crones had inhabited. They paused only mo-

mentarily before Aonghus and Cairell led the way in,
followed by Aige. Perhaps it was nervousness, a fear of
encountering some other monstrous manifestation, but
they moved swiftly, swords held ready in their hands,
eyes flickering from side to side, ready for any threatening danger. Aige guided them through a maze of pas-
sages, some crossing through large caverns, worn out of
the bowels of the mountains by the movement of long-
forgotten rivers—rivers that had hewn winding corri-
dors through the granite. The Dési followed as Aonghus,
Cairell and Aige ascended steep inclines or moved down
gradual gradients, twisting and moving onwards until
they broke out into the late afternoon light in a large
valley, surrounded on all sides by towering peaks.

Aonghus and Cairell halted, eyes wide, while behind
them the Dési came spilling out of the cave, blinking
in the light.

"This is the land of Balor," whispered Aige as she
held out a slender arm to encompass the scene.

Chapter Sixteen

Before them lay a large and magnificent valley, surrounded by mountains on every side. Unlike the country outside, the valley was a scene of pastoral beauty—a green plain crossed by the winding blue ribbon of a river and dotted by a riot of bright colors where vegetation erupted into flower. Here and there were stretches of woodland and blossoming trees.

"Why, it is beautiful," breathed Aonghus.

"It is Balor's country," replied Aige, as if that explained everything.

She pointed across the valley floor to a spot where they could see the sun dazzling white on what appeared to be a group of buildings or a wall. "The Forbidden City of Balor."

Cairell heard the fear that underlined her voice and smiled reassurance at her.

"Where is the tower in which your lady Eithne is imprisoned?" asked Aonghus.

Aige raised a hand again to indicate a different direction.

In the distance they could see a structure rising skyward, sparkling and flashing with many lights.

"What is it?" breathed Cairell in amazement.

"Balor's Tower of Crystal, which he purposely built for the imprisonment of his daughter," replied the girl.

The tower seemed alight, dancing with innumerable flashes of color as the slanting rays of the dying sun played over it. It was as if the structure were on fire, a flame piercing the heavens.

"Let's get nearer to it," suggested Aonghus.

"It's best to get into the shelter of the woods," said Aige, landing them down from the base of the mountain toward a thickly wooded area.

Aonghus gazed around him with wide eyes. It seemed so strange that outside the tall ring of mountains the countryside was bare and desolate. Yet here, within the ring, the landscape presented such a luxuriant picture of pastoral paradise that he could be in Bregia itself.

It was not long before they reached the edge of the forest, scarcely a hundred yards or so from the cluster of small buildings that surrounded the tall tower whose walls were of milky opaqueness. Now that the sun had lowered itself over the mountains and the sharp clear light of pre-twilight had settled in the valley, the tower no longer danced with fire. It was but a momentary stillness before the swift onset of night.

The tower was one of the tallest structures Aonghus had ever seen, rising some six stories into the air. It was about twenty-five feet in diameter and built of highly polished crystal blocks. The workmanship was incredible.

Crouching in the shelter of the leafy foliage, Aige

drew his attention to the half dozen crudely constructed buildings of stone that clustered at the base of the tower.

"In those the guards and servants live," she whispered. "Only they and my lady's personal servants have access to the tower."

"And where dwells this lady Eithne of yours?" asked Aonghus.

"Her apartments occupy the top two floors of the tower. Below that is . . . was my room."

"And who dwells in the other stories?"

"Those are storerooms."

Aonghus examined the tower carefully. There was but one door—a massive, iron-studded affair. Before it stood two tall warriors. They were slim of build, even though their black cloaks enveloped most of their figures, hanging from shoulders to ankles. Each held a heavy war shield and carried a slim lance. It was only by glancing closely at them that Aonghus realized they were women, for their heads were covered in their war helmets and their visors were pulled closely down across their faces.

Aige saw his close examination.

"I told you—Balor has ordered that no man may be set near his daughter for fear of the prophecy. There are twelve women warriors who guard her, each one a champion trained in battle. No male warrior has ever bested them."

"And what of the servants?" asked Aonghus. "How many are there?"

"Five others, consisting of maids and a cook."

Cairell was staring at the top of the tower. It rose at least sixty or seventy feet in the air. He could see nothing but the reflection of the dying light against the glass of the upper windows.

"It would be impossible to scale those walls," he murmured.

"Then we will have to enter through the door," replied Aonghus with a grin.

Each-Tiarna, behind them, said: "There are fifteen of us to those twelve females. It's odds in our favor."

Aige gave him a pitying glance.

"Did I not tell you that these are no ordinary women?"

"The girl is right," Aonghus said. "The tower is impregnable, for by the time we fight the guards, even if we overcome them, the entire army of Balor will have heard the commotion and be upon us. No, we must attempt our rescue by cunning, not brute strength."

Abruptly, the door of one of the buildings swung open and two women came out, chattering softly together, and began to walk along the path that led toward the distant, white-walled city of Balor.

"Two maids," explained Aige, when Aonghus glanced at her. "They work in the kitchen."

"Why are they leaving?"

"All except my lady Eithne's personal maid have free access to the city. They work only for set periods and are free to come and go. Only I . . . as personal maid . . . was kept imprisoned with my lady."

"Are the maids replaced?"

"Yes."

"When?"

The girl pointed after the two women.

"See for yourself."

Aonghus saw two other women walking toward the tower. They halted when they came abreast of the two maids heading for the city and their voices rose in an exchange of gossip. An idea began to form rapidly in Aonghus' mind.

"Come, we must take them prisoner."

He moved quickly in the shelter of the forest, keeping parallel to the path. The two maids were already proceeding on their way while their two replacements

had paused to bid them farewell before continuing on
to the tower. It was over in a minute. Aonghus and
Cairell were upon the hapless women before they were
aware of danger. Their cries were stifled and they were
bound and trussed in an instant, and carried into the
shelter of the wood.

"You need have no fear," Aonghus told them in a low
voice, as their eyes bulged in terror above their gags.
"We will detain you only for a short while."

Aige was frowning in bewilderment.

"But these maids have no access to the tower," she
protested.

Aonghus had removed the women's cloaks and shawls
and handed one set to Cairell.

"You'll make an attractive maid, Cairell Mac Fios,"
he grinned, wrapping the shawl around his head.

Aige shook her head in disbelief.

"This will avail you nothing. Not even with the gloom
of fallen dusk will anyone be taken in by such a disguise."

"All we need is the element of surprise," Aonghus
smiled.

Turning to the others he said: "Cairell and I will
go to the kitchens. From there we will see if there is
any way of getting to the tower itself. Be ready for
anything."

Each-Tiarna nodded morosely.

"A frontal attack is best," he muttered.

"Do not precipitate anything," warned Aonghus.

Aige caught his arm.

"Shall I come too?"

"We shall need you," Aonghus agreed.

The three of them, walking in the gloom of dusk,
moved onto the pathway toward the tower. Aige walked
with Cairell while Aonghus shuffled behind. The sen-
tries by the tower stared indifferently. There was no
challenge. They went straight toward the kitchen build-

ings. The door was ajar and beyond, Aonghus caught sight of a broad-boned woman bending over a cauldron that simmered on a fire.

Aonghus pushed the door open and moved quietly in.

The draft from the door caused the woman to glance up. Her eyes widened and her mouth opened to scream a warning. Without compunction, Aonghus struck the woman cleanly on the jaw and she sank to the floor without a sound.

Cairell and Aige stepped in quickly behind him and closed the door.

"What now?" demanded the charioteer.

Aonghus was gazing at the simmering stew.

"It must be near to the time of the evening meal," he said thoughtfully.

Aige shrugged.

"That should be obvious."

"Do all the guards eat together?"

"All except those guarding the doors of the tower."

A look of hope crossed Aonghus' face.

"But all except those will eat of this meal?" He gestured to the cauldron.

"Yes."

Aonghus smiled wickedly at Cairell.

"You know enough druid tricks to ensure their meal will be interesting?"

Cairell did not understand.

"The druids mix herbs to induce sleep. I have seen it done. Buckthorn and Mandrake and Mountain Flax," amplified Aonghus.

Cairell stared at him: "You wish me to mix such a potion as to send the guards to sleep?"

"And quickly."

"I am no druid," protested Cairell.

"But you can do it," Aonghus pressed.

Cairell went to the shelves on which the herbs were kept and glanced along the rows of bottles. Then he found a mortar and pestle and began taking down jars while the others watched in silence. Mistletoe, poppy, henbane, bugleweed and several others were pounded into a paste and introduced into the simmering cauldron.

"If I have the recipe correct," he said, almost to himself, "then one spoonful should induce a deep sleep."

"Pray to the Dagda that you have it correct," Aonghus said anxiously.

A voice suddenly called from without: "Where is the food, Arnica? Must we all starve?"

Aonghus glanced around.

"Pull your shawl over your head, Aige, and carry this cauldron to them."

"What if they recognize me?" protested the girl.

"It is a chance we must take, for they will certainly see through our disguises."

Without another word, Aige did as he had bidden her. Covering her head with the shawl, she picked up the cauldron and carried it carefully before her.

The feasting room of the warriors and the rest of those detailed to look after the crystal tower prison was situated next to the kitchen. Most of the warriors and maids were already seated, tearing impatiently at the bread while awaiting the succulent stew. They did not even glance at Aige. As soon as she had set the cauldron in the center of the table they scrambled to grab the ladle in order to be first to fill their bowls.

Aige was turning back to the door when one of the warriors suddenly glanced at her.

"Where is Arnica?"

Aonghus and Cairell, waiting outside, heard the girl's voice falter.

"She is preparing another dish."

"I have seen you somewhere before . . ." The female warrior's voice became suspicious.

"I often work in the kitchen," came Aige's reply.

"No. You are no kitchen maid. You . . ." The voice paused. "Strange . . . I feel . . ."

They heard a thump.

"What is it?" cried another woman's voice. There was the sound of scraping chairs, a bang, and then Aige came hurrying through the door. She was trembling.

"It worked!" she hissed. "They have all fallen asleep."

Cairell grinned. "Let my father's shade be praised!"

"Not before time," muttered Aonghus dryly, as he pushed into the feasting chamber to ensure all were asleep. He counted the stretched-out forms.

"There were nine warriors here and two maids, plus the cook and the two women we took captive. That means there are three warriors, by Aige's reckoning, who are unaccounted for."

Aige nodded. "Two stand at the door of the tower and hold the keys. The third guards the inner door."

"Then those we will have to subdue by force," Aonghus said reluctantly. "But as silently as possible."

They left the sleeping guards and moved quietly to the edge of the buildings, within sight of the two guards outside the tower door. The female warriors stood still, statue-like, lances and shields in hand.

Aonghus pointed to Cairell's sling.

The young charioteer took it out and inserted a shot, whirling it with a soft hissing sound around his head. Even as the first missile fled the sling he had inserted a second and sent it speeding after it. The first slingshot hit the head of the nearest warrior with a sharp crack and she went down without a sound. The second stone arrived a fraction later but too late to catch the next warrior, who had jumped forward before her companion had reached the ground.

"Guards! An attack! An attack!" Her powerful voice

would have been enough to wake the dead. She swung around, her lance ready.

Aonghus was already moving forward. As he emerged from the darkness, shaking free of the woman's cloak, the female warrior's arm went back. The lance flew with dead accuracy toward him. Had he no warrior training he would have been a dead man. Instead, he flung himself to one side, bringing up his shield, which deflected the weapon's deadly path. Then he closed in with his sword. The Fomorii woman already had her own weapon out. Unlike the warrior he had encountered earlier that afternoon, the woman was an expert sword fighter. The flickering blades circled wickedly. Sparks flashed as metal spoke against metal. Back and forth the two circled, until the woman grunted and fell at Aonghus' feet.

Cairell replaced his slingshot.

"We cannot afford to waste time heeding the code of single combat now," he grunted.

Aonghus hesitated, glancing down at his fallen foe. It was not according to the warrior's code, but Cairell was right. There could be no code of honor or quarter given.

Aige was already bending over the first warrior and extracting a bunch of keys from her belt. She inserted one into the great, iron-studded door of the tower. It turned and she threw her weight against it. It creaked slowly open.

She would have gone directly in had not Cairell grabbed her back.

A split second later a javelin embedded itself into the door jamb.

The third female warrior was scrambling up the stairwell inside to turn and stand ready at the head of the stairs.

Aonghus moved forward, watching her with grudging approval.

One person could hold back an army on the stairway. The warrior had divested herself of her cloak. She stood clad in body armor and a short kirtle, her muscular limbs well balanced to meet the attack.

"We cannot afford to waste time," cried Cairell. "Let me finish her off with my sling."

The female Fomorii jeered at them.

"So you have no honor code, but are simply thieves in the night!"

The jibe aroused Aonghus' anger.

"I have an honor code, Fomorii," he replied between his teeth as he moved quickly up the stairs to meet her challenge.

She crouched with sword at the ready to meet him.

Just as he reached her she suddenly stumbled backwards and Aonghus heard the sharp report of stone on metal. For a second the warrior looked surprised and then collapsed on the floor.

Behind Aonghus, Cairell came swiftly up the stairs, calmly replacing his sling.

"Didn't I say that there was no time for playing the hero?" the charioteer snapped. "Let's find this lady Eithne and leave before all of Balor's warriors are unleashed upon us."

Aonghus started to protest. It was not right for the warrior to have been slain by a slingshot from Cairell after he had accepted her challenge to single combat. It was against the honor code that had been instilled in him during his warrior's training. He felt guilt at this deed. But Cairell was practical. And right. There was no time for heroics.

Aige was already at the next door and using the keys.

They moved rapidly up the inner flights of steps to the third floor. The doors were locked here, and Aige soon had them undone.

"This was my prison for two years," she explained, bitterness in her voice as she led them through a series of rooms to another flight of stairs, which ended at another iron-studded door.

She bent, fumbling with the key, but it would not turn.

Cairell gently thrust her aside and tried. His more powerful grip turned the key immediately and he pushed the door open.

Inside were richly furnished apartments—apartments fitting for the High King's own daughter. But what caught their immediate attention was the slim figure standing in the center of the room. One hand raised to her mouth, eyes wide with fear, stood a young girl.

Chapter Seventeen

Aonghus stood still, mouth slightly open, staring at the pale-faced girl. Her hair was dark—not the black of Aige's frizzy curls, but the glorious color of jet, sheened with blue—a tumble of curls that spilled to her shapely shoulders. Her skin was the color of cream, pale from lack of contact with the sun, which Aonghus realized was the result of her lifetime of confinement. She had a broad forehead, high cheekbones and gently chiselled features, with a delicately shaped nose and a well-shaped mouth. Her mouth was attractive; the lips seemed made for laughter. Her figure was small and well proportioned, the waist slender. In Aonghus' eyes the girl was beautiful.

Aonghus shook himself from his contemplation as he realized that her eyes beheld him in fear.

"I mean you no harm," he mumbled, somewhat incoherent in her presence.

Aige was pushing by him.

"Lady, I have returned with these warriors to rescue you."

The girl's face changed to astonishment and then joy as she beheld Aige. The girls clasped each other in a warm embrace.

"Is it true? Can it be true?" she gasped.

Aige, laughing happily, turned to Aonghus and Cairell.

"Lady, these are warriors of Éireann. This is Aonghus Mac Orba of Hy-Nia and his charioteer, Cairell."

The girl disengaged herself from Aige and stepped toward them, smiling and holding out a hand to each.

"I am Eithne, daughter of Balor. I bid you welcomes, sirs, to my poor prison. You must forgive my anxiety. I have not beheld men so close before, saving my father, Balor."

Aonghus and Cairell bowed over the girl's hands.

"Eithne, there is little time for formalities. We must proceed at once, for Balor's guards will soon be alarmed," Aonghus said gruffly.

Aige nodded eagerly.

"Come, lady, they have ships waiting. Better fly from this land, or die of unhappiness or worse."

Eithne hesitated, glancing around her.

"These rooms are all I know of the world. It is hard . . ." Then she bit her lip and squared her shoulders. "Is there aught I should bring with me?"

Aige was already gathering a few articles of toiletry, throwing them into a bundle.

"We must travel light, lady. Is that not so?"

She threw an appeal to Aonghus and Cairell.

"They who travel lightest travel fastest," said Cairell solemnly.

"Then I am ready," replied Eithne.

Aonghus led the way down the stairs, over the bodies of the warrior women. Outside the tower Each-Tiarna was waiting impatiently with the rest of the Dési.

"I think the alarm has been raised," he greeted

Aonghus. "A moment ago I heard a shrill trumpet sounding from the city."

"Then we must move swiftly," cried Aonghus.

He took Eithne by the arm and led her off through the forest with Cairell and Aige behind, and Each-Tiarna with the rest of the Dési bringing up the rear. They moved at a rapid pace through he woods toward the dark, shadowy mountains.

"I am sorry we must hasten," muttered Aonghus to the girl. "If your father's warriors overtake us . . ." He left the sentence unfinished.

She smiled trustingly up at him.

"I understand. Anything is better than the years of confinement I have endured, even if it is only a brief few moments under the stars, hastening through this marvelously fragrant forest." After a few moments of silence she asked: "Where are we going?"

"Back to our ships."

"But then where? To Éireann, your country?"

Aonghus shook his head.

"Alas, we are not bound for Éireann, lady."

"Why not?"

He frowned a little at her disconcerting way of asking questions. Briefly, he told her the story of the struggle against Cormac Mac Art.

"So the Dési are doomed to wander the world in search of a new home?" she asked at the end of his short tale.

"We believe that we may find sanctuary in the land of Alba, across the northern sea. That is where we were bound when we were blown off our course and landed here."

"Will your chieftain allow Aige and myself to join you in your wanderings? In truth, I do not know the world outside the walls of my prison. Even this forest is something I have not experienced before."

Aonghus felt an inexplicable joy.

"I am sure my chieftain will welcome you and Aige as Dési born and you will find Aonghus of Hy-Nia yours to command forever."

He tried to make the statement lightly but it came out with such a serious tone that Eithne glanced at him oddly, her brows drawn together. Aonghus colored and was thankful that the gloom hid the blush on his cheeks.

Each-Tiarna called from behind: "I hear riders, Aonghus."

They were not far from the walls of the cliffs.

"How far to the cave entrance, Aige?" Aonghus called over his shoulder.

"Not far," replied the girl.

Aonghus stared into the darkness but could see nothing. He knew that Each-Tiarna, with his great knowledge of horses, had better eyes and ears to spot riders from afar.

"How many riders, Each-Tiarna, and how far off are they?"

Each-Tiarna halted and bent to the ground.

"Two fifties of horsemen. Not far off," he replied, catching up with the still hurriedly moving column of Dési.

They did not pause and soon came to the shadow of the mountain walls, rising cliff-like above them. Aige moved forward to lead the way.

"Here is the entrance!" she called after a moment or two.

There came a cry behind them. An arrow hissed out of the darkness and broke against a boulder nearby.

"Inside!" yelled Aonghus, turning his shield forward. "Inside the cave, quickly."

Cairell seized both Eithne and Aige and pushed them into the darkness. Each-Tiarna stood with Aonghus until all the Dési had passed inside. In the gloom of the forest they could see shadows moving, and more arrows hissed their way unseen through the air to break against the rocks around them. One actually struck Aonghus' shield. Then, with everyone inside, Each-Tiarna and Aonghus turned into the cave. The party was hastening up the passageway with Aige leading. Cairell had already fashioned a torch, lighting the way forward. It soon became obvious that Balor's warriors were following closely, leaving their horses behind them. They could hear the sound of their feet, and now and again someone gave a hoarse cry of command.

The rapid movement through the stone passageways seemed endless. Time seemed to have no meaning. When Aige gave a cry that the exit was in sight, they felt that they had been travelling for weeks rather than hours. Soon they were able to see for themselves the faint, predawn light ahead.

The Fomorii had been unable to catch up with the Dési, although they could still be heard following close behind. Yet the sight of the exit gave the Dési and their charges a fresh burst of energy. Most of them had been ready to throw themselves to the ground in exhaustion, but the nearness of the end of their journey renewed their vigor and they increased their pace.

Cairell reached the exit first and stood, motioning the others out, while surveying the surrounding rocks. Then, with a cry to Each-Tiarna to help him, he started to scramble up a rough incline to the side of the cave entrance.

"What are you doing?" yelled Aonghus, as he came through the exit and caught sight of Cairell in the half light.

"The Fomorii will overtake us easily in the open. We must try to stop them," replied Cairell, not pausing in his upward scramble, Each-Tiarna at his heels. "You go on. Get to the ships before Eochaidh gives the orders to sail."

Aonghus hesitated and then, without a further word,

took Eithne and a protesting Aige by the arm and
hurried them forward.

Cairell and Each-Tiarna had reached the ledge that
Cairell had spotted about thirty feet above the cave
mouth. Gasping, the young charioteer pointed to a
boulder that stood on the ledge. There was no need for
him to explain what he wanted done. Together the two
of them placed their backs against the rocky wall, their
feet on the boulder, and began to push. The veins stood
out on their necks, and their faces went red with the
effort.

Below, within the cave, they could hear the hoarse
shouts as the Fomorii caught sight of the entrance.

They pushed again. The boulder slowly began to
move, and then toppled. It bounced away down the
rock face, its weight gathering small boulders and rocks
until a veritable landslide hit the entrance.

They heard a scream. At least one Fomorii was buried under the falling debris.

Hanging onto the ledge, Cairell and Each-Tiarna fought
to recover their breath.

The din of falling rocks ceased.

Slowly they stood up and peered down into the rising
dust. They could see nothing. Cairell signalled Each-
Tiarna to follow him downwards. Soon they could see
that the boulder had created a landslide which had
covered the entrance of the cave; covered it enough to
cause the Fomorii several hours of digging to get out.

Cairell was grinning in triumph when Each-Tiarna
cried a warning.

He had time to duck the first blow aimed at him by a
bloodstained Fomorii warrior. The man held a sword in
his hand and was raising it again. He knew he would
have no time to draw his own weapon before the blow
fell. It was Each-Tiarna who threw the dagger that
embedded itself in the Fomorii's chest. The man collapsed across the rubble without a sound.

They spared but a moment more to inspect their handiwork before hastening after their companions. Already they could hear cries and the smash of metal on rock as the entombed Fomorii began to work at the debris.

A short while afterwards, Cairell and Each-Tiarna stood above the small cove where the three Dési ships still rode at anchor. Below them, on the sandy beach, Aonghus was loading his party into the boats.

Cairell cupped his hands together and shouted.

He saw the tiny figures below look up, and he waved.

There rose an answering shout and they started down toward the cove.

Aige was waiting for Cairell, her face animated.

"Are you safe, lord?" she demanded, her anxious eyes searching him for wounds.

Cairell shifted his weight in embarrassment.

"Safe enough," he replied gruffly. "But, Aige, please do not call me 'lord.' It is a word that has no currency among the men of Éireann. The saying goes that we are all the sons of kings, for no man is higher than another— not even our chieftains and High Kings. It is the people who ordain a king, not the king who ordains the people."

The girl smiled.

"I will obey your customs, Cairell. But if I call you 'lord' it serves only to express my respect for you."

"Then call me by name," grunted the charioteer, face burning.

"That I will do and gladly," replied the girl solemnly.

Aonghus went straight to Eochaidh's ship, the *Cúr*, while Cairell conducted Aige and Eithne to their own *Spioróg*.

Eochaidh and Iolar, the druid, greeted him with pleasure.

"We were getting worried," Eochaidh said. "Did you lose any men?"

"Yes," Aonghus said heavily. "One—Slibire. But we must hurry, for the Fomorii are on our heels."

Eochaidh nodded. "Iolar has supervised the supply of water. We shall make straight for Alba."

Within half an hour the Dési ships were straining toward the entrance of the cove, sails cracking in the wind.

On the *Spioróg*, Aige and Eithne stood, gazing in wonder.

"It is hard to take in so much," whispered Eithne to Aonghus. "I have heard of the great ships that ride the waters, but to actually be in one . . . to see the vast expanse of the sea . . . it is hard to believe when one has spent a lifetime imprisoned."

Smiling, Aonghus conducted the two girls to a more sheltered spot toward the stern of the *Spioróg*, while Maraí, grinning, ordered his crew to trim the sails in order to get the maximum speed out of the dipping vessel as he hauled down after the *Cúr* and *Méirliún*. Soon the three ships were racing for the open sea with the dark humped island of the Land of Towers receding behind them.

"Well," Aonghus remarked to Cairell as they stood watching the dark hump vanishing on the horizon, "I am not sorry to forgo further acquaintance with Balor and his Fomorii."

"But equally glad that we landed on that shore," grinned Cairell.

For a moment Aonghus blushed, and then he said: "Well, at least you have found an admirer . . . *lord*!"

Cairell glanced in mock anger.

"I . . ."

"Sail! A sail!" The harsh cry of the lookout caused them to peer upward. The man was pointing astern of them.

Immediately all eyes strained from those on deck. It was some moments before the tip of a sail could be seen from the lower elevation of the deck as well as from the masthead. Then the lookout was calling: "Four, five . . . six sails coming from the southwest!"

"Fomorii?" asked Cairell.

"From the wrong direction," rejoined Aonghus, running up the rigging and shading his eyes to gaze across the waves.

"The ships of Cormac Mac Art," he cried, amazed.

Lookouts on the other Dési ships had given a similar recognition. Signals were being exchanged between Eochaidh and his captains.

Maraí looked worried. He was no longer boastful about *Spioróg's* speed.

"I think they will overtake us, Aonghus. I recognize the big ship standing out in front. It is the High King's own vessel, the *Díoltas*—a fitting name in the circumstances."

Díoltas meant vengeance, but the joke did not amuse Aonghus. He had heard of the ship before. It was said that it could spread more canvas than any three ships of Éireann put together.

Aonghus bit his lip. He had underestimated Cormac Mac Art. That his navigators had been able to chase the Dési ships through the thick sea mists to the shores of the Land of Towers was a truly astonishing feat.

"Eochaidh is signalling!" cried Cairell.

Maraí squinted at the *Cúr* and then sniffed disgustedly.

"He only demands that we put on more canvas and run before the wind. We won't be able to escape the High King's fleet in this fashion."

Cairell had suddenly stiffened, his hands showing white at the knuckles where he grasped the railing.

"Don't you feel it?" he whispered.

The girl Aige, constantly at his side, glanced at him with a worried frown.

"Feel what, Cairell?"

"The chill . . . the evil . . . by the wings of the Mórrígan! Look!"

He thrust his hand toward the pursuing vessels.

Where the ships had been ploughing through the waters, silhouettes of large, gruesome monsters with swanlike necks and ugly, flat heads were swimming after them.

There was consternation among the Dési.

Eithne gave a scream, catching at Aige's arm.

"Do such beasts exist in the seas?" she gasped.

"What manner of witchcraft is this, Cairell?" Aonghus said. "How did the ships of Cormac turn into such beasts?"

Cairell shook his head.

"Witchcraft is right, Aonghus. Didn't I tell you once before that Indech was a great magician. It is his thoughts we are seeing, not the reality."

"Those beasts are real enough," snapped Maraí from the tiller. "I can see them and so can we all. Can you not smell their fearsome odors, borne on the breath of the sea winds?"

Aonghus nodded.

"They are like the monsters that attacked us in the mist," he said.

Cairell shook his head.

"Don't you see that if you deny that you see those beasts, then you will not see them?" he said. His voice held a tone of desperation.

"I can only see what I see, Cairell," said Aonghus.

"On the island of the Fomorii, you saw three beautiful women. They were three crones who could change into serpents and spiders. You accepted that."

Aonghus took the point, but he could not apply it.

"Can't Iolar work some magic to change the monsters back to ships?"

Cairell heaved a sigh.

"The change must come within you," he urged.

"The druid will protect us," muttered Aonghus uneasily.

Cairell turned toward the *Cúr* and bent his brow in concentration.

Aige went forward toward him, but Aonghus reached out and drew him back.

"I have seen him do this before," he whispered to the girl. "The druids have a way—telepathy, they call it—of communicating with each other over distances. He is trying to contact Iolar, our druid, on the *Cúr*."

Aige's eyes grew round.

"Is Cairell a druid?"

"The son of a druid, but he has some of the druid's arts."

Cairell startled them by suddenly letting forth a scream. This time Aige ran to his side and grabbed his hands. The young charioteer's face was sweating. His eyes were wild. For a moment he did not see them.

"Cairell, what is it?" demanded Aonghus.

"Iolar! He is dead!"

Aonghus frowned. "How can you be sure?"

"I was in contact with him. He was trying to fight Indech, but Indech's mind is powerful. Iolar was old and tired. He had not the strength. Indech has slain him."

Aonghus gazed at his companion in disbelief.

"Don't you see?" cried Cairell in alarm. "We have no druid to protect us now."

He began to hasten uncertainly across the deck, as if unsure of his surroundings. They watched him go in bewilderment. It was too much to accept for those unused to the ways of the druidic brotherhood.

Cairell's mind, however, was racing. He knew that Indech's evil mind was probing forward. He had met the mind of Iolar, but Iolar had not been strong enough to combat him. Soon Indech's probing thoughts would seek out Aonghus and destroy him too. Then all the Dési would perish.

He was halfway across the deck when he realized
what he must do. Only he among the Dési knew the
forbidden knowledge, even though he was not of the
brotherhood. He turned and swung himself swiftly up
the rigging of the *Spioróg* to the center masthead and
squatted down on the tiny lookout's platform.

He turned his head, eyes closed, toward the oncoming black shapes.

Cross-legged he began to breathe deeply.

"The truth against the world. The truth against the
world."

Slowly he began to intone the chant so beloved of the
druids. Slowly, closing his mind to all else, to everything else, he repeated the words over and over again.

He felt the chill of evil, of the projection of alien
thoughts, but he kept his inward chanting until they
receded.

Then he heard the soft, coaxing voice of someone—of
Aige, he thought. It was strange that she had climbed
into the crow's nest with him. She was telling him not
to mind the beasts. She would look after him. There
was nothing to fear. He smiled. No, nothing to fear.
Then, for a moment, he felt the return of the chill
atmosphere and knew that he was being tempted. He
returned to his feverish chanting and Aige was gone.

A familiar voice echoed within him. It seemed as if
his father, Fios, was there, congratulating him, re-
minding him of the incantation to the Storm Lord:

I am the wind which blows across the sea.
I am a wave of the ocean.
I am the white foam of the breaking seas.
I am the bubbles on the surface.
I am the strength of countless millions.
I am the storm clouds hurrying thus and thus.
I am the dangerous lightning.
I am the angry tempest, the roar of thunder.

And I hold destruction in my grasp.
Beware all who are false for I am. I AM!

He found himself chanting the ancient words that
Amairgen, the first druid and chief of all the ancient
druids of Éireann, uttered to conjure a storm with
which to destroy the enemies of the children of Éireann—
a storm that not even the gods could prevent. Cairell
found himself caught in the excitement of the wild
chant. His whole body vibrated with power, chanting,
chanting, chanting, until he began to realize that the
elements themselves were joining in to the roaring of
his voice. Great flashes of lightning were bursting low
across the sea, followed by the angry din of thunder.
The sea itself was stirring restlessly and giant waves
were beginning to curl and roar around the ships of the
Dési.

For a moment Cairell felt awe. He had found the
power and conjured it to his aid. But would that very
power destroy him?

Beware all who are false for I am. I AM!

Chapter Eighteen

The storm whipped the seas, tossing them into high mountains and deep valleys. Cairell clung to the mast-head, appalled by the power he had unleashed. Below him he heard the cries of his companions and began to struggle down the rigging with the wind beating at him and tearing at his clothes. Aonghus clutched at the rail, watching him in awe.

"Get everyone below and secure yourselves," yelled the charioteer to him and then, turning to Maraí: "Trust me with the tiller of your ship until this storm has passed."

Maraí shook his head.

"I'll trust no man with my ship," he replied. Then, with less obstinacy: "But I'll share the tiller with you."

Cairell did not argue, and when Aige, pale-faced, reached for his hand, he pressed her back, saying roughly: "Get below with the others."

He took a stand by Maraí with the tiller between them.

A great black wall of cloud that seemed to cover the eastern sky was moving rapidly toward the *Spioróg*. It was an intense blackness, solid and threatening like a line of cliffs standing out of the sea, rather than a mass of vapor blown forward at the command of the winds.

"What new devilment is this, Cairell?" grunted Maraí.

"The storm will prove our friend, Maraí," replied the young man, gazing at the blackness. It was strange how calm he felt now, how elated. He, who had never sailed the seas in his life, was able to calm a sailor-born, for he had found the power. Twenty long years did a postulent have to study the ancient craft before he could be admitted to the druidic order, and yet he, Cairell, had been able to conjure the elements as his friends.

Around them the sea was bubbling, hurling up strange mounds of foam that spread in circles, with the *Spioróg* in the center. The ship began to roll heavily, and with each roll, water sprayed across the deck. Even the howling wind did not dull the creaks and groans from the timbers of the vessel, and the uneasy chorus from the masts, sails and gears were like a thousand groaning souls in pain. The sea was leaping up beneath them in a great hammock of water.

"May Manannán Mac Lir, god of the oceans, protect us!" cried Maraí. "Hold on for your life!"

Between them they gripped the tiller firmly while before them the seas seemed to be torn apart with clouds of monstrous spray, swamping the bows of the vessels as Maraí tried to turn her head into the storm. The *Spioróg* heeled over at a terrible angle. For a moment, Cairell almost lost courage and thought the ship was going to keel over entirely.

"Steady, the tiller!" yelled Maraí.

Landbound as Cairell had been all his life, he realized that in spite of the aid of the elements, with the seas rising to such formidable heights, a mistake with the tiller would result in the ship being hurled broad-

side into the seas with capsizing an inevitable consequence. The pressure of the wind had grown painful
and exhausting, and it was all they could do to keep
their balance.

Everything was in darkness now, the gloom alleviated only by the flash of lightning, accompanied by the
dull crack of thunder.

To be able to breathe they had to turn away from the
face of the wind, so powerful it was. Everywhere around
came the incessant howling of the storm. They were
conscious that time was passing, but the pounding noise
and the constant whip of the sea spray caused a vague
lethargy to descend. The foam was licking at the ship,
making a shrill, hissing sound as the sea boiled and
burst in thunderous motion. Again and again the great
tongues of water lashed at the vessel, seeming, at one
point, to rise on every side.

Finally, as if by some miracle, the skies began to
lighten.

The seas started to subside, the wind to die away
and, as if the hand of Manannán Mac Lir, the great
ocean god himself, had passed across the broad stretch
of water, all was eventually quiet. The seas were still,
but on every side appeared the tumbled, interminable
chaos that marked the passing of the storm. Not far
away, like wrecks more than rigged vessels, the *Cúr*
and *Méirliún* stood amazingly together. There was no
sign of any other ship on the horizon.

Aonghus and the others emerged on deck, gazing
about them in cautious bewilderment. At once he began to ply Cairell with questions, but the young charioteer could not answer him. "Call it druidic magic, if you
like," was all he would say.

After a while—after they had cleaned up the wreckage caused by the storm, a sea breeze rose, as evening
was fading into night. The three Dési ships turned their
bows to the northeast, catching the breeze at their

backs. Everyone was subdued after witnessing the power of the ocean. Their spirits were not lightened when they heard confirmation that Iolar, Eochaidh Allmuir's druid, had died before the storm, even as Cairell had said. Eochaidh ascribed the death to age and exhaustion. Only Cairell knew the real reason for the druid's death, as Aonghus could not accept Cairell's explanation. He refused to believe the power of Indech.

That same evening, in the dark of night, as Aonghus stood leaning on the stern rail, he found Eithne at his side.

"I have no knowledge of the sea," she said reflectively. "Should I have felt fear during the storm?"

Aonghus smiled at her.

"Fear is a great killer," he said. "But I felt enough fear for all of us."

She turned her face in surprise.

"Fear? But you are a man."

"You will learn, Eithne, that men are always frightened, if they but admit it. Most of them don't admit it, even to themselves, and those who don't admit it are worse than cowards."

Eithne turned her gaze to the dark night sky and the silver points twinkling down. She changed the subject.

"It is truly a miracle that I stand here, hearing the soft whisper of the sea and watching the great canopy above, unhindered and free. The world is truly wonderful."

Smiling at the girl, Aonghus could not explain the curious sensation he felt in his chest and throat as the moon flitted from behind a cloud and dappled her perfect features. For the moment he was content to stand happy at the girl's nearness and friendship.

The sun was standing at its zenith when the lookout shouted.

"Land! Land dead ahead!"

Through the haze of heat a line appeared barely

visible between the sky and the sea. It was not long before the soft breeze had brought the Dési ships close in toward the shore. They could see no natural harbors yet, only a line of rocks, grey and threatening. The tides had caught the ships and Maraí, a worried frown on his face, shouted orders to the crew to adjust the sails while he bent his strength to the tiller.

His seamen were experienced, using the combinations of wind and swell and the leeway of the tide and backwash to guide the ship through the rocks and ragged surf. They could see reefs not far below the surface, but the Dési built their ships shallow-bottomed and there was no danger. Fronds of seaweed swirled around, floating on the surface of the waters. They clung tenaciously to the occasional rock that thrust above the surface, while here and there seals slid into the protection of the waves as they approached. One or two, bolder than the rest, returned the stares of the people on the vessels with an almost human curiosity.

The breeze cracked the sails as the ships surged forward over the dark lines of kelp, charging across the reefs. Then they were in safer waters, amid calm, flat seas that were protected by the reefs. The three ships turned along the coastline and eventually an inlet was spotted that gave access to a natural harbor. From the rocks, which provided a ready jetty, ran a broad stretch of white sand behind which green and purple mountains rose majestically.

Maraí smiled with satisfaction: "This must be Alba of the high hills."

Eochaidh Allmuir had signalled his chieftains to meet him on the shore and Aonghus and Cairell disembarked in the lazy afternoon sun. Razorbills, guillemots and the inevitable herring gull cried out their cacophonous welcome, but there seemed no other signs of life as the Dési chieftains gathered on the shore.

Eochaidh Allmuir was looking old and tired, more

strained than he had ever looked during the days of the battle against Cormac Mac Art. The loss of Iolar had hit him hard.

"Mairnéalach, the captain of the *Cúr*, tells me that we have landed on the seaboard of the Gael on the western shore of Alba," Eochaidh told them. "My plan is to make contact with whoever is chieftain of this land so that we may ask for sanctuary here." He glanced anxiously toward Aonghus and Cairell and added: "Did anyone see what befell the ships of Cormac?"

It was Biobal who answered.

"Perhaps they perished in the storm?"

"Let us hope so," interposed Each-Tiarna, scowling.

No one seemed willing to mention the transformation of the ships into sea serpents, yet all had witnessed it. Everyone was beginning to doubt their vision. Cairell kept silent. If Aonghus rejected his explanation, there was little hope the others would accept it.

"Well, even if Cormac did survive, he will not be able to find us now," Biobal said brightly. "It was a stroke of luck that he was able to follow us to the Land of Towers. Bádóir, the captain of the *Méirliún*, said so. Such luck cannot hold twice. I think we are rid of Cormac Mac Art."

"We can only hope so," Eochaidh sighed. "Peace is what I crave above all things. To see my people decimated, to see a once-great clan dwindle to nothing, grieves me sorely."

Biobal was squinting at the afternoon sun.

"Little we can do today, Eochaidh," he said. "We ought to encamp here tonight and go inland tomorrow in search of habitation."

"Is it safe to camp on the shore?" Aonghus questioned. "Better to rest on our ships tonight until we are sure of a safe welcome."

Eochaidh hesitated but Biobal chuckled. "If this land was inhabited, we would have people flocking to this shore to demand our business. The place is surely deserted . . ."

"Deserted?" Cairell gestured across the sands. "Then that is an apparition."

They turned in the direction he pointed. Farther along the sandy shore, where a gently sloping path moved up toward the top of the dunes and hillocks beyond, they could see a chariot moving in their direction. It was a war chariot, pulled by a team of four milk-white horses.

Biobal glanced nervously around: "Should we take a defensive stand?"

Eochaidh Allmuir shook his head. "Since when are Dési warriors afraid of a single war chariot?"

They stood watching its approach. They could see only one figure in the chariot—a slight figure that seemed to handle the horses with expert ease. The car of the chariot was sparkling with beaten silver. Its great wheels were hubbed with scythes that sparkled wickedly in the sun. The trappings and harness were of white leather. It was truly impressive, and yet it seemed to be driven by a boy, so slight was the figure that controlled the massive beasts. It rumbled across the strand to halt twenty yards from the Dési chieftains.

The driver was a woman.

They gazed upon her with astonishment, for her beauty was beyond question. Her face was oval and her white skin was clear and unblemished. Her hair was black— black as the raven's wing—and tumbled freely around her head. Her figure was exquisite and it was hardly concealed from their astonished eyes, for she wore only a short kirtle fastened around the waist by a leather belt, from which a long sword and dagger hung. A simple twist of cloth covered her breasts. Around her neck was a twisted golden torque that denoted her warrior status. She stood staring at them with deep, dark eyes, in critical examination, totally unself-conscious.

"Who are you?" she demanded. Although the voice was accented, she spoke in the language of the children of Éireann.

"I am Eochaidh Allmuir, chieftain of the clan Dési of Bregia in the country of Éireann."

A quick expression of recognition flitted across the woman's face as if she had heard of Eochaidh and the Dési.

"And why have you landed on this shore?"

"Is this the shore of Alba?"

The woman inclined her head. "This is the Land of Shadows in the country of Alba," she confirmed. "Why do you come here?"

"We come in peace, in search of peace," replied Eochaidh.

The woman threw back her raven locks.

"I am Scáthach. Here, in the Land of Shadows, I rule."

Her dark eyes took in the three ships anchored in the bay before returning to the group of chieftains before her. Her gaze moved from Eochaidh to Each-Tiarna, to Biobal, to Cairell, and then to Aonghus. They hesitated a moment on the young chieftain of Hy-Nia and her mouth widened slightly at the hint of a smile.

"We ask hospitality of you, Scáthach," Eochaidh was saying. "We ask this of right."

She raised an eyebrow disdainfully.

"In the Land of Shadows there are no rights unless I, Scáthach, decree them."

"Do not the Brehons dwell here in Alba?" demanded Each-Tiarna querulously.

"In Alba, yes," Scáthach shrugged. "This is my domain. And yes . . ." Her glance returned to Aonghus for a moment. "I grant you hospitality. It is my desire. Your people may encamp on this shore tonight. There is fresh water from the springs and you may hunt fresh meat on the left shore for a mile inland, no more. But to the chieftains and leaders of your people, Eochaidh, I grant you the hospitality of my fortress for a feasting this evening. There you may explain to me what has driven you from Éireann, and why you seek sanctuary in my land."

She began to turn her chariot and then glanced back: "My fortress lies over the hills on the next headland." She flung up a well-shaped arm. "Come there at the set of the sun."

Before Eochaidh could say another word, the woman had expertly turned her chariot within its own length and whipped her team into a gallop across the sands. They stood watching the silver chariot until it vanished over the dunes.

"A magnificent woman," breathed Biobal.

"Scáthach of the Land of Shadows," Each-Tiarna said reflectively. "I am sure that I have heard the name spoken before."

"Her beauty is such that it would spring from lip to ear of many a bard traveling the world," smiled Eochaidh.

Under his orders, the Dési disembarked from their ships and established a small stockade on the foreshore, the men cutting down saplings to build a rough perimeter fence to protect them from any disturbance during the night. Soon, cooking fires were crackling and makeshift shelters were built. Hunting parties were sent out in search of fresh meat.

Aige was watching Cairell set up a shelter for her and Eithne.

"Is it true that this Scáthach is a woman of great beauty?" She pouted slightly in asking the question.

"There is beauty and beauty," grinned Cairell. "There is the beauty of the gentle seas compared with the beauty of the mountains, the beauty of a garden seen in the midday sun and a garden seen at dusk with its muted perfumes."

"I should like to go to this feast tonight."

Cairell shook his head.

"Only the Dési chieftains have been invited."

"But you are going," she pointed out.

"I go in place of Iolar," Cairell sighed. "I alone among the Dési have some knowledge of the druids, for I learned it at my father's knee. Now that the Dési are without a druid, any knowledge is better than none."

"But are you not the servant of Aonghus Mac Orba?" frowned the girl.

"Among the Dési we have no servants—all are equal," rebuked Cairell. "A charioteer and his warrior are like two brothers—each supports the other; each depends on the other in time of war."

"Your people have some strange customs, Cairell. But then everything is strange to me since I broke out of the crystal tower of Balor. It is like being born again, breaking out of a shell and finding the world is new. I can live with your customs, Cairell, if you will help me."

Cairell smiled happily. In the days since they had sailed from the brooding Island of Towers, he had come to delight in the girl's company. The pain of Áine's death had ceased to be sharp. Her memory was to be sad shadow.

"Of course I shall teach you our ways and be pleased that you will share our lives."

Aige looked at him, a hopeful expression on her face as if expecting him to say more, but Cairell had turned to speak with Maraí.

It was arranged that the crews were to remain aboard the ships that night to protect them while the others remained in their stockade encampment. There was no general unloading from the ships until Eochaidh Allmuir had sought and obtained the permission of Scáthach to allow the Dési to settle in her lands, if such a thing were possible. While the chieftains of the Dési were being entertained at Scáthach's fortress, it was Maraí

who would take charge of the encampment and ensure
it was well-guarded in case of any trouble.

Toward sunset Eochaidh Allmuir, with Biobal, Each-
Tiarna, Aonghus, and Cairell, set off for the headland,
bearing the customary gifts that those seeking hospitality dispense among their hosts. Walking together they
climbed out of the bay and found no difficulty in following the path, for the towering black silhouette of Dún
Scáthach on the next headland was visible for miles.

Chapter Nineteen

Dún Scáthach stood perched on the top of a jutting headland, standing aggressively out, thrusting, dominating, toward the sea. It was a dark grey stone-built fortress with round towers fully fifty feet in height and ramparts rising to twenty feet. There was only one entrance, which ended the roadway that led up the headland.

As was the custom, Scáthach stood at the gates with her sub-chieftains to greet the Dési. Gifts were presented and accepted. Then Scáthach took them inside the sombre ramparts to the feasting hall. She reclined at the head of the table, graceful and aware of her beauty and power. The mead was circulated and the traditional toasts were drunk. Then she invited Eochaidh Allmuir to tell his story. The chieftain recited it simply and without the customary embellishments. As he did so Scáthach's speculative eyes swept across the Dési chieftains and alighted on Aonghus. Her gaze remained on the chieftain of Hy-Nia, smiling as if at some hidden knowledge, until a faint tinge of red touched the young warrior's cheeks and he dropped his gaze. Scáthach's smile broadened. Cairell bent forward and whispered: "It seems that the ruler of the Land of Shadows is taken with you, Aonghus."

Eochaidh's story had ended and the Dési chieftain made his formal request that the clan be allowed to settle among Scáthach's people. To this request, Scáthach shrugged a shapely shoulder.

"Time enough to discuss that after the feasting," she replied, and nodded toward an attendant. At once the attendant clapped his hands and others came into the hall, bringing dishes of varied and exotic quality. Two attendants came in bearing a great silver platter on which was a roast pig. They placed it before Scáthach, who stood up, knife in hand, and smiled around at the assembly.

"And who will claim the hero's portion?" she asked softly.

Her gaze swept from her own chieftains to those of the Dési, and finally fell on Aonghus.

"Will no one contest for the hero's portion?" she smiled.

Eochaidh Allmuir spoke for the Dési. "In Éireann, it is the custom for a warrior to claim the hero's portion. But such custom has long been out of use among the Dési for we, in our war against Cormac, have fought shoulder to shoulder as brothers and deem all as worthy as his kin."

Scáthach threw back her head and gave a peal of laughter.

"Now that is a quaint notion. Here we judge warrior's mettle in other ways."

A tall, scowling warrior rose from his seat on Scáthach's right. He grinned in an ugly fashion at the Dési.

"Find me a man among the Dési and I will contend with him, or leave the hero's portion to me," he growled.

"For I am Mag, son of Cet, captain of those who guard the lands of Scáthach."

Eochaidh smiled gently, laying a hand on Each-Tiarna, who was about to rise in answer to the challenge.

"We are content to leave the division to you."

Mag's eyes went wide in disbelief.

"Is there no man among you?" he sneered.

"When there is food aplenty, why fight for it?" soothed Eochaidh.

"By the gods!" Mag cried. "I swear by that which my people swear by. Since I took a spear in my hand as a boy, I have never been a day without shedding blood or a night without plundering and burning, and I have never slept without the head of an enemy beneath my foot."

"Then it is a brave warrior you are," replied Eochaidh evenly, ignoring the other's ritual attempt to goad the Dési into combat.

Scáthach remained slightly amused during the exchange, her eyes still observing Aonghus, watching his reactions. Then she said quietly: "I will take the hero's portion, Mag, unless you wish to contend with me?"

Mag grew sullen and sat down.

Scáthach began the ritual of carving the pig. She cut a special portion, laid it on a plate, and turned to an attendant.

"Take this portion to the young warrior with the fair hair," she said, indicating Aonghus. "For I believe only modesty in the presence of his chieftain prevented him from claiming what is his."

Eochaidh—indeed, all the Dési chieftains—looked startled by Scáthach's remark for, under the laws of hospitality, it was a gross affront to Eochaidh. Aonghus, crimson, rose in his place.

"You mistakenly honor me, Scáthach," he said, trying to find the right words in his embarrassment. "My chieftain has told you that it is no longer the custom among the Dési to claim hero's portions. Were it so, then there are many among us who have a better claim than I."

"A modest man is usually admired," replied Scáthach, ". . . if people ever hear of him."

"You still misjudge me," replied Aonghus. "I am not modest. To declaim one's ability and demean oneself is not modesty but folly. To undervalue oneself is pusilla-nimity and hypocrisy." He gestured to the portion of meat on his plate. "This gift is wrongly given."

"A gift once given can never be taken back." Scáthach met his gaze with a challenge.

"Then, accepting this gift, it is mine and I can give it to one whom I admire," replied Aonghus.

Turning, he gave it to Cairell. There was a gasp from Scáthach's chieftains. Mag was on his feet, hand on his sword, but Scáthach was smiling. She reached out to hold back the captain of her guard. That Aonghus had given the hero's portion to his charioteer, even though he was acting as the Désis advisor because of his druidic knowledge, could be interpreted as a deliberate affront. No charioteer was eligible for the hero's portion. Only warriors and chieftains might contend for it. Aonghus, however, turned and met Scáthach's challenging gaze, and to his surprise, he saw amusement in her eyes.

"You are indeed a man of bravery, Aonghus Mac Orba," she said softly. Then, glancing at the others, as if becoming aware for the first time of the uneasy atmo-sphere, she said: "Come, let us eat and drink while my musicians play."

As Aonghus sat down, Cairell leaned toward him and whispered: "It is best not to provoke this lady, Aonghus. For all her beauty is but a sheath to a will of sharpened steel."

Aonghus nodded slowly.

"Perhaps it is unwise for Eochaidh to contemplate the settlement of our people in her domain. We would never live free of fear of her moods."

They fell silent as the meal progressed but every so often Aonghus felt Scáthach's gaze upon him. The feasting lasted for some time and musicians and bards vied with one another to entertain. As the hour grew late the Dési began to grow restless, yet Eochaidh could not suggest the time had come for leaving while the ruler of the Land of Shadows insisted on showering hospitality upon them.

In the middle of one recital, Scáthach slipped surreptitiously out of the feasting hall, and a short while later the scowling warrior, Mag, came to Aonghus.

"Scáthach wishes to speak to you alone," he said softly, so that only Aonghus could hear.

He glanced at Cairell, but he and the others of the Dési were all attention as a bard recited one of the high deeds of Fionn Mac Cumhail. No one noticed as he rose and followed Mag from the hall. The warrior was curt and uncommunicative as he preceded Aonghus down a corridor into an eloquent apartment.

"Wait," the man grunted and left him.

A moment passed and then the soft voice of Scáthach said: "Welcome, Aonghus Mac Orba."

The ruler of the Land of Shadows stood on the threshold of a small door on the far side of the chamber. She motioned him with her slim hand. There was a smile on her lips as she backed into the room. Frowning, Aonghus followed. He stepped into a small chamber whose walls were hung with brightly colored tapestries. A single lantern provided illumination. Aonghus saw that it was a bedchamber. The furniture was luxurious and the rugs and tapestries were of a rich quality. There was a soft fragrance of perfume in the air.

"You wished to see me, Scáthach?" asked Aonghus, stating the obvious.

Scáthach moved to the soft wool tapestry that over-laid the couch and sat down. Her battle harness had been discarded for a single flowing robe of sheer silk that left nothing about the contours of her perfectly shaped body to the imagination.

"Sit here, Aonghus," she said, her voice little more than a whisper. She patted the tapestry next to her.

Aonghus hesitated and was met by a chuckle.

"Why, you are nervous. Why be nervous when you are a strong warrior and I am but a weak woman?"

Aonghus bit his lip, non-plussed, and did as he was bid.

"What is it that you wanted to see me about?" he asked woodenly.

"Can it be that there is granite beneath the flesh of your skin?" she asked, chuckling lasciviously and reaching out to lay a hand on his thigh.

Aonghus trembled slightly in discomfiture, which brought forth another chuckle.

Gone was the commanding ruler of the Land of Shadows; gone, too, was the allure of beauty, for there was something slightly different about Scáthach now—about the way she carried herself, the way she responded to him. There was a self-assured voluptuousness. It created a seductive grossness that made Aonghus ill-at-ease, like an untutored youth before her glittering, speculative gaze.

"You do not know what it is like to be a ruler, Aonghus," she sighed. "I have been so lonely in this place, for there is none who can sit at my side as my equal. None that I would want . . . until I saw you."

Aonghus shifted uneasily.

There would have been a time when he would have been flattered, when he would have been bedazzled by her beauty and the lewd, suggestive posturing. But now she was no more than a wanton creature, a selfish, cunning woman. Even though she stirred against him, he felt unable to respond.

"I am yours, Aonghus. Let me make you consort in my Land of Shadows."

He tried to restrain her gently.

"Stop, Scáthach. You do not know me; therefore, you can have no feeling for me."

"I know enough. My eyes have taken in your image, my ears have heard your wit, and my nostrils have absorbed the odor of your body. Is there aught else that I should know?"

"You do not mention love," Aonghus replied. "And loving someone is knowing them."

Scáthach screeched with laughter.

"Love? I am Scáthach! I have chosen you above all men to lie with me. Are you a babe to want coaxing by tales of love?"

Aonghus smiled gently.

"I do not want you, Scáthach. I am sorry."

Scáthach blinked, not understanding.

"I am a ruler of this land. No man is my equal in war for the heads of enemies that I have slain in battle would encircle a million chariots. I can have my pick of any man within or without my kingdom. Yet I have chosen you, Aonghus Mac Orba. If it's love you demand, then I will give it to you."

He shook his head.

"Love is a gift that cannot be simply given. It must wait to be accepted. I do not want what passes for love with you."

An ugly look appeared on her face.

"Ah, you desire another?"

Aonghus shook his head, but he was thinking suddenly of Eithne. The thought surprised him.

Scáthach, watching his face, read the truth of her

accusation there, even if Aonghus was not certain of his own mind.

"Do you think that you can cast me aside so lightly, little man of Éireann? Mag was right. You are no man." Her voice was venomous.

Aonghus stood up and backed away from her unbridled anger. The fury of her face was unnerving.

"You shall pay for this insult," she hissed.

"I do not mean to insult you, Scáthach," he replied calmly. "But would you have me to lie to you? You seek to do me an honor, which I cannot enjoy."

Scáthach's face was flushed now, the eyes flashing with fury. Never had Aonghus seen such fury in the face of so beautiful a woman. He could not believe that one so lovely could harbor such malevolence.

A sad smile touched his lips.

"I am sorry for you, Scáthach."

She leapt to her feet. Aonghus felt that if she had had a weapon to hand he would have been a dead man.

"Sorry you will be," she replied, murder in her eyes. "By rejecting me, you have condemned yourself and your people. Get out!" She swung away. "Get out!"

He paused a moment, shrugged and left. Outside the door the surly Mag was frowning as he brushed by.

When Aonghus returned to the feasting hall he felt anger with himself. Had he been too blunt with Scáthach? Should he not have been more diplomatic and remembered that Eochaidh wanted to settle in peace in this land of Alba? He should not have aroused her ire without attempting a more diplomatic response. Wisdom is always wasted after the event.

Cairell noticed his return and smiled.

"Why so miserable? We are being well treated. In fact, too well. The hour grows late and still Scáthach showers us with drink and song."

Aonghus found that he had no words of explanation.

At that moment, Scáthach returned to her place at the head of the table. Her face was an expressionless mask, and she was once more clad in her battle harness. Aonghus glanced up and saw her whispering to Mag, who had followed her in. The captain of the guard had a sly smile.

Scáthach now rose, her voice once more melodious.

"The hour grows late," she announced, "so let me propose health and long life to our guests."

The goblet was in her hand.

Th toasting momentarily distracted Aonghus. Suddenly he heard Cairell utter a curse at his side. He glanced to his charioteer in surprise and found Cairell's face dripping in mead. Cairell was staring angrily at Mag and the ugly-faced warrior was chuckling.

"That was done deliberately," Cairell accused.

"Deliberately, little man?" sneered the warrior. "Why should I spill good mead over you?"

"You can answer that!" exclaimed Cairell with barely controlled anger.

"Explain? Perhaps you'd best apologize for insulting me in the hall of my ruler. I say you tripped me and now you have insulted me. No man insults Mag son of Cet!"

Without a further word, Mag pulled his dagger and struck at Cairell. It was done before anyone could recover from their surprise at the way the incident had turned into a deadly combat.

Cairell was shocked but his reflexes were still swift enough to move aside, seizing the man's right arm and twisting it so that the dagger jerked up behind his back. For a moment or two they struggled, and then Mag's left hand came up.

Aonghus was about to cry a warning but Cairell had seen it and thrust the warrior backwards. Mag staggered a few paces and fell over, measuring his full length on his back. His right hand was still behind him. He gave a gasp, convulsed a moment on the floor and was still.

There was a silence in the feasting hall. No one moved for a moment. Then one of Scáthach's warriors came forward, bent beside Mag's body, and turned it over. The knife that Mag had held in his right hand was protruding from his back.

The warrior gazed up at Cairell. His eyes were cold.

"He is dead," he said. "You have killed Mag Mac Cet, captain of Scáthach's bodyguard."

Chapter Twenty

The silence that followed was interminable. Everyone in the feasting hall knew the laws of hospitality and the penalties for transgressing them.

"Cairell was provoked," Aonghus protested, breaking the heavy silence.

"It is a grave matter." Scáthach had risen, and her voice was icy.

"Mag deliberately provoked Cairell," replied Aonghus, anger creeping into his voice.

"Has Cairell no tongue?" mocked Scáthach.

The charioteer flushed.

"I have a tongue right enough. And Aonghus is right. Mag deliberately poured wine on me and provoked this fight. He would not be dead now had he not tried to kill me by underhanded means."

There was a roar of anger from Scáthach's warriors.

"Are you compounding your crime by accusing him who cannot answer?" sneered the ruler of the Land of Shadows.

"A truth is a truth whether a man is dead or not," retorted Cairell, recalling the scene in the High King's hall at Temuir when Aonghus used those very words.

"Then put the truth to a test."

At first Cairell did not understand Scáthach's meaning.

"The truth of the sword," Scáthach went on, "is surely known among even the Dési?"

"Only a warrior may contest in such a manner," interposed Eochaidh. "Cairell is no warrior. He is charioteer and advisor in the stead of my druid."

Scáthach merely smiled.

"He ate of the hero's portion at this feasting and was warrior enough to slay the captain of my guards."

There was a silence and then Scáthach spoke again.

"Are you admitting your guilt and cowardice, or do you accept the challenge?"

"I accept!" snapped Cairell. "Whom do I fight?"

"Why," chuckled Scáthach, "me, of course."

Cairell stared at her in astonishment.

"I can't fight a woman."

The ruler of the Land of Shadows' eyes flashed.

"I am Scáthach. I am champion of all the peoples of the Land of Shadows," she cried harshly. "Now prepare to defend yourself."

She turned and gestured to an attendant, who came forward with her long sword. It gleamed flashing gold in the light of the torches of the feasting hall. An attendant came to Cairell and offered him a sword.

Aonghus had caught at Cairell's arm.

"You are no swordsman, Cairell," he said, his voice low. "It is your right to appoint a substitute. Let me accept the challenge for you."

Cairell shook his head.

"I am not old or infirm. That is the only reason for a substitution."

"Lack of knowledge of weaponry is also a reason," replied Aonghus.

But Cairell shook him off his arm and turned toward the warrior ruler. The tables were pushed aside to make space in the hall. Aonghus looked pleadingly at his young friend. He knew Cairell could handle a sword in an amateurish way, but not the way he handled his sling or his team of horses. He could not fight as a warrior might fight. The young charioteer shaped up valiantly enough, swinging the sword to test its balance.

Scáthach had thrown aside her cloak and stood in leather harness and kirtle, revealing her glorious brown, near-naked body. Her limbs were well-shaped and supple. Yet there was no doubting that beneath her graceful, feminine figure the muscles were hardened to the warrior's calling. In her left hand she held a short dagger, while in her right hand the long sword seemed an extension of her being. She dropped to a fighting crouch, every inch a champion. She seemed to be at one with both weapons, gliding smoothly across the floor, the wicked blades flickering.

A few lunges showed that Cairell was outclassed. Whatever his skills, the outcome would be inevitable. He backed a few paces, parrying the quick blows with which Scáthach engaged him. The warriors grunted their approval as their ruler came catlike to the affray. Her dagger touched Cairell lightly on the arm, so lightly that it did not pierce to any degree but simply drew blood. It was a demonstration, to show Cairell her superiority over him rather than to hurt him. He fell back a pace.

Her face was a smiling mask. She came on, slashing and lunging with a force that drove him backwards in surprise until he tripped and fell before her. The long sword swept up to the ceiling. There was a tense silence while they waited for the fatal blow to fall.

A firm, muscular hand closed around the slender wrist of Scáthach, staying the sword from commencing its fatal journey.

"No more," said Aonghus softly. "No more. If you want revenge against me, then fight me."

There was a gasp of astonishment as Aonghus twisted the sword from her hand and threw it to the floor. Some of Scáthach's guards drew their weapons and advanced on the chieftain of Hy-Nia.

Cairell scrambled from the floor while Eochaidh looked on with pale face.

"Aonghus Mac Orba, it is not permitted to interfere . . ." he began.

Staring straight into Scáthach's face, Aonghus said: "It is not you she wishes to kill, Cairell. She wishes to revenge herself on me. You are but a means to do so."

For a moment Scáthach stared back, her face a contorted mask of hatred. Then she broke into a smile. It was a smile of triumph. In that moment Aonghus knew how devious the woman was. She had planned this, planned even his very intervention. Yet for what purpose, he did not know.

"This is an insult, Aonghus Mac Orba," she said without emotion. "You have insulted the ruler of the Land of Shadows."

Eochaidh was pressing forward in concern.

"This thing was done unintentionally," he said defensively.

Scáthach raised an eyebrow.

"Unintentionally? Have you no control over your chieftains, Eochaidh Allmuir? You come to my land demanding hospitality, a refuge, and it is offered. Yet I am insulted by this warrior whom you call Aonghus of Hy-Nia. He insults me when I offer him the hero's portion. His charioteer slays and insults the reputation of my warrior, Mag. Now, during the ritual of the truth of combat, Aonghus of Hy-Nia intervenes and insults me again."

Aonghus stood staring into Scáthach's dark, fathomless eyes. Could a woman's hatred be so deep because her advances had been rejected?

Scáthach turned back to her seat and sprawled in it, her brows drawn together.

"Reparation must be made for this insult," she said slowly.

Eochaidh bowed to the inevitable.

"In fixing reparation, according to the Brehons, I am sure your wisdom and knowledge of the spirit of justice will take into account that no insult was intended. The generous impulse to save a life was the spirit that moved Aonghus of Hy-Nia to act as he did."

Scáthach's mouth twisted in humor.

"I am interested to hear that Eochaidh of the Dési supports and excuses the actions of Aonghus of Hy-Nia. Do you excuse his guilt?"

"If there is guilt here, it is because the Dési have no wish to shed wasteful blood," replied Eochaidh.

"Since Eochaidh has assumed guilt for the insult," Scáthach said, "the punishment of the Dési will be a portion of your punishment should you fail to accept the task of reparation, Aonghus Mac Orba."

Aonghus stood silent. He did not drop his gaze from the dark malevolence of her eyes.

"What task of reparation?" asked Eochaidh.

"All in good time," smiled Scáthach. "First let me tell you the penalty. To repay the insult done by the Dési to the peace of this land, they will be gathered up as slaves to work for the welfare of the people they have insulted. The old men shall be sent to the iron fields to work at extracting the metal. The young men shall be sent to the stone quarries to keep our highways in repair. The old women shall find work in the households of our chieftains, for it is not seemly that the wives and daughters of chieftains should be forced to menial tasks. The young women . . ."

Scáthach stretched languorously in her chair and stared at Aonghus.

"The young women shall be kept to propagate our race and will be sent as concubines to our bravest chieftains."

Eochaidh and the other Désí chieftains were appalled.

"This is unjust!" cried Eochaidh. "No Brehon would sanction such a punishment."

Scáthach turned angrily on him.

"I have already told you that I dispense justice in the Land of Shadows, not the Brehons. My will shall be done."

Each-Tiarna, Biobal and Cairell drew nearer to Eochaidh. There was a threatening murmur from them but Aonghus held up a hand and called for quiet.

"Wait. Scáthach has told us the penalty if I fail to accept this task of reparation. She has not yet told me what the task is."

Scáthach smiled.

"Several days' ride to the north of here is a great range of mountains, so tall that they almost black out the skies. That is why this land has become known as the Land of Shadows. Beyond their bounds, completely surrounded by them, is a large valley. It is called Gleann na Scanradh, the Glen of Terror. Since time immemorial the bards have told stories about it, but none have we met who came from there nor, save one, who have travelled there and returned.

"According to the bards the glen is populated. But the population is kept in fear and bondage by a great beast which has existed in the glen since the beginning of time. The beast . . . the Oillipheist . . . haunts the land, destroying all who encounter it. Its cry pierces the heart like a whetted spear. At its sound, young men lose their vigor, old men their senses, while beauty and health are driven from maidens. The animals are slain and the trees and crops wither. The land lies desolate and barren. Many have been the youthful warriors of the Land of Shadows who have set out on a quest to find the Glen of Terror, but only one has returned . . . and he returned without his senses and died of fear within a moon."

Scáthach paused, her eyes narrowed on Aonghus' face.

"If you go to the Glen of Terror, Aonghus Mac Orba, and slay this Oillipheist, and do this thing in the service of Scáthach, bringing me proof that the deed is done, and further bringing me the thanks and fealty of the people who dwell there in payment of this service done to them, then I will release the Dési. You and your people will be free to leave the Land of Shadows in peace."

"Stories by bards, an insane warrior returning . . ." Cairell's voice was skeptical. "What proof have you that this Glen of Terror even exists, let alone that there is an Oillipheist, or that people suffer from its oppression?"

Scáthach smiled grimly.

"You are possessed of knowledge, young druid. The young warrior who returned from the Glen of Terror had been touched by the gods and uttered inspired prophecy before his death. Is there not a proverb that the insane cannot deceive? The young warrior had seen the Oillipheist and thus was his sanity cast from him. He . . . he was my brother."

"And what manner of beast is this Oillipheist?" demanded Aonghus, intrigued by the woman's story, in spite of Cairell's skepticism.

"A beast from the Otherworld," replied Scáthach.

"Why does it haunt only this one glen and not the rest of your lands?" demanded Cairell, still cynical.

"Because the beast is imprisoned by his bulk in the glen and cannot get out, so the bards tell. It was thought that there was no way in or out of the glen until . . . until my brother returned."

"And did he tell you how he entered the glen?" Cairell asked.

Scáthach shook her head.

"Nevertheless, there is a way. It will be for you to find it."

Eochaidh intervened for the first time.

"What manner of reparation is this?" he began, but Aonghus glanced at him and shook his head.

"I am willing to undertake the task," he said quietly.

"What if the glen and Oillipheist do not exist?" Cairell said.

"It exists," Scáthach replied quickly.

"Then I will find it," Aonghus said.

"You will need your charioteer, Aonghus," Cairell sighed, stepping forward. "Perhaps Scáthach will give us the loan of a chariot and team?"

Scáthach nodded, a slow smile spreading across her features. "You will have the gift of my best chariot and team and a choice of our best crafted weapons."

Aonghus half nodded.

"And do I have your solemn word before this assembly that, should I perform the task, you will let all of us continue our journey in peace?"

"I have said so."

"Your word on it?"

"My word."

"Very well. Point the way to where this Glen of Terror is supposed to lie, but remember this . . . should I return and find any of my people harmed, or given into slavery before I am back, then I give you my word that I shall seek you out and slay you."

Scáthach met his eyes boldly and her smile was grim.

"Brave words, Aonghus Mac Orba. Rest assured that I shall make no attempt to enslave the Dési until a full moon has passed from this night. The Dési may return to their encampment on the shore and await the moon. But one thing more: my warriors shall watch, and if any attempt is made to break on your ships, my vengeance shall be swifter than the flight of the eagle on its prey."

"Is there no other way to resolve this?" demanded Eochaidh.

Aonghus smiled and shook his head.

"It is not my destiny to die in the Glen of Terror," he smiled. "Keep our people safe, Eochaidh, and watch for my return."

Eochaidh, Each-Tiarna and Biobal returned to the Dési encampment with the news of what had transpired, but Aonghus and Cairell were kept at Dún Scáthach until sun-up. In the courtyard of the fortress Scáthach had left the gift of a chariot and a selection of weapons that had been polished and sharpened.

Not long afterwards, Cairell urged the horses forward and took the chariot out into the road that Scáthach indicated. It meandered through rolling hills, twisted among great forests and on toward the distant blue mountains. Cairell and Aonghus spoke little as they rode along; little enough there was to speak of. It was no use speculating on what manner of creature the Oillipheist would be or wishing that events of the previous evening might have taken a different course.

For five days they drove onward until the mountains grew close and the highway disappeared into a stony-ground that began to rise sharply toward the broad shoulders of the peaks.

Three further days they spent searching for some pass through the mountains.

"No lie Scáthach told us when she said there was no way in or out of the Glen of Terror," Cairell commented bitterly toward the end of the third day, when the search had proved fruitless.

"Well, we cannot go back," observed Aonghus. "Tomorrow, I will attempt to climb the mountains, leaving the chariot here."

That evening Cairell climbed to a high rock at dusk and seated himself cross-legged, closing his eyes.

"The truth against the world. The truth against the world." He began to mutter the druidic chant, letting his mind go blank to all else save the rhythm of the words until his whole being vibrated with them.

A path opened up before his mind's eye, almost as if he had his eyes wide open and had risen to follow it. On and upward it moved through rock and crevice, through darkened passageway, twisting and moving until . . . his eyes snapped open and he rose with a smile.

"I know the way," he told Aonghus as they prepared for sleep that night.

The next morning Cairell moved off without hesitation, guiding the chariot toward the base of a tall peak. The way seemed impassable. Nevertheless, Aonghus made no comment. He did not question Cairell's perception. Soon the sides of the chariot were brushing the walls of a deep cleft. At one point it grew so narrow that they decided the only way forward was to unharness the chariot and leave it, mounting the horses and moving in single file. Even then the path narrowed again and the last part of the journey was made by dismounting and leading the horses by the bridle through the darkness of the cleft.

Then they were through the pass and gazing on a large, wild valley.

Chapter Twenty-one

Passing into the Gleann na Scanradh, the Glen of Terror, was like going through a door from a sunny garden into a dank, gloomy house. As Aonghus and Cairell passed through the narrow defile between the tall mountains, it seemed that the sun was immediately hidden, that dark clouds billowed through the sky, shutting off the limpid blue of morning and turning the day into chilly gloom. Across the glen the mountain sides rose steeply, the high tops ragged. Their walls were unclimbable and wisps of mist floated across many of them, obscuring several peaks.

The glen was dark in color, with scarcely any vegetation. The earth was burnt and like a wasteland. No flowers, no trees, not even a wild grassland alleviated the scene in any direction. Yet here and there a tree stump did survive, a crumbling, rotting piece of decayed wood. Pools of stagnant, stinking water stood like cesspits. The scene of utter desolation stretched as far as the eye could see.

"Whoever named this the Glen of Terror had the right of it," Cairell observed, easing forward on his horse.

Aonghus suddenly lifted his head. Somewhere in the far distance came the roar of some animal—a strange, high-pitched cry that was oddly alien and disturbing. It rumbled in the chill air and died away. In spite of himself Aonghus shivered.

Motioning Cairell, he led the way forward, horses picking their way cautiously, their eyes showing the whites as they rolled in terror from side to side. The beasts' nostrils were flaring, their ears bent flat to their heads. It was obvious that they sensed danger.

They moved down the gloomy glen some way before Cairell called softly to attract Aonghus' attention and pointed his hand away up a mountain slope to their right. Some way up Aonghus saw some cave entrances, and in the darkness of one of them he saw a fire flickering and smoke dribbling into the air.

"People," Cairell said.

"Let's find out who they are," replied Aonghus, turning his horse in the direction of the caves.

The gloom seemed to increase as they grew near the craggy rocks. The cave mouth was moderately large but across it, rising out of the mud, someone had built a wall of stone and rotting pieces of wood. If it were meant to be a stockade designed to protect those who dwelt within, it was worthless. Aonghus could see that all he had to do was give a hefty kick and the wood would simply crumble into nothing. Yet within the stockade a turf fire crackled and silhouetted a group of figures crouched around it. A sudden cry of alarm told him that he had been spotted.

"We are friends!" he cried. "Travellers wishing to take hospitality."

Shadows flitted this way and that as the figures ran in terror into the furthermost recesses of the cave.

"Maybe we should pass on," whispered Cairell, a feeling of anxiety descending on him.

Then a figure came forward, advancing slowly to the wall of the makeshift stockade. A crude wooden spear was held protectively before it.

"Travellers? No one travels through the glen," said a wheezy voice suspiciously. "Yet I have no recognition of you. You are not of the folk of the glen. How did you come here and what do you want? Are you shades from the Otherworld?"

"You need have no fear," Aonghus replied. "We are men of flesh and blood."

"If you be men, then we do not fear you."

Suddenly another figure moved across to the stockade and emerged into the gloomy light. She was a hideous woman, bent almost double, with one eye closed, hair matted across her dirty face. She stared up at Aonghus, her toothless gums bared. Her voice was a harsh cackle.

"They be men! Ask how they came into the glen. There is no way in or out."

"There is a path," said Aonghus, "and we followed it."

"Lies!" screamed the old woman. "There is no path. They are servants of the Oillipheist, come to lure us to it."

"We come in peace!" protested Aonghus as the first figure stood hesitating, the crude spear raised.

"There is no peace in the Glen of Terror. Kill them!" hissed the old woman.

The first figure emerged from the shadows now. It was a man as matted of hair and as dirty as the old woman. A simple skin, wrapped around his middle, was the only garment he had. He was of indeterminate age. He stood a moment and then, as the old woman yelled once more "Kill them!" raised his spear and came running forward. Aonghus merely drew his sword and lopped at the rotting haft of the spear, cutting it neatly in two. Then his sword point was at the man's chest.

"Move and you die," he snapped. "Tell your people to lay aside any weapons that they might have."

The man sniffed like a bad-tempered child.

"You have destroyed the only weapon we possessed," he said, his voice petulant.

Aonghus swung down from his horse, his sword still ready.

"Tell me who you are?"

"My name is Lag, and this is my family," the man replied, attempting some semblance of dignity.

The old woman started to curse him.

"Be quiet!" snapped Aonghus. "I have no time to deal with meddlesome old witches."

The old woman started to curse him as well as Lag, but Aonghus swung at her with his sword. It was only a gesture, but sufficient to shut the crone up immediately.

"Good. If you wish to take another breath, remain silent."

He turned his eyes back to the man.

"Who is she?" he asked, indicating the old woman.

"She is Glao," shrugged Lag. "She is one of the wise women of the glen. I am not related to her, but she lives with whoever will feed her."

"How many live in this glen?"

"I don't know. Many who escape from the attentions of the Oillipheist. That's how I know. At its coming we crawl up the mountainside or hide in our caves. Sometimes we escape from it, sometimes not. Once, long ago, at a time before the coming of the Oillipheist, it was said that there were buildings throughout the glen. It was a happy place. But that was long, long ago. I have only heard the story from my father and his father before him. It is a legend. Perhaps it is not true, for we have never known an existence within living memory."

Aonghus frowned. "Why do the people here put up with such an existence? Why don't you simply leave this glen?"

The man Lag gazed at him blankly.

"Leave? But this is our land, the land of our ancestors. We cannot abandon it."

"Besides," cackled the crone, daring the sharpness of Aonghus' sword, "there is no way to leave."

Aonghus glanced at Cairell and shrugged. How could one persuade people that something existed if they were not prepared to accept it in the first place?

"Let us rest ourselves by your fire for a moment, Lag. We will not hurt you if you do not threaten us. We would talk to you about the Oillipheist and the customs of your people."

Lag shot the old crone a look and then shrugged. He turned back into the entrance of the cave.

The light of the smoky fire showed that Lag's family consisted of his wife, a middle-aged woman, and four daughters. They were a wild, tousle-haired group, their bodies clung with mud and their hair matted and streaked with it. They wore the crudest of garments—sleeveless vests of animal fur—and they went barefoot. Their features held a certain animal cast—a suspicious, brutish quality that made both Aonghus and Cairell feel wary of them.

Lag squatted down at the fire while his wife went back to attending a smoking pot that hung over it. The old woman, Glao, spat silently, and disappeared into the darkness at the back of the cave.

Only one of Lag's daughters showed interest in the newcomers. She was about eighteen, or so Aonghus judged, though it was difficult to tell with the smeared and dirty face. Underneath it the girl seemed to possess a quality of attractiveness. Perhaps it was a simple animal magnetism. She came close and stretched her near-naked limbs languorously toward the heat of the fire and bared her teeth in what was an attempt at a friendly gesture. Aonghus wondered how such brutish-looking parents could give birth to an attractive daughter.

"Tell me about the Oillipheist," he invited, seating himself down, aware of the girl's wanton appraisal.

"What is there to tell?" asked Lag. "The beast comes, the beast goes. Sometimes we survive. More often, we perish."

"What manner of beast is it?" pressed Cairell.

"A creature from the Otherworld, that is all."

The daughter bent to her father and whispered.

"Hold your tongue, Druth!" snapped the man. "Get ale for these strangers."

Ale? Aonghus exchanged a glance with Cairell and smiled.

"That would be welcome," he said, "we are parched from our journey."

The girl, Druth, stood up and moved across the stockade, returning moments later with a stone pitcher and drinking vessels of fire-hardened clay. The ale was strong. Very strong.

"You brew this yourself?" asked Cairell, blinking at its potency.

"No. We barter for it. Only one man in the Glen of Terror is allowed by custom to brew ale."

"One man?"

"Bríbhéir, the brewer, who dwells farther up in the valley. He has vast vats in the caves where he dwells and he brews ale for all the people of the glen."

"But from what does he brew this mixture?" demanded Cairell. "I see no crops. He cannot brew it from wheat or barley."

Lag shrugged indifferently.

"He brews from root crops—roots that grow under the poor soil."

"He is a sorcerer," added the girl, Druth, smiling at Aonghus.

"But about this beast . . .?"

The girl filled his drinking vessel, bending so close that her slender shoulder touched his arm. She looked at him with a coquettishness that could not be misinterpreted.

"You will see the beast soon enough," replied Lag dismissively

Aonghus sighed.

"In that case, we will press on. Perhaps this man Bríbhéir will be able to give us information."

The girl pouted in annoyance, but Aonghus ignored her. As Aonghus and Cairell finished their drinks and rose, she said:

"I will come with you."

"It is dangerous," Aonghus said in astonishment.

The girl sniffed.

"I am used to danger. You are without a woman to cook for you and keep you warm at night. I will come. I will be your mate."

Aonghus' mouth dropped. Cairell started to chuckle but stopped himself at the look on his companion's face.

"Such is not the custom of my people," Aonghus said. "There should be love between a man and woman under the blanket."

The girl frowned. "You do not find me attractive?"

"Yes," admitted Aonghus.

"Then why don't you want me?"

Aonghus glanced at Lag and his wife, who sat indifferent to their daughter's behavior.

Lag met his eye.

"It is the custom in the glen that the daughters of a house may choose to sleep with any male they feel attracted to. Thus are the people of the glen propagated. So has it been since the coming of the great beast."

"Well, such is not the way of my people," muttered Aonghus in embarrassment.

"If you refuse me," snapped Druth angrily, "then you insult me and my father's house."

Aonghus shrugged and turned. He was not prepared for the way the girl launched herself upon him, clawing, scratching and biting with all the strength of her lithe young body. Aonghus twisted away, clutching at her wrists. Cairell stood shaking with silent laughter as Aonghus pushed the girl back into the arms of her father.

They rode away with the curses of Druth ringing in their ears.

"What are you grinning at?" demanded Aonghus after a while.

"I never knew you had such a fatal way with women. First Scáthach. Now this girl Druth. By the gods, I believe you were well named, Aonghus. Aonghus Óg, the love god."

"Keep your mind on your task, Cairell Mac Fios," muttered Aonghus in annoyance. "Leave jests to the fools and clowns."

Cairell made a face but continued to grin broadly.

They were approaching a rise when, with a startling abruptness, a loud cry echoed from nearby. It began as slow moaning sound that grew in volume and ended in a loud, barking scream. The horses reared up, terrified, hitting out at the air with their forelegs. It took all Aongus and Cairell's strength to pacify their mounts.

As soon as he was able, Aonghus nudged his horse to the rise. He froze at what he saw on the other side.

At that moment came another deafening roar. The creature who emitted it loomed terrifyingly large before him. It stood full twenty feet in height at the shoulder where a bony hood encircled its neck, like a bizarre bonnet rising around the back of its head. It was a dirty greyish blue color, not unlike slate, although its face was yellow, with thin bands of pure grey encircling its eyes. The eyes were startling. They were blood red.

The yellow was repeated along its belly and underside. From the neck down to its long tail ran three parallel lines of bony protuberances. In front of the broad forehead were two large horns, and a further median horn rose from its snout. The stubby, tree-trunk legs ended in three talonlike toes. In all, Aonghus guessed that the towering bulk of the creature was something like seventy-five feet from snout to tail and its strength must surely be colossal.

This was the Oillipheist.

The beast suddenly swung around and was staring full into Aonghus' face with its wicked, tiny blood-colored eyes.

It opened its mouth, disclosing powerful carnivore teeth, and let out a further scream.

Aonghus kicked his horse into motion.

"Away!" he yelled to Cairell. "Away for your life!"

The Oillipheist lumbered swiftly over the rise and paused a moment, glaring down at the men and horses fleeing from it. It roared out its challenge again and set off at a speed which, because of its bulk, seemed incredible.

Heads against their horses' necks, Aonghus and Cairell raced for the side of the glen. Both were intent on reaching the caves, which provided the only shelter through the entire valley.

They had not gone far when Aonghus saw a small figure to his right—a running figure that suddenly checked and halted. It had obviously spied the oncoming beast and was standing frozen with fear. Aonghus took into his racing mind that it was the figure of a girl. He yelled to Cairell to keep going while he turned his horse and rode toward her.

The girl saw him coming and gazed from him to the beast in fright. Aonghus was only a matter of seconds ahead. He bent forward, reaching out with one powerful arm and praying the girl would not be too frightened

to know what she should do. His fingers met the girl's
extended arm. With a muscle-wrenching jerk, Aonghus
swung her around onto the back of his horse without
slackening speed. Calling to her to hold on tightly, he
turned the horse again, so sharply that it nearly
overbalanced. Then he was racing away after Cairell.

Aonghus could feel the hot breath of the beast on his
neck. Up the long, shelving valley he urged his mount.
As good as the beast was he knew that it would not be
able to keep up the pace for any length of time. Sooner
or later the Oillipheist would overtake him.

Cairell, just in front, had already realized the problem and was casting his eyes feverishly about for a
suitable shelter. Along the gloomy valley, where the
mountains started to rise, he saw some outcrops of rock
and patches of blackness. Caves! He urged his horse
toward them, hoping Aonghus was following.

It was not long before he was able to confirm his wild
hope. Caves, indeed—caves big enough to take horse
and man. Big enough . . . but would they be deep
enough to save them from the scratching talons of the
Oillipheist? He ran his horse for the cave, ducking his
head, for there was scarcely room for man and beast
together. Then he halted, slid from the saddle and ran
back into the darkness, leading the horse.

Aonghus was already behind him. They halted in the
comforting darkness, shivering. They could hear the
grunting sound of the Oillipheist coming to a halt,
could hear its raking talons scratching at the rocky
entrance. The horses stood trembling with fear. There
came a baffled roar as the beast realized it could not
enter.

"The gods be praised!" whispered Cairell. "It cannot
reach us here."

Cairell felt in the darkness and found a few dry twigs.
A moment later he had struck a light and found rotting
wood enough to start a fire. It was obvious that the cave

had been used before for there were signs of previous occupation and enough materials to keep a fire going for some time. It was only then that Aonghus turned to the girl he had rescued. He stared in astonishment at the face of Druth.

"You! What are you doing here?"

The girl was recovering from her fear. Her chin thrust forward.

"I followed you."

Aonghus did not know whether to be angry or sorry for her. She had nearly lost her life through her willful pursuit of him.

He drew her to the warmth of the fire.

"Why did you follow me, Druth?" he asked kindly.

The girl sniffed in annoyance.

"No man rejected me before."

Cairell smothered a chuckle

"Well," said Aonghus, eyeing him grimly, "unless we can find a way out of here, Druth, it will be a unique experience for you."

Outside the Oillipheist roared with impatient anger.

Chapter Twenty-two

A large, sleek-looking ship was moving closely into the bay under the high stone walls of Dún Scáthach. Even as it drifted to anchor, its great oceangoing sails were being furled and signals were exchanged with the fortress high on the headland. It appeared that a storm had ravaged the great ship, for its crew was still engaged in cutting away wreckage, broken spars and twisted rigging. On the stern deck a druid, with skull-like features, stood at the side of an elderly man with one malevolent eye and a grim face. Cormac Mac Art, High King of Éireann, stared up at the ramparts above him.

"The fortress of Scáthach, Cormac," murmured Indech the druid. "A woman whose temper is as evil as her features are beautiful."

Cormac's single eye flickered dangerously.

"I have no time for beauty. I need only a safe anchorage in which to repair the *Dioltas* and make her seaworthy again. Then I will not rest until I have found those Dési jackals."

Indech smiled thinly.

"Have no fear, Cormac. They will not escape your vengeance."

"Yet they escaped your magic in the storm," snapped the High King.

Indech paled slightly.

"A miscalculation, that is all. I underestimated the strength of the youth, Cairell. His father, Fios, had a reputation among the brotherhood for his skill and knowledge. Little did I know that his son had learned some of his father's art."

"That underestimation has cost me dearly. I have lost my fleet—five ships lost and eight fifties of warriors drowned."

Indech was about to say something when Gorta Mac Goll gave a cry.

"There is a group of warriors coming down to the shore, Cormac, with a woman at their head."

Indech squinted shoreward.

"Scáthach in person," he whispered.

Cormac signalled for a boat to be lowered and he, with Indech and Gorta, were rowed through the surf to the shore below Dún Scáthach.

The warrior queen of the Land of Shadows stood waiting for them, flanked by her chieftains.

"You are welcome, Cormac of Éireann," she greeted the High King.

Cormac was momentarily disconcerted.

"How do you know who I am?"

Scáthach chuckled.

"I have only to examine the markings on the sails of your ship yonder to know that it is the ship of the High King of Éireann," she said. Then she paused and added softly, "And news that Cormac bears only one eye has long since spread from the boundaries of your country."

Cormac's face tightened angrily.

"Since you know who I am, and since you know why

I bear a single eye, you may also know that I am in search of the rebellious clan called the Dési."

"It is known that you pursued them from Éireann in six great ships with twelve fifties of warriors." She paused and gazed at the *Dioltas*. "Yet it looks as if you have encountered hardships."

"The other ships were wrecked in a terrible storm," muttered Cormac. "I need a safe shelter in which to carry out repairs."

"You have it," Scáthach replied, gesturing at the bay before them.

Indech coughed slightly.

"Excuse me, queen. But since you are all-knowing, maybe you would know if the Dési weathered the storm?"

Scáthach laughed hollowly.

"One would expect that the druid of the High King would have knowledge enough of his arts to know this?" she sneered.

Indech blinked at the insult.

"Well, I am in a generous mood this day," Scáthach continued. "The three ships of the Dési are safely at anchor but a short distance from here."

Cormac's jaw dropped.

"By the gods! Do you tell me so?"

"By the gods" mocked Scáthach. "I do. But do not fly into a rage, for the Dési are mine."

"How so?"

"I have taken them into slavery."

Cormac bit his lip and then said: "Then let me buy but one of the Dési. Let me have Aonghus Mac Orba and you may do as you will with the rest of them."

Scáthach gazed meditatively at the High King.

"So Aonghus Mac Orba is the cause of your misfortunes?"

Cormac's face convulsed in anger but he did not speak. Eventually Scáthach said: "Sorry I am to disappoint you, but this same Aonghus has undertaken a task for me. He has gone to the Glen of Terror to slay Oillipheist. In the unlikelihood that he accomplishes this task and returns . . . his fate is yours." She smiled wickedly. "I promised him that should he fulfill the task, then he had my word that all the Desi would go free from my bondage. In which case I am not breaking my word in giving you the right to dispense with them." For a moment a curious blaze shone in her fathomless eyes and she muttered fiercely, almost beneath her breath: "No one insults Scáthach with impunity!"

Cormac clenched his fist with a smile of joy.

"Then I pray to the gods that Aonghus Mac Orba is successful in slaying this Oillipheist of yours."

Scáthach laughed.

"Vain that prayer, Cormac. There is no power in this world or in the Otherworld that will make Aonghus successful in his quest."

While Cairell tended to the fire, for the cave was extremely chill, Aonghus went cautiously to the cave mouth to observe the Oillipheist, which had taken up a stand outside, casting its baleful red eyes now and again in their general direction. It seemed that the beast had settled down for a long stay. Aonghus regarded its grey, scaling skin distastefully, wondering how such a creature could be destroyed. There seemed no weak chink in its thick hide, no vulnerable spot where one might cast a spear or send an arrow. After a while he returned to where Druth and Cairell sat huddled over the fire.

"Is it still there?" whispered the girl nervously.

Aonghus nodded. The girl sighed as if she had expected no other answer.

"It will always be there," she said reflectively. "It never gives up once it has decided on its prey."

"Is there no way of killing it?" demanded Cairell.

There came an unexpected peal of laughter which caused them all to start to their feet with pounding hearts. A dark shadow hovered in the back of the cave.

"Who is it?" demanded Aonghus, drawing his sword.

"No need for a sword, stranger."

A figure shuffled into the light of the fire. It was the old woman Glao from Lag's encampment, or so he thought.

"How did you get here?" he demanded.

The old woman chuckled, her rough, aging vocal cords creating a cacophonic discord.

"I have always lived here. I am Osna."

Aonghus frowned.

"I thought your name was Glao.'

This caused more merriment.

"Glao is my sister. I am Osna, chieftainess of the wise women of Gleann na Scanradh," she announced with cackling pride.

"How long have you been hiding in this cave?" asked Cairell. "I am sure you were not here when we entered.".

"You are perceptive, young man. This cave connects with many other caves and passageways in which the people of this glen dwell. It is a sanctuary in which they hide from the attentions of the Oillipheist."

"So we can move freely from this cave?" Aonghus asked, a hope dawning in his mind.

"Only yourselves—not your horses—for the tunnels are too low and narrow. Horses, however, will provide us with fresh meat."

"By the gods, they won't!" snapped Cairell. "We need them to return to Dún Scáthach."

"Return? No one leaves the Glen of Terror," cackled the old woman.

"Then we will be the exception," replied Aonghus firmly.

The old woman gazed at him thoughtfully across the fire.

"Perhaps you will," she said thoughtfully.

Cairell turned to Aonghus.

"Did you find a way of killing the Oillipheist?"

"No." Aonghus shook his head. "Perhaps there is no way."

"If you were to pierce its throat exactly in the center, then it would die."

They turned to stare at the old woman who made the statement.

"How do you know this?" demanded Aonghus.

"Because it is an ancient knowledge handed down among the wise women," wheezed the old woman, Osna. "Once the Oillipheist had a mate . . . so the story goes. Not long after the two beasts arrived in Gleann na Scanradh. That was when there were real men in the glen, not the spineless animals that exist now. There was one such warrior . . . ah, but I forget his name. He matched his steel with one of the Oillipheist and thrust his spear into its throat. He died, of course, but so did the Oillipheist. Its mate has lived on, age after age, and no other man has dared offer his life to destroy the beast. Only by self-sacrifice can the beast be killed, for one must approach close to it if one is going to be able to cast a spear into its throat."

Aonghus bit his lips thoughtfully.

"You are sure of this?"

"Yes. But no one would be able to get near enough to cast his spear without coming into range of the raking talons of the creature. Therefore, one avoids the Oillipheist or one commits suicide."

"That does not sound like a choice," Cairell grimaced.

The old woman cackled again.

"It is a choice only for the brave."

"The brave or foolhardy," rejoined Cairell.

The woman laughed again and then subsided with a sniff.

"Have you no ale here?" she asked querulously.

Aonghus shook his head absently. He was wondering how he could approach the beast close enough to stab it in the throat without being raked by its talons or torn apart in its powerful jaws.

"This is no hospitality," Osna grumbled. "I am off to the cave of Bríbhéir."

She stood up and began to shuffle off into the darkness.

"Wait!" Cairell sprang up. "Can we get to the cave of the brewer from here?"

It was the young girl Druth who answered.

"Of course. All the caves in which my people dwell are connected."

"Then," said Cairell to Aonghus, "let us leave the horses here and go to see this Bríbhéir the brewer. We may be able to learn something from him."

Aonghus nodded. Osna had already vanished and so it was left to Druth to guide them. They took a handle of wood as a makeshift torch and followed her through the twisting passage. Now and again they were surprised to enter an occupied cave and find people crouched around fires.

"This is where the people live," Druth told them. "There is a story that once we lived out in the glen itself under the sky, which was bright and warm during the day and dark with silver lights at night. But that is a story. . . ."

Finally they came to a large cave—a cave of incredible vaulted heights that was filled with a smoky light from countless burning torches. The stench of alcohol was overpowering.

"This is the cave of Bríbhéir," the girl said.

Everywhere stood large pottery jars, each the size of a man, while in the center of the cave stood vast vats of simmering alcohol whose fumes made Aonghus and Cairell feel dizzy by their pungency.

Druth looked at Aonghus speculatively.

"Let us drink ale, warrior, and retire to some secluded cave."

Aonghus shook his head impatiently.

"Listen, Druth, I have explained before that the customs of your people are not those of mine."

"But I have followed you across the glen," protested the girl, sulkily. "You have saved me from Oillipheist."

"I do not love you."

"Love again? We live short lives in the glen because of the Oillipheist. Therefore, our law is to enjoy the life we have—drink when we can and partake of the enjoyment of our bodies while we can. What other law is there?"

Aonghus sighed deeply.

"Maybe the gods will one day let you discover the answer to that question. One day, once the Oillipheist is gone."

The girl pouted.

"The Oillipheist is—is now and has always been. There can be no life without it."

Aonghus became aware of a jovial-faced fat man threading his way unsteadily through the vats.

"Greetings, friends. I had heard rumors that there were strangers in the glen, yet I did not credit it. There is no way in or out to my knowledge."

Aonghus sighed impatiently and was about to comment when the fat man went on: "Have you come in search of my ale?"

The girl stepped forward with a smile. "Why else should we seek out the cave of Bríbhéir?"

The brewer stroked the side of his nose with a pudgy forefinger.

"What can you give me in return?" He glanced at Aonghus and Cairell. "Fine shields and swords will buy you much ale."

"They are not for barter," replied Aonghus coldly.

The joviality vanished from the fat man's face.

"I say what is for barter in Gleann na Scanradh!"

"We are here to kill the Oillipheist. We need our weapons," explained Cairell.

Bríbhéir stared at him in surprise for a moment and then threw back his head and began to roar with laughter. So hard did he laugh that he staggered back to the edge of one of his vats, sunken into the floor of the cave, and would have toppled in had not Cairell leapt forward and dragged him back. The action promptly sobered the brewer.

"Forgive me," he said. "It is little enough humor there is in the glen." He wiped his forehead. "If I had fallen into my vat I would either drown or be so overcome with fumes that I would have slept a thousand years."

Cairell shrugged. "It was nothing."

But the brewer was full of gratitude.

"No, no. For that you will have a jug of my best ale."

Aonghus was staring at the fat brewer with a frown of concentration. He looked from Bríbhéir to the vat and back again.

"Is it known if the Oillipheist drinks?" he asked slowly.

They looked at him, not understanding.

Old Osna, who had come to the cave before them, poked her scrawny neck out from behind a barrel.

"Of course it drinks, stranger. And it eats . . ." She gave a high-pitched cackle. "It eats well."

Aonghus was looking at Bríbhéir now.

"How much ale do you have?"

The brewer grinned uncertainly.

"I could drown the entire glen if I so wished," he said proudly

"What are you thinking?" asked Cairell.

"If we could get the creature to drink Bríbhéir's ale, perhaps it would go into a sleep—a sleep deep enough for me to approach and pierce its throat as the old woman said."

"What if the old woman's wrong about the way to kill the beast?"

"It's a chance one has to take, for there is no other option."

"But where will we be able to find a vat of sufficient

proportions to fill with enough ale to make a suitable potion for the beast?" protested Cairell. "And how will we be able to hold the beast at bay while it is being filled? And how will we be able to entice the beast . . .?"

Aonghus waved him to silence and turned to Bríbhéir again.

"Do you know any place in the glen that is large enough to provide a drinking well for the animal, and one we could fill without endangering ourselves?"

A hint of respect was sitting on Bríbhéir's face as he regarded Aonghus.

"I know of such a place, warrior. You have a marvelous idea. Not even the wise women of the glen ever thought of such a thing . . ."

"Where is this place?" interrupted Aonghus impatiently.

"Not far from here. It used to be a small lake in the days before the coming of the Oillipheist. It dried up. It is simply a great hollow now of hard dried clay. That could easily be filled."

"How easily?"

"The lake used to be fed from the mountain. The rains used to seep through the mountains, gather in subterranean streams and pools. These very streams and pools I have dried and now use to store my ale when I brew it. All I have to do is remove the obstructions from the main vats and the ale will go plunging through the underground passage, through which the subterranean stream ran, and empty out into the bed of the stream that fed into the lake."

Aonghus smiled. It sounded too easy.

"How are you going to entice the Oillipheist away from the cave to the lake?" demanded Cairell.

"The Oillipheist is waiting at the cave where you left your horses," Druth nodded. "It won't leave there until it thinks you are dead or gone."

Aonghus thought a moment.

"Then I will make it follow me." He turned to Bríbhéir again. "You are sure you have enough ale to fill the lake?"

Bríbhéir chuckled. "I have enough ale to fill ten such lakes. What else in life have I to do except brew ale?"

"Cairell, you will take charge of filling the lake with Bríbhéir. I will go to lure the Oillipheist toward the lake."

"But you don't know the way," protested Cairell.

"Bríbhéir must tell me."

The brewer tugged at his ear. "I'm no good at directions . . ."

The girl Druth drew herself up.

"I will go with you, warrior, and show you the way."

"No," Aonghus said at once. "It's too dangerous."

Druth tossed her head scornfully

"If it is dangerous for me then it is as dangerous for you."

Aonghus sighed.

"We cannot spend our time arguing," he said. "Let us go." He hesitated and turned back to Cairell. "Remember, if anything happens to me, it will be up to you to free our people."

Cairell watched them vanish from the cave of the brewer and then turned with a sigh. "Come, Bríbhéir, let us start filling this lake of yours. And let us hope the Oillipheist likes strong ale!"

Chapter Twenty-three

Aonghus was glad that Druth had come with him for he would have missed several turnings in the passageways back to the cave where they had left the horses. He had forgotten what a sinuous, twisted route they had come by. It was strange that the people of the glen seemed to possess an uncanny knowledge of the paths through the caves, even in total darkness. Druth led the way with a firm, sure step and before long they were back in the cave. The two horses stood trembling and fearful. They whinnied and came nuzzling at Aonghus. He talked coaxingly to them for a while before moving to the mouth of the cave. The great Oillipheist was lying two hundred yards from the entrance, its red eyes half closed. At Aonghus' movement, the eyes widened and it let forth a low rumble.

Aonghus, having seen the speed of its great bulk, knew that there was little room to maneuver if they were to attempt to get past its scaly body.

"Can you ride a horse?" he demanded, returning to Druth.

"What you can do, I can do also," replied the girl with spirit.

"But it will take speed and skill to get by the Oillipheist, and then we must keep ahead of it until we reach the lake."

"You lead and I will follow."

"But where is the lake from the cave mouth?"

"To the right and along the foot of the high cliffs. It is about a mile across the hillocks."

Aonghus whistled.

"As much as a mile? I would have sworn that we had gone not more than a few hundred yards through the caves to Bríbhéir."

He calmed the horses again and led them to the mouth of the cave. Still keeping within the shadows, he helped the girl mount and then climbed onto his own steed. He hesitated a moment, gathering his courage, and then motioned with his hand, urging his mount forward.

The horses sprang out of the cave. Simultaneously there came a roar and Aonghus, glancing quickly over his shoulder, saw the mighty muscles of the Oillipheist rippling as it lumbered to its squat legs. The creature gave a bestial snarl of rage and then began to move forward.

Crouching low, Aonghus urged his horse to greater speed, glancing sideways to make sure Druth was keeping pace. The girl's horse was doing most of the work, for she had let it have its head and it was merely following the lead that Aonghus' mount had set it. They raced across the squelching, mud-soaked land. Yet behind them the reptilian beast seemed to be gaining on them in spite of its colossal bulk.

Onward they raced until, coming to the top of a rise, Aonghus saw a bubbling lake not far away. A group of

figures stood at its edge, Cairell among them. The filling
of the lake had been accomplished and Aonghus breathed
a short prayer of thanks as he urged his horse toward it.
He heard a cry on the air and saw one of the figures
point in their direction. All but Cairell were running
toward the shelter of the black caves beyond. This was
the shelter to which he and Druth must head.

He gave a cry of encouragement to the girl and dug
his heels firmly into his horse's flanks. Down they went
toward the lake. Cairell was moving rapidly in the wake
of Bríbhéir and the others, having satisfied himself that
all was well—that the lake was filled and that Aonghus
and the girl were in advance of the creature.

A moment later Aonghus heard a faint cry, the squeal
of a frightened animal. He glanced behind.

Druth's horse had stumbled and fallen and lay on its
side, kicking feebly in the air, squealing in pain. The
girl had tumbled off but was coming to her feet, shaking
her head as if to clear it.

Behind her emerged the mighty form of the Oillipheist.

Aonghus did not hesitate, futile as the gesture was.
He heaved his horse around in a tight circle and began
to make for the girl. He had hardly gone a few paces
when he realized that it was too late to save her.

The beast was upon her before she knew it. One snap
of its terrible jaws ended the girl's existence. The
Oillipheist threw back its head, sending the bloody
body into the air before it caught it again in its cavern-
ous mouth. For a few moments the beast halted, quiv-
ering and panting as it proceeded to devour its gruesome
meal.

Sickened, Aonghus turned away, realizing, in spite of
the moment, that the incident had given him time to
turn and spur away for the lake again.

Reaching the cave he threw himself from his horse.
Cairell was waiting, white-faced, with the others. No
one said a word. From the shelter of the caves they

watched as the beast finished its meal and came trotting down toward the lake, sniffing suspiciously.

"Even as you suggested, the lake is filled," Bríbhéir muttered.

"Let us hope the beast will drink," said Cairell quietly.

Osna, the old woman, cackled mirthlessly in the background.

"It always drinks after a meal."

Aonghus bit his lip. Had these people no feelings? One of their own had been killed before their eyes and no one seemed to mind.

Bríbhéir seemed to read his mind.

"We have grown accustomed to such scenes, warrior," he said defensively. "Life goes on. What point in lamenting?"

The beast was moving slowly to the edge of the lake, hissing in pleasure. It sniffed suspiciously and then stood staring at the bubbling liquid with its blood-red, malignant eyes. A long, flickering red tongue washed over its bloodstained jowl. Slowly it lowered its massive, scaly head to the lake. Its snaky tongue flickered out to test the liquid. It paused. Those watching held their breath, wondering what the creature would do. Then the Oillipheist put its head down in earnest and began to drink long and deeply. After a while, as they watched, the beast began to lurch a little, becoming unsteady on its massive legs. It raised its head and began to shake it in an odd fashion. However, it continued to drink. Then, after several moments more, it tottered forward several paces into the lake. The level was now distinctly lower than before. It peered around, almost in a bewildered fashion. Slowly, almost gently, it lowered its bulk into the remaining level of alcohol, rolled on its side and a heavy snoring began to rise from its recumbent body.

A smile spread across Bríbhéir's face. "By the gods of

terror and fear, your plan has worked. The Oillipheist is asleep."

Cairell silently clapped Aonghus on the back.

Aonghus drew his long sword.

"Well, let us put old Osna's information to the test."

Cairell started to come with him but Aonghus shook his head.

"No need for both of us to taste danger. I will go. You stay here, and if I fail, it will be up to you to perform the deed and free our people from Scáthach."

Cairell was about to protest but he realized Aonghus was right. Silently he watched the chieftain of Hy-Nia walk slowly from the cave toward the massive sleeping form in the center of the lake.

The stale smell of ale and the putrid smell of the creature were vile. Aonghus moved cautiously around the edge of the lake and came to the shallows where the beast had entered. The Oillipheist was lying in perhaps two or three feet of ale. Its great head was stretched forth and Aonghus saw that its long neck was unprotected. He realized that Osna was probably right—the neck was not covered in hard scales like the rest of its grey body. Indeed, the underside of the neck was a dirty white color, and below its putrid, fleshy exterior a large pulse throbbed.

It required all Aonghus' nerve to move toward the terrible beast. Long sword in hand, he waded through the stench of alcohol and moved cautiously to where the pulse of the sleeping beast throbbed in its neck.

Grasping the hilt of his sword, daggerlike, he raised his hands on a level with his own head, leaning backwards a little, then threw his entire weight behind the thrust, sinking the blade into the pulsing mass.

There was a piercing shriek from the beast. It was fear more than anything that now controlled Aonghus' actions. He drew out his blade and thrust it into the neck again, right to the hilt, and then he stabbed at the animal a third time. Out spurted a dirty purple liquid, spraying like a geyser. It soaked Aonghus, covering him with its loathsome color and its even viler smell. He had no time to feel disgust. The beast was shrieking and threshing about.

Panic-stricken now, he turned and went scrambling back through the reeking liquid, sword still in hand. He half glanced across his shoulder as he reached the shore. He expected to see that the beast had risen and was at his shoulder, but it still lay on its side, the terrible purple liquid spraying from its throat. Its limbs were jerking in the final spasmic muscular reaction of death.

He stood watching. It was several minutes before the beast finally died.

Cairell was the first to reach him. Wordlessly, the young charioteer gripped his arm. Then, taking out his own sword, he moved to the beast and began to cut the central tusk from its snout.

"Scáthach wants proof," he said shortly.

Bríbhéir and Osna had several other people come slowly from the cave to stare in wonder at the dead Oillipheist, which had been central to their existence from time immemorial. It was Bríbhéir who expressed their thoughts.

"What shall we do now that the beast is dead?" he asked wonderingly.

"That is for the people of the glen to decide," Aonghus replied. "But this deed was done in the name of Scáthach, ruler of the Land of Shadows. In return for its accomplishment, she asks the people of the glen to swear allegiance to her."

"That we will do," Bríbhéir replied readily.

"I must take her a token of your oath."

"Old Osna will cut an Ogham stick for you to take to Scáthach."

"Then we will rest with you a day and commence our journey back to Dún Scáthach tomorrow," Aonghus said. Suddenly he realized that he felt very tired. Perhaps it was the fumes of the alcohol, or the putrid smell of the beast. He closed his eyes and swayed. Cairell caught him by the arm. He found himself being led, half carried, toward the caves. He tried not to think about the fate of the girl, Druth. He didn't want to think about anything—not for a long, long time.

Chapter Twenty-four

It took Aonghus and Cairell a week to approach the
hills around Dún Scáthach. The journey had been a
slow one, mainly due to the fact that they had to share
the surviving horse, for nowhere could they find a
second mount. It had been futile to try to harness the
solitary beast to the chariot and so they had discarded
it. In spite of the irritations at the delay, they had to
move in a slow and leisurely pace to ensure that the
animal was not worn out by the extra burden it carried.
In other circumstances the journey would have been a
pleasant one, passing through green, welcoming glens
with gushing streams and verdant surroundings, populated with wild game, fowl and fish.

Cairell had estimated that Scáthach's fortress was
about half a day's ride ahead of them. They were passing through a glen covered in tall conifers—a pleasant
valley where countless birds trilled in the branches of
the trees. Cairell was walking beside the horse with

Aonghus taking his turn at riding when the young charioteer halted and tugged at Aonghus' leg.

Ahead of them on the pathway stood a young warrior,
his shield hitched over his shoulder. His weapons were
sheathed.

"By his bearing he is a Désí warrior," frowned
Cairell. "Do you recognize him, Aonghus?"

Aonghus shook his head and nudged the horse forward.

They drew closer and saw that he was a young man
with pleasant features. He saluted them gravely.

"Greetings, Aonghus of Hy-Nia."

"Who are you?" replied Aonghus, puzzled, for Cairell
was right—the plaid the man wore proclaimed him to
be of the clan Désí.

"I am Meallaim of Hy-Macalla. I was sent to find you
by Eochaidh Allmuir."

"What has happened?" demanded Aonghus, a tingle
of fear in his spine as he realized that Eochaidh would
not send a warrior in search of them, risking Scáthach's
fury, if there was nothing wrong.

"Eithne was abducted from our midst while we were
waiting for you by Dún Scáthach."

Eithne! His heart lurched. He had been thinking
much of the Fomorii princess since he had departed on
Scáthach's errand. While he felt indifferent to the advances of the queen of the Land of the Shadows and
poor little Druth of the Glen of Terror, he realized that
his emotions were not impassive when he thought of
Eithne.

"Scáthach? Did she abduct Eithne?" His voice was
harsh.

Meallaim shrugged.

"We do not know who was behind it. All I know is
that she is held in a fortress nearby this very spot and I
was sent to show you to the place."

Aonghus already had his sword in hand. His face was
grim.

"Show me the way!" he demanded.

Cairell opened his mouth as if to protest, then closed it. He was puzzled but, without consulting him, Aonghus was already moving swiftly behind the young warrior, leaving the broad path into the dark forest. He had dismounted and was leading the horse. The way through the trees seemed incredibly short. They emerged from their enveloping darkness into a rocky clearing in the middle of which rose a tall, impressive-looking fortress. It looked bleak and forbidding.

"This is the place in which she is held," the young warrior said, standing aside.

Aonghus stared at the silent ramparts.

"How many guard her?" he asked.

"Alas, I do not know," Meallaim replied. "Not many, I think."

"Are you sure that this is the place, Meallaim?" asked Cairell suspiciously. "It gives the impression of being deserted."

"By my ancestors," vowed the young warrior. "This is the place."

Aonghus pressed his lips together as he gazed over the barren-looking, windswept stone of the fortress with its black, eyeless windows. The tall gates stood open.

"Well, we will not find her standing here," muttered Aonghus. "Let's enter."

Cairell laid a cautious hand on his arm.

"Surely there is something amiss, Aonghus," he began.

"Something will surely be amiss if we do not effect Eithne's rescue," replied Aonghus, pushing on toward the gates.

Meallaim followed, his own sword drawn, but Cairell could not shake his feeling of disquiet. There was something wrong about the situation.

They came through the gates into a gloomy, darkened hallway. Aonghus could just make out several doorways leading off to left and right. He stood uncertain. The atmosphere was damp and he felt an oppressive coldness hanging in the air.

A hollow laugh echoed through the hall.

Cairell, who had followed behind Meallaim, drew his own sword. In the movement of the shadows he lost sight of Aonghus and the young warrior.

"Aonghus!"

There was no answer. He began to run toward the shadows to his right. Then a scream halted him. It was a high-pitched, feminine scream.

"Beware a trap, Aonghus!" he called desperately, peering around to try to spot his companion.

Aonghus had heard the scream. With the cry "Eithne!" on his lips he had pushed through a portal to his right, into the darkened bowels of the fortress. He stood blinking a moment, aware that there was a faint light emanating from a strange substance that clung to the stonework. He appeared to be in a large hall, one that would have made the Great Hall of Temuir seem like a cattle shed. It was a vaulted chamber that ran endlessly into the distance. Again the hollow laughter seemed to echo out of every dark cranny in its structure.

The coldness Aonghus had felt was more marked.

He took a pace forward and at once found himself enmeshed in a cold, sticky substance. He tore at it with his free hand. It was like a mesh of silk. It seemed to be festooned everywhere, a curious gossamer, fine and almost invisible, shimmering like strands of thread in the soft light that fell on it. The substance was surprisingly strong. Eventually Aonghus sheathed his sword, took out his dagger and hacked at it until he was free.

It was then he noticed that Cairell and Meallaim were no longer with him. He called out to them but received no reply.

Then he felt a movement in the air. He glanced about him and stifled a cry of disgust in his throat.

High up on the wall, moving slowly down the gossa-

mer threads, was a nightmare of a creature, large and
venomous in appearance, and almost as big as a man.
Its dozen legs clung to the threads while four more
limbs flexed and unflexed like gigantic claws. It was
moving easily down the strands toward him.

Aonghus struggled to free his long sword from its
sheath. As the thing moved near he made a slashing
motion. The creature halted, its forelegs waving in curious patterns, as if to mesmerize him. Aonghus slashed
again, severing one of its limbs. The thing opened its
hideous slit of a mouth and let forth a cry that froze
Aonghus' very blood, so hideous a scream he had never
heard before.

It was fear and no other motivation that made Aonghus
rush forward, slashing and stabbing at the creature until
a terrible yellow pus sprayed from its punctured body.
The thing, pierced in a dozen places, with many of its
limbs severed, fell from its perch on the web and hit
the floor on its back, where it lay with its remaining
limbs kicking feebly at the air.

Aonghus stood shaking.

The female scream came again, even more piercing
than the terrible moaning sounds of the creature's dying.

Aonghus glanced up.

Farther along the vast hallway he could see a raised
platform. On it, her arms manacled to two stone pillars,
was Eithne. She struggled and screamed in frenzy while
nearby, sewing their gossamer nets ever more closely
to her, came two fellow creatures of the thing that he
had slain.

"Help me, Aonghus!" came her soft cry of fear.

Aonghus began to move forward, horror and desperation on his brow as he realized that he could never cover
the distance to her before one of the creatures reached
her.

He realized that the entire hall was filled with the
loathsome things and he moved forward in a frenzy of

slashing and cutting. An unearthly chorus seemed to well up around him as the things began to swarm on him.

Behind him Cairell had found the door through which Aonghus had gone. He threw it open and stood in a ruined hallway. Before him in the gloom he saw Aonghus moving, yelling, cutting and slashing at seemingly invisible enemies. There was nothing else in the deserted hall. He heard a hollow chuckle behind him and swung around.

At the door stood the skull-faced druid.

"Indech!"

The druid's smile was malicious.

"Too late to save your friend now, little charioteer," Indech sneered. "I have planted the seed and your chieftain's imagination will encompass his own death."

"Not if the gods are still with us!" cried Cairell.

"You need more than gods to help you," laughed the druid and vanished where he stood.

Cairell swung back to where Aonghus was continuing his frenzied battle.

"Aonghus! Stop! It is all in your imagination! Indech has done this thing!"

But Aonghus, stabbing as another creature came dangerously close, did not understand.

"Eithne!" he cried, his eyes on the vision ahead of him. The girl was struggling and twisting in her bonds as the creatures come nearer. "We must rescue Eithne!"

Cairell saw Aonghus' fear-crazed eyes and knew his task was hopeless.

Aonghus felt a slimy touch on his arm, turned, and saw a grinning creature, claws waving in the air. He stabbed swiftly.

Cairell dodged under the sword, throwing himself to one side to avoid the blade. Then the young charioteer, quickly reversing his own weapon, sent the pommel smashing down on his friend's head.

Aonghus Mac Orba of Hy-Nia collapsed slowly to the ground.

Sheathing his sword, Cairell picked up the inert body and carried Aonghus out of the ruined hall—out of the ruins of the grey fortress.

There was a pool in the clearing nearby. He carried Aonghus across and laid him down by its side.

"You dare meddle, little charioteer?"

The threatening figure of Indech stood on the other side of the pool. The druid's face was creased in anger.

Cairell's sword was in his hand immediately.

"Stay back, Indech. Druid or not, I shall kill you."

"You can't harm me, you little fool!"

"No?"

Cairell suddenly felt calm as he gazed on Indech's ugly, skull-like features.

He let his sword drop to the ground.

"You are right. I cannot slay you with a warrior's ways."

Indech gave a smile of triumph. Then he noticed the sling in Cairell's hand.

"Fios, my father, taught me many things, Indech. He once gave me the *uball-clis*—the feat-apple—made from the blood of toads and bears, with hardened sea-sand. He told me its secret. This slingshot is a brain ball, blessed by my father, and with a druid's blessing I can pierce your head with it and shatter your brain to pieces."

Indech gazed into Cairell's eyes and saw the truth in them.

"We will meet again, Cairell Mac Fios," Indech said hollowly. "And when we do, beware. You'd best have your *uball-clis* ready."

A mist began to envelop him. For a moment Cairell wondered whether to release his brain ball. The hesitation gave Indech his chance. He was gone and a moment later, so was the mist.

By the pool Aonghus was groaning as he recovered consciousness.

Cairell bent and began to bathe his head from the water in the pool.

"What happened? Where's Eithne? Those creatures . . . ?"

"Peace, Aonghus," urged Cairell. "It was all in your imagination. This was Indech's doing."

Aonghus frowned in bewilderment.

"Indech?"

"He was here, if not in flesh, then in projection. Did I not say that Indech was a powerful sorcerer? He can control the minds of others to perform his will."

"But I saw Eithne!" protested Aonghus, sitting up and gazing around him.

"You thought you saw Eithne. It was merely an image in your imagination."

"Then what has happened to Meallaim? He led us here."

"That was no more than Indech himself, or an image he conjured."

Aonghus bit his lip.

"You were suspicious all along," he sighed. "I was simply foolish. As soon as I heard the Eithne was in trouble, I ran blindly after Meallaim, like some fool."

"It wasn't just the fact that I had never seen a warrior among us like Meallaim, but consider his tale. Why would Eochaidh have sent a single warrior to find us? How would Meallaim know the exact spot where Eithne had been taken . . . which just happened to be where he met us on the road?"

Aonghus shook his head.

"I have much to learn about Indech's sorcery."

"He has several times been able to fool you with his magic, Aonghus . . . By the gods!" Cairell suddenly swore. "My brain works slowly! This means that Cormac and Indech have followed us to this place! It means that they must have formed some agreement with Scáthach to encompass our deaths."

Aonghus rose to his feet.

"Then the Dési. Eithne and Aige and the others, are in danger!"

They exchanged no further word but mounted the horse and began to move as swiftly as they could toward Dún Scáthach.

By late afternoon Dún Scáthach was a black silhouette on the horizon, standing out against the western sky.

There was no more warning than a hiss in the air.

Three arrows embedded themselves in the horse, causing it to collapse without a sound. Aonghus and Cairell sprung from it as it crashed down beneath them and managed to roll away before they were pinned under its bulk.

More arrows hissed and shattered against the rocks around them.

"More imaginings?" grunted Aonghus.

"These are real enough," replied Cairell, nodding to the arrows. "I know the markings well. Those are of Clan Morna."

"So as Indech failed with his magic, Cormac hopes to succeed with his warriors."

Feeling more confident in his ability to handle the tangible, Aonghus smiled. "Let's find out how many and where they are."

Crouching low, he moved through the shelter of the boulders up a nearby rise to gain some high ground. The rocks gave them good cover for a while. When they halted and peered back they saw that a bowman had emerged into the open on the far side of the narrow valley through which the road wound. Raising himself, Cairell reached for a shot and set his sling into motion. The bowman yelled, flung his weapon from him and fell to the ground.

"How many do you reckon, Cairell?" asked Aonghus as they peered at the rocks opposite for sign of the rest of the attackers.

"At least three," Cairell replied. "Perhaps more."

Hardly were the words out of his mouth when two men, arrows already aligned to their bows, came running from cover. Cairell's hands worked like lightning with his sling. The two fell to his speeding missiles. As they did so, there came the sound of horses galloping and two more men, crouching low over their horses's necks, went swiftly off down the valley. Three riderless horses went wildly after them.

Cairell rose to his feet and grimaced in annoyance.

"A pity. We could have used those horses."

"No matter," Aonghus said, standing and brushing himself down. "We will be at Dún Scáthach soon."

They moved back down the hill and, walking swiftly, eyes constantly alert, toward the darkening silhouette of Scáthach's fortress. As they neared it they saw no guards on the outer walls, no sign of women, children or old men about its deserted ramparts.

Before they reached the gates, Aonghus had unsheathed his sword and swung his shield before him.

"Have they fled before Cormac?" wondered Cairell.

"I do not think it is in Scáthach's nature to flee before an enemy, if enemy Cormac has turned out to be to her."

They moved through the gates. The fortress seemed deserted. Curiously, they went to the feasting hall where the beautiful warrior queen had entertained them on their arrival in the Land of Shadows.

Aonghus placed his foot against one of the doors and shoved it open.

Scáthach sat on the chair of office in the feasting hall. She was alone. She watched Aonghus and Cairell with a half smile as they came warily in.

"So, Aonghus Mac Orba of Hy-Nia, you have succeeded in spite of the odds."

Aonghus grimaced.

"As you see, I still live."

Cairell untied the bag he carried at his waist and threw it on the floor before Scáthach.

"Here is proof that the Oillipheist is slain. Behold its horn, Scáthach. And with it is an Ogham stick, cut by Osna, the wise woman of the Glen of Terror, which swears fealty to you. The task is accomplished."

Scáthach did not glance at the sack.

"I have no need of such proof. I need only your word, Aonghus of Hy-Nia."

"Truly?" There was a harshness in Aonghus' voice. "The task is done."

"In offering to place you at my side, you do not realize what honor I do you," went on the ruler of the Land of Shadows.

"It is an honor that I can't live with," replied Aonghus. "What has happened to the Dési? Why is this place deserted?"

Scáthach ignored the questions.

"There is still time to change your mind," she urged. "Come and live here with me at Dún Scáthach. Forget all other women; forget the Dési. If you continue your path with them, you will be destroyed."

"By you?"

She shook her head.

"By Cormac and Indech. You know that well."

"You do not understand, Scáthach. I do not wish to harm you. Yet while I live I am true to my chieftain and my clan."

"Very well, Aonghus of Hy-Nia," sighed the woman. Tears lay on her eyes as she looked at him. "It is your fate. You may join your chieftain and your clan. There is nothing that you or they may fear from me."

"On your soul?"

"On my soul, Aonghus."

"Where are Cormac and Indech?" demanded Cairell. "Why is your fortress deserted?"

"While Cormac and Indech raged on my shores I have ordered my people to remove themselves to the interior," replied Scáthach.

"Rage . . ." began Cairell. Anxiety crossed his face as he glanced at Aonghus. "We must get to our encampment."

"Provide us with horses or a chariot," demanded Aonghus. "Give us this one last gift."

Scáthach rose gracefully and waved them to follow her. In the courtyard stood her own silver chariot with four milk-white horses yoked to it.

"Take my chariot as a parting gift, Aonghus."

Cairell was already in the car holding the reins.

As Aonghus made to climb up beside him, Scáthach said softly: "Health to you, Aonghus of Hy-Nia. Yet my wishes cannot change your fate now. Death and destruction are still written in the heavens. Indech and Cormac will dog your path until they have destroyed you . . . or you have destroyed them."

Aonghus climbed aboard and gazed down at her beautiful features for a moment.

"Health to you, Scáthach, I hope you find a happiness that exists in reality and not in shadows."

As the chariot moved out of the courtyard of Dún Scáthach, he did not notice the tears rolling from the dark eyes of the ruler of the Land of Shadows.

Chapter Twenty-five

Cairell drove the chariot rapidly, sending it swaying along the highway over the hills toward the bay in which the Dési ships were anchored. Even before they reached the heights overlooking the long stretch of sand, they saw a wreath of smoke above the encampment on the shore.

"That's no cooking fire," muttered Cairell.

He sent the horses careening down the path. As they thundered across the sands they could see the stockade, charred and smoldering in places. Several bodies were strewn in bloodied heaps across the sands. Figures were moving behind the stockade and, without warning, a shower of arrows hissed through the air toward them. Only Cairell's expertise with his team avoided them.

Then came a shout. The gates opened and Each-Tiarna waved wildly for them to drive through into the protection of the stockade.

As they halted, people crowded around with shouted questions. There was Aige, thrusting her way forward to throw herself in Cairell's arms. There was no embarrassment in her as she hugged him to her.

"I thought you had been killed, lord!" She was laughing and crying at the same time.

Ignoring the company, Cairell bent to kiss her.

Hands were applauding Aonghus as he dismounted. He turned, searching the crowd, but Each-Tiarna and Biobal were grasping his hands and Eochaidh Allmuir, looking incredibly old and tired now, came limping forward. His arm was bandaged and he had a fresh cut, still bleeding, on his forehead.

"By the gods, Aonghus! It's good to see you alive."

"What has happened?" demanded Aonghus, gazing around at the scene of the destruction.

"Cormac Mac Art," replied Eochaidh laconically.

Each-Tiarna nodded.

"Soon after you left, the *Díoltas*, Cormac's ship, entered the next bay under the walls of Dún Scáthach. Cormac must have made some deal with Scáthach. Last night he attacked the encampment. We had no warning. However, we gave a good account of ourselves."

Aonghus bit his lip.

"You say the *Díoltas* arrived. What of Cormac's other ships?"

"They perished in the storm," Eochaidh said. "We discovered that much when we took one of Cormac's men prisoner. But he died before he could give us more exact information."

"Where is Cormac now?"

It was Biobal who replied, with a coarse chuckle.

"Fled back to his ship to lick his wounds."

Aonghus had made a swift estimate of the Dési warriors crowding around him

"Then let us use Cormac's weapon," he said earnestly. "Let fifty warriors come with me and we will attack Cormac's ship and destroy it so that he will haunt our wake no more."

"By the Mórrígán!" yelled Each-Tiarna. "I'm with you!"

"And I!" cried Biobal.

Eochaidh held up his hand in protest.

"Better to let him go, Aonghus. He is a wounded beast of prey. There is no telling what he will do. We were lucky to survive the attack."

Aonghus pressed his case.

"A wounded beast of prey, indeed. That is why he must be destroyed—he is even more dangerous than he was before. Better to have done with him now."

Eochaidh raised his arms helplessly.

Already Each-Tiarna and Biobal were organizing their men.

It was then that Aonghus saw Eithne and his heart leapt. The girl was standing in the shade of one of the shelters watching the joyous warriors milling about Aonghus. He pushed them aside and came to her.

She said nothing but stood smiling sadly up at his face.

He made to speak but she leaned forward and pressed a solitary finger against his lips.

"We will talk later. Now you must do what you must do."

He hesitated, then nodded and turned back to where the fifty warriors had gathered. They moved swiftly to the hills overlooking the bay and strained their eyes across it in search of *Díoltas*.

"It's gone!"

It did not need Each-Tiarna's comment to tell them.

Aonghus swore softly.

"He and Indech must have feared pursuit and gone into hiding."

Cairell pursed his lips.

"Perhaps he has fled back to Éireann?"

Aonghus barked with sarcastic laughter.

"Knowing Cormac and Indech, do you think it likely they would give up so easily?"

Cairell did not bother to reply.

The Dési warriors returned to the encampment immediately and Eochaidh called his depleted council of chieftains together. His wounds were troubling him and exhaustion sat on his grey features.

"We cannot stay here—that much is obvious. My dream of settling in peace among the people of Alba is not to be," he began.

"Let us sail south," suggested Biobal, at once. "I have heard tales from our seamen that there are rich and pleasant lands to the south of us."

Eochaidh turned to Each-Tiarna.

"One direction is as good as another to me," shrugged the chieftain.

"And you, Aonghus? What do you say?"

"Whichever path we take, Cormac and Indech will be there. I feel it. Sooner or later we will have to have a final confrontation with them." He paused. "Let it be south. As Each-Tiarna says, one direction is as good as another."

"It is settled. But there is one other matter."

They looked at the chieftain of the Dési in expectation.

"I have grown old in recent times," Eochaidh said. "Age is not only a physical matter, it is also a thing of the mind. Responsibility has left me weak. Seeing the destruction of many people, seeing them driven from the lands of our ancestors, seeing my friends, my relatives, my kinsmen, pursued to death, has set bonds of iron over my soul. I am old and wounded. Soon I may no longer be able to lead you."

They protested at that but Eochaidh smiled and raised a hand to quiet them.

"Once I could count fifty chieftains at my council. Now I count but you three." He grew morose. "Ah, if only Iolar, my druid, were here."

There was silence for a while.

"Gabur of Dún Glas has gone, too. He was my *tánaiste*. Had he lived, the chieftainship of the Dési would have been his. But he fell before the vengeance of Cormac Mac Art."

Eochaidh raised his head and looked at them each in turn.

"The time has come when I must appoint a new *tánaiste*—one who will lead this remnant of the Dési when I have journeyed on to the Otherworld. Who shall it be?"

They looked at each other in embarrassment. What Eochaidh said was true. The clan needed a *tánaiste* to guide it as well as the chieftain.

"There is only one man fitted for such a task," Each-Tiarna said, standing up slowly. "I nominate Aonghus Mac Orba of Hy-Nia."

Biobal was on his feet.

"I, too, pledge my loyalty to Aonghus of Hy-Nia."

Eochaidh smiled gently at Aonghus. "You have confirmed what was already in my mind. Subject to the acceptance of the people of the Dési, will you receive the office as my nominated successor, Aonghus of Hy-Nia?"

Aonghus swallowed and nodded, not trusting his voice.

"Then when we sail south tomorrow, you shall be *tánaiste* of the Dési."

Maraí, of the three captains of the Dési, had once conducted trade among the Britons and the Gauls whose countries lay to the south of Alba. He recalled one peninsula which, interpreted from the native name, meant "the land of comrades." It jutted to the south-west some three days' sail from the coast of Alba. He assured Eochaidh that while certain customs and laws differed, the druids and the Brehons were found in equivalent among its pleasant valleys and mountains. So it was that daybreak found the three ships, *Cúr*, *Méirliún* and *Spioróg*, straining their sails away from the shores of the Land of Shadows into calm blue seas before a southerly and pleasant breeze.

Only Aonghus paced the deck of the *Spioróg*, watching anxiously for signs of Cormac's ship. But the seas were clear around them. Nevertheless, Aonghus remained nervous and worried. Cairell began to grow anxious for his friend and spoke to Aige about him.

"Can't you talk to Eithne?" he asked. "He is in love with Eithne, though he tries to hide it."

Aige made a face.

"Eithne certainly cares for him, and yet she feels that he only sees her as a friend, and for this she is sad."

Cairell shook his head.

"It is more than friendship, so I believe. And he needs both love as well as friendship, for I suspect that he has imprisoned himself in the burden of guilt he feels for what has befallen the Dési because of his actions."

"To find fault one must trace events back to the first fault," observed the girl.

"If only Aonghus saw that," smiled Cairell.

But even Eithne could not persuade Aonghus to give up his troubled thoughts. Nor could she draw aside the veil over which he now guarded his emotions. He felt the responsibility more now that Eochaidh had made him *tánaiste*. He felt the strain of duty heavy on his soul. He grew more introspective, going back again and again in his mind to the events of Temuir when his spearthrust had been the destruction of the Dési.

The three ships ploughed through the seas, chasing the southerly sun. There were no storms, or mists, or monsters to make their journey one of anxiety. Only

the cry of circling seabirds interrupted the idyll of the
voyage. The days were warm, the skies were blue, and
the golden sunshine bathed a sky that saw no clouds. At
night the warmth continued with the fragrant smell of
the soft sea.

Maraí knew the waters well. By dawn on the fourth
day, the Dési ships approached a twisted and sinuous
peninsula, jutting like some crooked finger into the sea.
But the area was one of a delightful variety of scenery,
covering the long backbone of sandstone that ridged
down its center. The ships found a natural anchorage in
a small sandy bay whose dazzling white beach was set
between moderately sized cliffs. Rising on either side
were thickly wooded areas of green and a stream ran
open to the sea. Everywhere it was lush and even from
the decks of their ships they could spot wildlife aplenty.

Eithne came to stand at Aonghus' side as he viewed
the land from the stern deck of the *Spioróg*.

"This is how I envisaged the shore of the Land of the
Ever Young," she whispered.

Aonghus shrugged. "Beauty can be deceptive, Eithne,"
he said curtly. "We must be on our guard."

Eochaidh called a council on the deck of the *Cúr* and
Aonghus took Cairell with him.

"It seems a pleasant enough corner of the world," the
chieftain observed. "Yet no one appears on the shore to
greet us."

"There are fish in the sea and animals on the shore,"
Biobal pointed out. "There is ripe fruit for the taking,
and beyond the woods I see pastureland, where cows
might graze. It seems a paradise without people."

"And that worries me," responded Aonghus.

Biobal frowned.

"Perhaps you see a threat that does not exist?"

Aonghus was about to reply when Eochaidh intervened.

"Unless the Dag da, father of the gods, has blessed us

with sudden good fortune, I share Aonghus' concern. Aonghus, you are my *tánaiste* now. If my wounds were not troubling me, I would undertake the task I will ask of you. Take twenty warriors and search the countryside. Find out if there be a king or chieftain of this land. Tell him that we desire to settle in this land in peace and amity with his people."

Aonghus turned to Each-Tiarna.

"Will you come with me?"

The chieftain smiled and nodded.

"I have seen some wild horses yonder. Perhaps I can catch a few for our use."

Eochaidh laid a hand on Aonghus' arm.

"I pray to the gods that the ruler of this land will accept our coming in peace. I would like to see the Dési at rest before I depart for the Otherworld."

Aonghus shook his head.

"Plenty of time then, Eochaidh. The time for your journey to the House of Donn, lord of death, is not yet."

They spent the morning establishing themselves on the shore. Each-Tiarna, the horse lord, and some of his men were able to catch several horses and, curiously, many of them proved to be already broken and used to humankind. Yet they had not been shod in a long time. It was as if they had been abandoned by their owners.

When Each-Tiarna showed them to Aonghus he shook his head with a puzzled air.

"There is something wrong here," he said softly.

Aonghus ran his hands over a grey that Each-Tiarna had just harnessed. Though the horse had not been groomed for years, it was obvious that it had been a trained and domesticated beast. It trembled slightly under his hands but certainly gave no other sign of skittishness that a wild horse would show.

"Are the others like this one?" Aonghus asked.

Each-Tiarna nodded.

"How long have they been abandoned?"

"Perhaps a year, no more. Perhaps less. Beyond the woods, I saw some buildings. Ruined, they were. Deserted. One of them had been fired in its destruction. They were small dwellings such as farmers live in."

"Perhaps the farmers simply moved on?" suggested Aonghus.

"And left good horses to run free?" Each-Tiarna shook his head. "No. There is something wrong here. I know it."

Chapter Twenty-six

It was mid-afternoon when the score of Dési warriors, led by Aonghus, Cairell and Each-Tiarna, mounted their horses and left the shore to commence a search of the interior of the peninsula. As the countryside was clearly deserted, Eochaidh Allmuir and Biobal had decided not to fortify their encampment on the shore. There was little to fear and such fortification would be a waste of time. It was decided that if Aonghus and his party found no sign of habitation within two or three days then they would return. His leave-taking from Eithne was a little subdued for he was still weighted down by depression, and no matter how the girl tried to reach out to him, he retreated into morose feelings of guilt. There was no reservation between Aige and Cairell as they said farewell and, indeed, it was hard to part the loving pair. But finally the group of horsemen moved away from the pleasant bay and up into the grasslands beyond the forests.

No sooner had they passed into the grasslands when

Cairell spied a stretch where the grass did not grow so thickly and it became obvious that once a broad highway had stretched along the peninsula, passing the ruins of several stone houses which, as Each-Tiarna had said, lay deserted, with some partially burnt.

It was Cairell who summed up the thought that had occurred to Aonghus.

"It looks like a land ravaged in war."

Indeed, as they moved on, the countryside seemed scarred and desolate of people. A sombre atmosphere began to hang around the group of Dési as they pressed onwards. The afternoon passed without incident and the misty fingers of twilight were approaching when Aonghus signalled for them to make camp for the night. They had come to the deserted buildings of what had been a farming community, all empty and shorn of roofs and parts of walls and doors. They stabled their horses in one of the deserted barns, lit a fire in the main building and settled for the night.

The cry came from the sentinel, whom Aonghus had set to keep watch, just as they were finishing their meal.

Sword in hand, Aonghus led the rush outside. The Dési warrior was struggling with a small, wiry figure who twisted and turned in a valiant effort to escape its captor. It was a youth.

They dragged him into the building to examine him by the light of the fire.

He was young, scarcely more than a boy—a slight, handsome youth with an intelligent face that he held high, his features proud, as he gazed at his captors. His limbs were well-muscled and despite the drabness of the farmer's clothes he wore, he looked every inch of warrior stock.

"Who are you?" demanded Aonghus. "Can you speak this language?"

The youth hesitated and then said in softly accented

tones: "Yes. But it is the language of Éireann. Do you
not speak the tongue of the Coranieid?"

Aonghus shook his head.

"Is this the land of the Coranieid?"

The youth was scornful.

"No; yet you and your like would make it so."

"I don't understand," Aonghus said.

The youth stared at Aonghus and for a moment there
was doubt in his eyes. Then he straightened, adopting
his scornful mask once more.

"You are jackals of the Coranieid, even if you be not
Coranieid yourselves."

Aonghus shrugged.

"I have little idea of what you are talking about. Tell
me who you are."

"I am Teg, son of . . ." began the youth, but paused
and said more softly, "I am Teg, a farmer."

Instinctively, Aonghus knew he lied.

"Tell me, Teg the farmer," he smiled, "in what country are we?"

Teg raised an eyebrow, expressing disbelief in Aonghus'
lack of knowledge.

"You are in the kingdom of Dyfed."

"Who rules here?"

"My . . ." again the boy paused. "My king is Ludd."

"Why is the countryside so devastated?" demanded
Cairell.

Teg glanced angrily at him.

"You should know the answer to that question."

"If I knew I would save my breath," snapped Cairell.

Again there was a passing bewilderment in the youth's
face.

"Because of the raids of buccaneers like yourselves,"
he said. "Because of the raids of the Coranieid whom
you serve."

"We serve no one but our chieftain, Eochaidh Allmuir

of the Dési," replied Aonghus calmly. "Tell me, Teg the farmer, where may we find Ludd?"

"So that you may destroy him as you have tried to do these past three years?" cried the boy. "Torture me—do your worst. I shall not tell you that!"

Aonghus sighed as the youth's mouth tightened. He had to admire the boy's courage, but it was a courage born of fears that were ill-founded.

He shrugged.

"Let him go."

Each-Tiarna protested, but Aonghus was adamant.

"The boy has obviously mistaken us for some enemy. He has courage. It is not worth trying to obtain information from him. We'll press on in the morning and search for this Ludd who rules here."

Each-Tiarna reluctantly took the boy to the doorway and shoved him into the night. For a moment Teg stood, his puzzlement clear on his features, then he vanished into the darkness.

Cairell plucked at his lower lip thoughtfully.

"If the youth is telling the truth—if there are continuous raids here—no wonder we have seen only ruins. Who are the Coranieid?"

"Perhaps Maraí would know," Aongus said. "He seems to know most things about the politics of the world beyond the shores of Éireann."

Far away to the west a tall ship with black sails was gliding slowly southward. On its deck stood the grim figure of Cormac Mac Art, his face ugly with its scars and its one unblinking eye, which never ceased its restless circle of the horizon.

Indech had just climbed onto the deck beside him.

"Well, do you bring me good news at last?"

The skull face of the druid smiled thinly.

"The auguries are auspicious, Cormac."

Cormac swore vilely.

"I need more than auguries! I want the life of Aonghus Mac Orba! I want the destruction of the Dési!"

"And you will have them," replied Indech calmly. "The Dési have even now landed in the kingdom of Ludd of Dyfed."

Cormac was momentarily startled.

"How do you know that?" he demanded.

Indech sniffed.

"I know. Accept this. It is not permitted that even a High King should know how I can do what I do."

"Then where is this place? How can we reach there and destroy them?"

Indech smiled again.

"The way of encompassing their destruction is at hand."

"Sails on the starboard beam!" cried a voice from the masthead.

Cormac cursed loudly and began to issue orders to keep the *Díoltas* hull-down on the horizon and out of sight of any inquisitive ships. But Indech shook his head.

"Those sails are the bearers of the tools by which you will destroy the Dési and Aonghus Mac Orba," he said. "Make for them and leave everything to me."

Cormac was perplexed.

"Who are they?"

"They are buccaneers from Gaul. They are on their way to raid the kingdom of Dyfed."

"I fail to see . . ."

"Trust me, Cormac. Make sail for them and I will show you what to do."

Within the hour the *Díoltas*, the High King's ship, whose very name meant vengeance, had been surrounded by half-a-dozen great ships full of armed men. They were broad-beamed ships with leather sails instead of canvas, and iron chains, and of a size that made even the *Díoltas* seem like a toy ship in comparison.

Indech ordered the captain of the *Díoltas* to run up a white flag, and then sail directly toward the leading ship.

A voice came echoing across the sea in challenge.

"This is the ship of Cormac Mac Art, High King of Éireann. We wish to come aboard and speak with you," replied Indech. "It will be to your advantage."

There was a pause before the voice instructed them to send a boat across, adding that any sign of hostility would cause their ship to be sunk immediately.

Cormac and Indech were rowed to the side of the vast Coranieid vessel and hauled aboard. They were seized roughly and shoved toward the stern deck, where a giant of a man stood, hands on hips. He was broad-shouldered, with yellow hair like dirty corn. It seemed to stick out everywhere and merged into a thick, curly beard. One lock of hair kept falling over his bright, sea-colored eyes and he flung it back occasionally with a toss of his head, as a lion might shake his mane. His face was dominated by a large nose that seemed to sit on his features like a beak. His posture was like that of a moody bear.

He stared from Indech to Cormac.

"I have heard of Cormac Mac Art of Éireann." He showed his teeth, black and decaying. "I have not heard that Cormac was so foolish as to travel the high seas without adequate bodyguards."

"I would not think of holding us for ransom, Drouk of the Coranieid," Indech said softly.

The big Gaul showed surprise that Indech knew his name.

"You know me?"

"I know many things, Drouk," Indech went on calmly. "I am chief druids of Éireann, and if you know the ways of the druid, you know the power I have."

The Gaul stood uncertain. Then a speculative light crossed his eyes.

It shone for an instant before he suddenly dropped to his knees with a cry of pain. His fellows stared at him in astonishment.

Indech was smiling gently.

"Foolish Gaul! You have forgotten the power. Are not the sons of Gaul sent to the islands to learn their art from the druids of Britain and Éireann? Think no more thoughts of harming the High King. Rise and listen to me, for I have a plan to put to you."

Pain and fear on his face, Drouk of the Coranieid rose slowly to his feet and stood in respectful silence before Indech. Cormac Mac Art looked on with a smile on his gaunt features.

Chapter Twenty-seven

The morning was bright and clear, without a cloud in the sky. The countryside looked lush and inviting as the Dési moved forward along the deserted highway toward the root of the peninsula. The land still stretched pleasantly before them, and here and there they could now see well-ordered plains with fields of golden wheat and corn. They even saw some people in the distance, but when they shouted to attract attention, the figures took to their heels.

"The Coranieid must have struck great fear into these people," murmured Cairell.

An hour passed before they came to the shoulder of a hill and, crossing it, saw a large valley dominated on the far side by a magnificent fortress. It was one of the most impressive strongholds that Aonghus had ever seen. No less than four great earthwork walls surrounded it, with the central wall enclosing, as he later learned, ten acres. The walls stood twelve feet in height and seemed invulnerable. Each wall followed the contours of the hill and was protected with ditches. Aonghus could appreciate the remarkable strength and defensibility of those walls. At the western end, which they were approaching, was a forbidding gateway, the gates shut, held in place by big timber posts.

Along the walls stood lines of bowmen.

Aonghus halted his companions just beyond arrow range and then, motioning Cairell to accompany him, he rode slowly up to the gates of the fortress.

"I am Aonghus Mac Orba of Hy-Nia, of the clan Dési. I and my people come in peace."

There was a movement on the walls and a warrior called down.

"Stay back, Coranieid. Leave our land of Dyfed or we shall shoot you down where you stand."

"I am of Éireann. I am not a Coranieid," replied Aonghus. "I am a chieftain of the Dési, who have landed on your shores seeking hospitality."

"We will have none of your subterfuge!" snapped the voice.

Aonghus saw an elderly man at the warrior's elbow. He wore a band of silver around his greying hair.

"We know your kind!" His voice was sharp. "Enough of this useless talk. Shoot the Coranieid!"

As one man the bowmen pulled back and Aonghus had barely time to raise his shield.

"Stop!"

He hesitated and glanced up at the young voice that cracked across the walls.

Teg, the youth who called himself a farmer, had appeared on the walls and pushed his way to the elderly man. The man turned and stared hard at Aonghus, then motioned for his warriors to lower their bows.

"Be prepared to shoot them down if they make a false move," he called, loudly enough for Aonghus to hear.

After a while the great gates opened and Teg emerged with several armed men at his side.

"You will come with me," he said to Aonghus without greeting. "The rest of your men will wait outside our fortress."

Aonghus frowned.

"Have I word of my safe conduct?"

"You have my word that there is no choice in the matter," Teg laughed. The boy was no longer clad in a poor farmer's clothes but dressed as a warrior of wealth and position.

Aonghus shrugged, dismounted and handed the reins to Cairell.

Teg and his men led Aonghus through the towering walls into a veritable city, the like of which few places in Éireann, not even Temuir, could emulate. In the center of this massive fortress was a smaller dún, or fortress, to which Teg conducted him. He was marched into a great hall, crowded with people, and at one end, Aonghus saw an elderly man with a silver circlet sitting on a chair of office waiting for him.

"What is this place?" Aonghus asked the youth.

"The capital of Dyfed," he replied proudly. "You asked last night where you might find Ludd, king of Dyfed. You are being taken to him."

Teg marched up to where the elderly man sat.

"Father, I bring you the man who calls himself Aonghus Mac Orba of Éireann."

A young man in the robes of a druid stood next to Ludd, ruler of Dyfed. It was he who spoke first.

"You claim you are not Coranieid?"

"Nor even heard of them until I was accused of being one by this boy, Teg, when he was in our camp last night."

The druid turned to Teg.

"And this you confirm? You were a captive and yet they let you go?"

Teg nodded seriously. "If they were Coranieid, or jackals of the Coranieid, they would not have done so."

The druid nodded.

"This man comes with the speech, manner and clothes of Éireann, Ludd," he said, turning to the elderly king. "We can at least hear his story."

Ludd gestured for a chair to be brought and placed before him, and then asked Aonghus to seat himself and recount why the Dési had come to the shores of Dyfed. The story was not long in the telling.

Soon Aonghus' men had been invited inside and offered hospitality in the feasting hall of Ludd.

"You must forgive our suspicions, my son," said the old king. "These are hard times for the land of Dyfed."

"Who are these people you fear, those you call the Coranieid?" asked Aonghus.

"Raiders from Gaul. Three years ago the kingdom of Dyfed was a peaceful and prosperous country. We are not a warlike people. We live by agriculture and fishing. We believe in the ways of Bel, harbinger of peace and love. Our life was happy. No one in the land wanted for food, nor went cold in winter. There was shelter for all. Then three years ago came Drouk and his Coranieid."

"Who is Drouk?"

"Drouk the Evil One is chieftain of the Coranieid. His are a fearsome, seafaring people who sail from the harbors of Armor, the land by the sea, which is in Gaul. They came as buccaneers, plundering our coast. They burnt our settlements, took slaves, stole our wealth and destroyed what they could not take away."

"Had you no defense against them?" queried Aonghus.

"As I have said, we are not warriors," sighed Ludd. "We do what we can. But farmers with scythes are no use against swordsmen and spearmen who are ruthless in the pursuit of our wealth. My son, Teg, has in recent months organized bands of bowmen, and this has afforded us a little protection. But our grain, our cattle, our sheep are still taken. And our women and children as well. The greed of the Coranieid is not yet assuaged. Still they come."

Aonghus pursed his lips in thought.

"How often do they raid and in what quantities? How many ships do they possess?"

"They raid as they want," replied the king. "As for ships, why I have seen whole fleets flying the black banners of Drouk."

Aonghus leaned forward, a plan in his mind.

"I have told you that my chieftain, Eochaidh Allmuir, wants refuge for our tribe. We, too, are a tribe that loves peace, but we are renowned and skilled in war. Let us settle among you, and then you can use us to help protect and train your people against the Coranieid."

Ludd smiled tiredly.

"It is a noble thought. But I doubt its merits in practical terms. Even yesterday my council advised that we should move farther into the interior of our lands— far enough away from the ravenous hordes of Coranieid. Only thus may we escape their murderous intent."

It was young Teg who spoke.

"I am against it, father. A people must make a stand to live free or perish entirely. Since the dawn of time, slave must rise against slavemaster."

Aonghus smiled his approval.

"I think your son is right, Ludd."

Ludd grimaced.

"The time will come for Teg to be heard in council when he is of an age qualified to speak," he said disapprovingly.

Aonghus was about to pursue the point when a man entered the feasting hall and came straight to Ludd.

"There is smoke on the horizon to the south."

"Coranieid!"

The cry was taken up but Aonghus, smiling, shook his head.

"No, no. Our encampment is to the south, on the

shores of the peninsula. It will be our campfire that you see."

The man who had entered shook his head.

"Unless you build campfires the size of a small fortress, then they are not campfires."

There arose speculation from the company as they quit the feasting hall and went out to the ramparts of Ludd's fortress. The pall of smoke could plainly be seen rising in the southerly sky. It was black and ominous.

Cairell gave Aonghus a glance of concern.

"It is true. That is no campfire, Aonghus."

Teg's eyes narrowed.

"Coranieid! They must have landed and attacked your camp."

"Coranieid . . ." Aonghus leaned close to Cairell and dropped his voice ". . . or else Cormac has followed us once more."

The old king of Dyfed looked helpless.

"We must prepare our defense. They may be marching this way."

"I and my men must get back to our encampment," Aonghus told him. "Do you have any warriors who can accompany us?"

Ludd shook his head.

"We will need every man to guard our fortress from attack."

"Not all, father," protested Teg. "Let me take some of the young men I have trained. The strangers need our help."

Ludd made to protest but already the boy was shouting orders, gathering his companions.

Within moments, the Dési were spurring their horses south again with half a dozen young men of Dyfed, led by Teg, behind them.

Chapter Twenty-eight

It was late afternoon before the column of horsemen led by Aonghus drew near the plume of black smoke. Aonghus had led them at a furious pace, scarcely pausing once to rest the horses. It was only after they drew near to the bay in which the Dési encampment had been set up that Aonghus eased the pace and ordered Each-Tiarna to send out scouts. If Cormac or the Coranieid were waiting to ambush them, then to rush helter skelter into the camp would be inviting a great slaughter. But no one waited in ambush, and when they crested the top of the hill overlooking the bay, a terrible sight met their eyes.

Only two of the Dési ships were still anchored in the bay, and one of these—they could see it was the *Cúr*—was on fire at its stern and listing badly. Of the *Méirliún* there was no sight at all. The *Spioróg* seemed undamaged. On the shore, the encampment was in flames and bodies lay scattered in profusion, staining the white sands red. He heard the wailing of women and the screams of young children.

In spite of the destruction, there seemed no sign of any enemy.

Cairell, his face white, was already sending his horse headlong to the shore with an agonized cry on his lips. Behind him streamed the rest of the Dési warriors.

Aonghus, for a moment, could not move as he stared down on the scene. He gave a low, animal whimper as he took in the death and destruction on the beach below. His body began to shake violently as if from cold, and his emotions tossed in him like a tumultuous sea, battering and pounding his sensitivities.

Once again the Dési had suffered slaughter and once again the responsibility was his. His was the fault. He should have ensured that they had been well protected before leaving. Eochaidh had been too tired, hurting from his wounds to think clearly on the matter. It had been his responsibility. And above all his jumbled, pain-racked thoughts, he kept seeing the face of Eithne.

By the gods! The feelings of guilt momentarily dispelled. If she had been hurt . . . if she was harmed . . . But it was his fault! *His* fault! Whoever had done this deed would pay a hundredfold! He gave a loud cry of anguish as he followed his companions down to the slaughter field on the beach below.

The first person he saw was Maraí, grim faced, standing among the dead.

"Eochaidh Allmuir is dead," were the seaman's first words.

Aonghus threw himself from his horse and gazed helplessly about him.

"Eithne?" he demanded. "Where is Eithne?"

Maraí's sea-colored eyes shone in compassion.

"The last I saw, she and Aige were alive. They were taken captive. Many of our people have been taken captive."

"Captive?" Cairell was standing at his side. The young charioteer was trembling slightly. "Taken captive by whom?"

Maraí shrugged.

"They were strange warriors. But Cormac is behind it."

Aonghus groaned slightly. He had been right. Cormac!

"You saw Cormac?"

Maraí shook his head.

"I saw the *Díoltas* standing off to sea."

"You'd better explain," Aonghus said, feeling suddenly weary. "Where is Biobal?"

Maraí paused.

"Biobal is dead; so is my brother Mairnéalach." He gestured farther up the beach. "Bádóir is badly wounded, and so are a great many others. We lost half of our warriors, and many of our women and children were slaughtered. About a third were taken captive."

"Tell me how it happened."

"They came just before dawn. Most of us were asleep. As you know, because the countryside was deserted, we thought we had nothing to fear and had not fortified the encampment. The first we knew was that the strange warriors were upon us, slaughtering everyone . . ." He paused again to gather his thoughts. "It seemed that they had landed under cover of darkness. Many of our people ran inland and found shelter. Others were rounded up and taken captive. Both Eithne and Aige were among them. However, Eochaidh Allmuir was killed immediately. Biobal gathered some warriors and managed to fight his way to the *Méirliún*, but six strange ships appeared in the bay and fired it."

Aonghus gazed out across the bay.

"Where is the *Méirliún* now?" He could see no sign of it.

"At the bottom of the bay," replied Maraí. "The *Cúr* was also attacked. She is disabled, and there is no hope of saving her."

"How was the *Spioróg* spared?"

"I managed to get my crew aboard and we beat for

the open sea. We managed to fend off one attack, and that was when I saw the *Díoltas*. It was with the strange ships. I managed to avoid the ships by sheltering behind a headland. It was all I could do. I hadn't enough men to counterattack. Their ships were big and fast." He gestured helplessly.

"You did what you could, Maraí," Cairell said.

"After a while the strange warriors, with those of our people they had taken captive, withdrew to their ships and sailed south. *Díoltas* was with them."

"South?" frowned Aonghus. "Who were they?"

"Coranieid!"

It was Teg who spoke. The young man had picked up the shield of a strangely clad warrior whose body lay on the shore.

"Look at these markings. Your encampment was attacked by Coranieid."

Aonghus' eyes narrowed.

"So Cormac is in league with the Coranieid now?"

Each-Tiarna joined them, having tried to gather the survivors.

"What are we to do, Aonghus?" he said helplessly. "You are *tánaiste* of the Dési. Now that Eochaidh is dead, you are chieftain. You must tell us what to do."

Aonghus stared at them for a moment. They were all turned to him, waiting expectantly.

A cold, fiery anger surged within him. He had no doubts at all. "We will follow the Coranieid and revenge ourselves."

They gazed at him blankly.

"We shall break the power of the Coranieid," he went on. "Aye, and Cormac. We shall follow them to Gaul and take back our people. And we shall find Cormac and destroy him. For he—he and Indech—are the evil architects of our misery!"

There was a fierce murmur of approval.

The youth Teg moved forward and grasped Aonghus' arm.

"And I, Teg, son of Ludd, will come with your Dési, Aonghus. For if we destroy the Coranieid, then, indeed, my father will welcome you to these shores in peace and friendship. You may settle here as you wish in the lands of Dyfed."

"Is it agreed?" asked Aonghus.

The air became filled with shouts in support of Aonghus as the survivors gathered around. Scarcely more than seventy warriors had survived the onslaught and Aonghus immediately took these, with Teg and his men, aboard the *Spioróg*. Teg had sent one of his men back to his father to tell him what they proposed. Soon the canvas began to strain before the wind as the *Spioróg* shuddered under her canvas and moved out of the bay, turning south in the vanished wake of the raiders. The ship ploughed through the grey, choppy seas, bobbing and dipping before the wind.

On the deck, Maraí was at his place by the tiller. Beside him were Aonghus, Cairell, Teg and Each-Tiarna.

"How long before we reach the land of the Coranieid?" asked Aonghus, impatient as he peered toward the horizon.

"A full day's sail, maybe two, depending on whether we catch a fast tide across the sea."

"The weather's behind us," Teg said confidently. "We'll reach the Gaulish coast tomorrow."

Maraí glanced at him.

"You know a lot for a landsman." His tone was cynical.

Teg smiled, unabashed.

"The men of Dyfed would be poor farmers if they did not know how to read the signs of the weather."

"And do you know anything about the coastline of Gaul?" demanded Maraí.

It was not meant as a serious question, but it brought forth an unexpected answer.

"Yes. I and some companions once tried to sail after the Coranieid ships to discover where their lair was. I

did not know what good that knowledge would do me
. . . now I have discovered a way to put it to use. I
know where Drouk and the Coranieid are to be found
once we sight the Gaulish coast."

"Do they have a fortress?" asked Aonghus.

"A formidable one," replied the youth. "It is so well
constructed that no man can break into it."

"No man can build anything that another man cannot
break down," smiled Cairell.

"A good druidic saying, Cairell," agreed Teg. "Yet
you have not seen the fortress of Drouk."

Aonghus let them talk on. He kept trying to still the
thoughts of Eithne that threatened to fire his brain. He
realized how stupid he was to have been reserved with
the girl, she who kept stirring his heart and emotions.
Yet he had been so preoccupied with his own selfish
anxieties. Now perhaps it was too late to declare his
love for her. He cursed himself silently.

It was on the following afternoon that Aonghus saw
the fortress of Drouk. They had sighted the coastline of
Gaul at midday, a vista of strange mauve cliffs, scarred,
rent and crumbled by a restless sea, protected by a
multitude of reefs and islands. Maraí turned the *Spioróg*
as Teg directed, sailing around headland atumble with
tremendous piles of rocks that stretched forbiddingly to
the heavens and seemed truly to mark the ends of the
earth. No sooner were the thrusting headlands gone
when gracious inlets, which shone forth with stretches
of white fine sand, met their gaze. There seemed many
desirable landing places. Soon the rosy and mauve colors of the rocks dappled and turned to grey as the
sandstone gave way to granite. At last, in a fairly sheltered part of the coast, Teg told Maraí to draw in his
sails and anchor.

"The fortress of Drouk is on the next headland,
Aonghus," the young son of Ludd said. "It would be
best if we put ashore here and climbed over the head so
that you can view it without being spotted."

Aonghus complimented him on his clear thinking and chose Cairell to accompany him. Each-Tiarna was to stay with Maraí. A small boat was lowered, and it was no effort to reach the white, sandy shoreline. Teg led the way up a granite-strewn pathway toward a rise. They came to the headland and stretched themselves in the long grass.

"There is the fortress of Drouk and the Coranieid."

Before them stretched a wide bay, a mass of heaving, restless water breaking onto a low, sandy shore.

The fortress stood on a huge granite outcrop that rose some two hundred fifty feet above the bay. A small island of granite it was, surrounded by the inconsistent sea, which ran with threatening currents. Teg told them there was no way of reaching the island except by water, for even at low tide it was surrounded by immense sandbanks, many of which were quicksands. Under the ceaseless motion of the waves, the sands were moving hither and thither. The tides were tremendous, the spring tide particularly so. It moved so fast that it was dangerous to the unwary trying to cross the sand to the island, if any were foolish enough to attempt to find a way through the quicksands.

From where they lay hidden Aonghus could see the back of the island, to the north, rising sheer up to where the ramparts of the fortress stood on the very top of the outcrop. There was no way of approaching the fortress from that angle. The front of the island had a more gentle incline, but it was well guarded. A small bay at the foot of the rocks provided a ready-made harbor, and he could see the tall ships of the Coranieid bobbing at anchor there. From the harbor a narrow and steep pathway, initially flanked by a few crude buildings, led upwards at a sharp angle, twisting on itself, until it came to the gates of the ramparts.

"If that is the only way in," Aonghus muttered, "then we must take it."

Cairell caught at Aonghus' arm.

"There's the *Díoltas*, Cormac's ship, among the rest."

Aonghus' jaw tightened. Then he allowed himself to relax and turned to Teg.

"Do you speak the language of the Coranieid?" he asked.

"It is a corrupt dialect of what we speak in Dyfed, but I can converse with them."

"We will try to gain admittance into the fortress, claiming to be envoys from Éireann in search of Cormac Mac Art." He was abruptly decisive.

Cairell was puzzled.

"What good will that do us?"

"Gain us admittance—a few of us only—but at least enough to find Eithne and Aige and the others of our people."

"That is no good plan," protested Cairell. "You cannot even begin to guess at the number of Coranieid inside and, indeed, Cormac's men are also within the fortress."

"You have a better plan?" demanded Aonghus.

Cairell shrugged. "No. But . . ."

"I am not afraid of another man's steel," snapped Aonghus.

Cairell shook his head sadly.

"That is an unjust remark. I'll fight with you to the gates of the Otherworld. But it is not steel you need fear. Where Cormac is, so, too, will be Indech. He is the person to be warned against."

Aonghus bit his lip. No sooner had he made his jibe than he knew it to be unworthy.

"I am sorry, Cairell, you are right. We must take Indech's sorcery into account."

"By first accepting that Indech is a sorcerer, one becomes free of his influence," Cairell observed.

"Yet how can one fight the supernatural?"

"The supernatural is the natural not yet understood. Remember that."

"Indech can perform miracles."

"He can create illusions. True miracles are the result of actions of men of courage. First accept Indech's sorcery, then realize that his sorcery relies on stirring in people's imaginations what they do not know they possess."

"I am not sure I understand."

"He preys on those who do not realize his power to create illusion, Aonghus. Know that power and you will best him."

Aonghus chewed his lip thoughtfully a moment, turning over in his mind what the young charioteer said. Then he nodded slightly.

"If I tell myself that Indech can create illusions, I can dispel the illusion. Is that your teaching?"

"Just so," Cairell nodded.

Aonghus turned back to study the fortress again, and finally he turned back.

"I can think of no other plan apart from the one I suggested. We need luck and audacity to gain admittance to the fortress. From then on, let us hope the gods are watching over us. But there is no other plan that I can conceive."

Cairell sighed. He knew that Aonghus was right. Drouk's fortress certainly looked impregnable. All they could do was trust to the benevolence of the gods to allow them to enter and try to save the Dési captives, as well as Eithne and Aige.

Chapter Twenty-nine

The moment the sun vanished below the sea's distant level, Aonghus gave the signal to Maraí to weigh anchor and hoist sail. The *Spioróg* moved slowly out of the sheltering bay and along the hazy coastline to where the tall black, jagged thrust of the granite island of the Coranieid lay silhouetted in the faint red embers of the dying day. By the time the ship reached the small harbor, and pushed its way a long the tall ships that lay jostling there, the day was dark.

On the quayside a giant brazier was burning and Coranieid guards stood suspiciously watching the *Spioróg* as it edged nearer.

A voice sang out.

"They are demanding to know who we are," whispered Teg.

Aonghus nodded. "Tell them what we arranged."

"We are the *Dreoilín* out of Éireann," shouted Teg. "We come in search of the High King, Cormac Mac Art, with urgent messages."

There was a pause.

"You are lucky," replied the voice. "This night Cormac feasts with our leader, Drouk, in the feasting hall of the Coranieid. Your envoy may come ashore."

It had been arranged that Aonghus and Cairell, with Teg and Each-Tiarna, would form the party to go ashore. Aonghus had given long and detailed instructions to Maraí. But to send more men would be inviting the suspicions of the guards. Even so, the burly Coranieid warrior who greeted them on the quayside sniffed his displeasure.

"It surely takes only one man to bear a message?" He spoke in the Éireann language.

"When a message is borne to the High King of Éireann," smiled Aonghus, disarmingly, "then it becomes an insult if it is not borne according to ancient custom."

The Coranieid spat.

"Custom! Custom and tradition make men prisoners of old men's whims."

He turned and motioned them to follow him.

Aonghus glanced at the dark outlines of the *Spioróg* and hoped Maraí, whom he had left in charge, would be prepared.

The Coranieid led them along the quayside, where a rowdy group of warriors were seated in the warmth of the brazier playing dice. Then they began to ascend the steep pathway that twisted up the granite outcrop to the grey stone walls of the Coranieid fortress. Atop the black, towering walls, torches burned and the shadows of several sentinels moved in the gloom. Aonghus noted that at the gates only two guards stood watch. He presumed that the Coranieid were confident that no surprise attack could be launched against them. However, the sentinels were watchful.

"Who is there?"

The Coranieid guide stopped. "It's Cai. I am conducting messengers from Éireann to the guest of Drouk."

"You may pass, Cai." The guard waved them inside the fortress gates. The great courtyard beyond seemed deserted. Aonghus could hear the sounds of music, shouting and laughter from one of the buildings.

"Everyone is in the feasting hall," Cai explained, leading the way in that direction.

A moment later, Aonghus' strong hand was at his throat, choking off any sound that the startled warrior might make. His sword was pressed against the small of Cai's back.

"If you want to live, Cai, take us to where the captives of the Dyfed are held," he hissed.

The Coranieid's eyes bulged above the hand of Aonghus.

"We have little time, Cai. Do you agree to show us or do you die now?"

The frightened warrior jerked his head in assent.

Aonghus relaxed his grip slightly.

"Lead on. If you play false, then your death will be immediate."

The hapless Coranieid took the group to the far side of the courtyard. A black hole loomed in the cobbled floor.

"What trick is this?" demanded Teg.

"No trick, by the gods! Look closer and you will see steps. They lead down into the caves beneath the fortress. That is where all our prisoners are kept."

"How many guards will we find down there?" demanded Aonghus.

Cai hesitated a moment and then, as Aonghus' sword pressed closer, he said: "More than you can deal with." He responded sullenly.

Teg bit his lip in the gloom. "I don't like it. It may be a trap."

"We will have to chance it," Aonghus said.

"We will need a torch or we'll break our legs down there." Cairell pointed out.

The momentary distraction caused Aonghus to loosen his hold on Cai. The man gave a sudden twist and struggled free, his lungs filled with air to shout, but the only sound he gave was a choking cry as he sunk to the ground. Each-Tiarna stood back, sword in hand.

Aonghus swore softly. He glanced around the court-yard to ensure that they had not been spotted.

"We'd best start down the steps," he said. "Move slowly and keep close together. I'll go first. Each-Tiarna, pick that up." He motioned to the dead Coranieid. "No need to warn people of our presence yet."

He stepped into the blackness and began to feel each step, one hand on the wall to guide him. The rock-hewn stairs were shallowly cut, at least, and curved gently downward under the fortress into the bowels of the island. It was a long time before Aonghus saw a light ahead. It turned out to be a torch set in the wall. The stairs continued downward, lit by another and another torch. He motioned Each-Tiarna to leave the body of the Coranieid. It was no use carrying it farther—the place was too well lit now. Eventually the stairs ended.

He paused. Ahead he could hear the low murmur of voices, punctuated now and then by an occasional despairing cry, followed quickly by laughter.

They came into a large cave, filled with numerous barrels and several boxes. On the far side was an opening into another cave. Aonghus led his three companions forward, keeping behind the cover of the barrels.

The second cave was extremely large. There were even more barrels stacked here, from floor to ceiling. They had a curious and rather unpleasant odor about them. Beyond this cave was yet another, and it was from this third cave that the cries and laughter were coming.

Aonghus moved to the entrance and glanced through. Once more he was looking into a large cavern, this one divided into sections by several iron cages, each containing people. In the center sprawled several Coranieid warriors, while others walked between the cages carrying whips, lashing out now and again at the occupants.

Aonghus' eyes widened. He could see several Dési prisoners. Others were prisoners, perhaps, from previous raids. Most of them were women and children. He began to search feverishly for signs of Eithne and Aige.

A scream drew his attention to a dark-haired warrior who was wrestling with a slim figure in the center of the cave where the guards sprawled about. They were cheering the dark man on with coarse laughter and lewd gestures. The slender figure in the man's arms was a woman. A low, brutish cry rumbled from Aonghus' throat as he recognized Eithne.

He started forward but felt a firm hand on his arm.

Cairell, taut-faced, shook his head. In silence he held up his sling and began fitting a missile to it. The weapon hissed through the air. There was a crack of impact and the warrior seemed to freeze a moment, then dropped silently to the floor. There was a sudden silence in the cave as the Coranieid guards stared at their companion in disbelief.

Cairell loosed several more deadly projectiles through the cave before Aonghus, Teg and Each-Tiarna, swords at the ready, ran forward to engage the remaining guards. In a matter of moments it was all over and the Coranieid lay sprawled in their own blood.

Eithne collapsed, sobbing, into Aonghus' arms.

"You have come! But why? Why did you come when there is no escape from this accursed place? They will surely kill you."

"They can try," Aonghus smiled grimly.

Eithne gazed at him through tears of happiness.

"You came even though the odds are against you?"

He kissed her upturned face while she clung trembling to him.

"My lord," she whispered. "My chieftain until death!"

"Aonghus!"

Cairell's voice was sharp with warning.

Aonghus spun around. The dark warrior against whom Cairell had sent his first missile while he had been struggling with Eithne was climbing unsteadily to his feet, blood gushing from his temple. He had his sword in hand and began approaching the chieftain of the Dési.

Aonghus drew back in astonishment.

"Gorta Mac Goll!"

Gorta Mac Goll of the Clan Morna drew his lips back in a grimace of hatred.

"So you still live, son of Orba!" he gasped. "Good. For when you slew my chieftain and friend, Cellach, at Temuir, I swore my hand would be the instrument of your death."

Aonghus waved Cairell, Each-Tiarna and Teg back as they moved to disarm Gorta.

"No. Leave him to me. He shall answer to me for the pillage of Dún Gorm. Release our people and leave Gorta to me."

With a cry of anger, Gorta rushed upon Aonghus, his sword flashing over his head. Aonghus moved in to meet his attack. Gorta had not become chieftain of Clan Morna and second-in-command of the High King's bodyguard without obtaining a considerable reputation as a warrior. Aonghus felt the power of his sword, saw the craftsmanship in the way he wielded it. Even though he was still dazed by Cairell's slingshot, Gorta was a formidable opponent.

The sharp clang of metal against metal reverberated in the cave. Hatred lent the two warriors a strength that seemed impossible. Back and forth they struggled, cursing each other and summoning the gods to their aid. Neither gave the other an opening.

Cairell, who had found and released Aige, gathered the former prisoners together. But now he glanced at the duelling pair with anxiety. Unless Aonghus ended the struggle soon, the escape would surely be discovered. Every second was precious.

The end came unexpectedly.

Gorta Mac Goll had swung violently with his sword—so violently that the blade of Aonghus' weapon was dashed against the iron bars of the nearby cages and broke in two, leaving only the cracked hilt in Aonghus' hand.

Gorta paused a second, a savage smile coming to his thin lips.

"Now," he said softly, "as I killed the father, so shall I destroy the son."

A wave of savage fury swept through Aonghus, even as Gorta lifted his weapon for the death stroke. He ducked forward, cutting with the broken sword straight across the face of Gorta. With a shriek, the warrior dropped his sword, his hands going to his seared and bloody face. While he stood swaying blindly, Aonghus grabbed the man's discarded weapon and drove it with full fury into his opponent's breast.

He paused a moment, shoulders heaving, and then turned away, sickened.

Cairell was already leading the prisoners from the cave.

"The only thing that will let us out of here is discipline," the young charioteer told them. "So walk quietly and be prepared to obey when we order."

Aonghus, casting Gorta's death from his mind, came after them and told Cairell to halt. Their exit would have to be carefully prepared.

"These caves lie just below the fortress," he frowned.

"Does anyone here know what is stored in the barrels in the next cave?"

One of the prisoners, a stocky man with a weather-beaten face, moved forward.

"I am Ur. I was a ship's captain before the Coranieid sacked my ship. The barrels are loot from ships that sailed out of the Middle Sea in the south. They contain the oil the Coranieid use to fuel their torches."

Aonghus reflected for a moment. Cairell was impatient.

"Each delay makes our chances of getting safe from this place even less, Aonghus," he protested.

"Yes. But if we can create a diversion . . ."

"By the gods!" It was Each-Tiarna who gave the cry. "The barrels are on fire—someone has set light to the oil. Get everyone out before the fire spreads!"

There was a cry of alarm from the prisoners.

Aonghus pushed his way between them. Each-Tiarna was right. The barrels were on fire, and even as he looked, the flames leaped from barrel to barrel, growing higher and crackling with intensity

He started back with a cry of fear. The flames had cut them off from the exit from the caves.

They were done for. Defeated! If only he had not delayed and taken savage satisfaction in fighting with Gorta. He was to blame . . . again, his was the guilt for the destruction of the Dési, of Aige and of Eithne! He found himself shaking with helpless fear.

"Aonghus!" He found Cairell's face near his, Cairell's firm hand on his arm. "Aonghus, this is no real fire."

He stared at his friend, not understanding.

"Think, think about Indech and look again."

Aonghus turned back to the leaping flames.

"It is in your mind. Recognize that he is the master of illusion and you will be the victor!" cried Cairell.

Aonghus blinked and stared.

The flames suddenly seemed translucent, glowing

with a curious, ethereal quality. Beyond the flames stood a shadowy figure. He concentrated, seeing the skull-like face and close-set eyes smiling evily at him. He had a wild hope. Cairell was right! He had to concentrate. He stared again. The flames seemed to be receding. A frown crossed the druid's face as he realized his power was waning.

Aonghus became aware that Cairell was fitting a stone in his sling and he stopped him with a gesture.

"No, Cairell. It is I who has to conquer Indech."

He took a step forward, confident at last.

The brightness in the druid's eyes increased. The flames vanished, but in the place of the druid stood a large lion, rearing back on its haunches and snarling. Its great forepaws hit the air in front of Aonghus' face.

"Do your worst, Indech," smiled Aonghus. "I finally recognize your sorcery. If you can deal in nothing worse than mere illusion, then you had best flee, because I am going to destroy you."

Sword in hand, Aonghus advanced toward the lion.

It vanished, and in its place stood Indech, his brows furrowed as he tried to concentrate his power against Aonghus.

The druid realized he had failed, for he suddenly gave a scream of rage and shouted: "Die!" He flung himself forward, a thin dagger in his hand.

Aonghus took a side-step and jerked up his weapon. It entered under the man's rib cage and buried itself in his heart. The druid stopped a moment, swaying slightly. Aonghus jerked out his sword and then . . . then Indech vanished.

"Another illusion?" he muttered.

Cairell had no answer.

"He is a powerful magician."

As Aonghus stood for a moment, sweat on his brow, Eithne came up and put her soft hand in his. She smiled up concernedly at him.

"With you to lead us, we will succeed in escaping, Aonghus," she whispered.

He answered her with a smile and then turned to Teg and Each-Tiarna.

"Take everyone up the stairs to the entrance of the courtyard and wait there for Cairell and myself. Prepare to move fast and to fight your way out if the plan does not succeed."

Teg and Each-Tiarna did not pause to question him but began to usher everyone through the caves and up the stairs beyond.

"Go, Eithne, and you, Aige; go with the others," Aonghus said, pushing the girls forward.

They were reluctant.

"We will stay with you," Aige said.

"No. We will be but a moment. Swiftly now. Time is precious."

Cairell glanced at Aonghus as they left.

"What now?"

"Indech has given me the inspiration I needed," smiled the warrior.

Cairell frowned.

"Indech?"

Aonghus nodded.

"I remember a story told by the bards of Éireann of how a great warrior led an army through mountain passes to attack his enemies. Moving through the passes the army was halted, unable to move, by a huge pile of rocks that blocked the narrowest part of the pass. The rockfall was so large that it towered over the pass, making it impossible to shift. The great warrior, whose name I forget, ordered his men to fell large quantities of trees and pile the timber around the rocks.

"As soon as a wind rose he ordered the wood to be kindled. For a day and a night he burned the wood against the rock until the great mass glowed bright red from the heat of the fire. Then he ordered his men to throw wine over the rock so that clouds of blinding steam billowed upwards. He ordered his warriors forward with iron axes and hammers and told them to deal blow after blow so that the rock split and crumbled. Days and nights passed and the process went on until the impassable obstacle had disappeared and the army went on to victory."

Cairell stared in bewilderment at Aonghus.

"I fail to see the analogy of your tale."

"We have barrels of combustible oil. These caves are directly below the fortress. We can give Drouk and Cormac something to think about."

"But we have no wine or hammers to crack the layers of rock between the cave and the fortress."

Aonghus shook his head impatiently.

"Rocks split under heat and all these barrels of oil will create the greatest fire ever seen—thanks to Indech, who provided me with the idea."

Aonghus turned and took down a torch.

"Be prepared to run when I give the word," he called. Then he knocked open the bung of the nearest barrel and allowed the oil to gush out. A moment later he threw the torch at the substance. The flames caught and spread at once, leaping upwards. "Run!" yelled Aonghus.

Together they raced up the steps.

As they came to the courtyard they heard the sounds of a struggle.

With Teg and Each-Tiarna at their head, the Dési were moving in a wedge-shaped formation across the courtyard. Some of them had armed themselves and were fighting desperately against the Coranieid sentinels who had been alerted. The darkness was an ally, for the Coranieid were unable to see exactly what was happening. The doors of the feasting room had been thrown open, but the silhouettes of the figures there presented a perfect target to some of the Dési, who had armed themselves with bows and slings.

Aonghus and Cairell ran to the head of the wedge and waved the phalanx toward the gates. The Coranieid stood confused. They did not even have the sense to swing the gates shut before their former prisoners swept through.

As soon as they were through, Aonghus ordered one of the bowmen to send a lighted arrow curving into the sky to alert Maraí, on the *Spioróg* in the harbor below. Aonghus prayed that Maraí had been able to carry out his instructions. The fiery sign curved high across the harbor. Soon there was movement below. One after another, the Coranieid ships abruptly burst into flame, becoming bright beacons in the harbor. Aonghus gave a fierce grin. Maraí had succeeded with his part of the plan.

"Come on!" he cried.

Leading the phalanx down the pathway, pushing the Coranieid back in confusion, they made good progress. Those warriors who were wounded by the Coranieid were gathered up by the women, and sometimes a woman would seize the weapons of a fallen warrior and take his place, fighting shoulder to shoulder with the man. Slowly, remorselessly, they made their way down the narrow, twisting pathway, away from the fortress, toward the harbor which now was ablaze with Coranieid ships.

The confusion worked to their advantage. Coranieid ran here and there, trying to put out the flames, or simply giving up in the hopeless disorder. The attempts to put out the blazing ships were futile.

The phalanx reached the quayside and Maraí drew the *Spioróg* close in, so the former prisoners could simply leap from quay to the deck of the ship. Aonghus and Cairell were the last to board, fighting off a few half-hearted Coranieid who tried to bar their way.

"Is all well, Aonghus?" came Maraí's voice.

"Yes," replied the Dési chieftain, moving swiftly to the tiller, where the imperturbable sea captain stood. "I can see that all went well with our plan."

Maraí grinned in the flickering light of the burning Coranieid ships surrounding them.

"Shall I cast off?"

"The sooner the better," agreed Aonghus. "Let's put some sea between here and the Coranieid."

Chapter Thirty

The *Spioróg* shuddered slightly under the canvas as
Maraí began to turn her head before the wind. Even as
they drew away from the quayside, a group of Coranieid,
finding fresh courage, ran onto the quay and set up a
desultory fire with their bows. No one was hit and few
arrows found a target in the darkness; most fell into the
widening gap between the guay and the ship. Maraí
steered carefully between the burning hulks of the formidable Coranieid vessels, which had brought fear and
destruction on the people of Dyfed. Beside him, Aonghus
peered through the flickering flames across the harbor.

"Where is the *Díoltas?*" he demanded. "Did you fire
Cormac's ship?"

Maraí hesitated.

"We could not act until you gave the signal," he said
defensively.

"Cormac's ship has escaped?"

"While we were waiting for the signal, Cormac and
several of his men came down from the fortress and

went on board. Almost immediately the sail was hoisted and the *Díoltas* stood out to sea."

Aonghus banged his fist into the palm of his hand in frustration.

"Cormac has escaped!"

"He was probably warned by Indech," Cairell observed. "The druid had sufficient power to sense our presence in the caves. He must have warned Cormac to leave."

Aonghus was bitter.

"While Cormac is free, our lives continue at risk. He will not rest until he has destroyed us all."

There came a sudden roar, the like of which no man on the *Spioróg* had heard before. It was a mighty crack like thunder, yet a thousand times more powerful. They turned their startled gaze toward the granite island of the Coranieid. It seemed to their incredulous gaze that the entire top of the fortress had blown off and, for a moment, was balanced on a pillar of blinding white flame. Then particles of rock were hurtled into the sea around them—red, glowing rocks that hissed and sizzled as they struck the water. The rain ended before they had time to realize how dangerous the missiles were. Every eye turned to the granite island that they had just left. A sheet of flame roared upward into the night sky from the center of the island, while several smaller fires blazed in many other parts.

Cairell clapped Aonghus on the shoulder enthusiastically.

"It seems the story of the bards was right."

Teg came forward to congratulate him.

"Dyfed need not fear the Coranieid anymore, thanks to you. It will be many generations before they recover from this blow. They are destroyed. We can return in peace to Dyfed."

Aonghus shook his head, his face taut.

"I fear not. All we of the Dési wish is peace, Teg. Yet

Cormac is still free upon the high seas, and while he is, I am fearful. He will continue to search us out to destroy us, and I have no wish to bring bloodshed to Dyfed because of our presence."

Teg threw back his head boastfully.

"Let this Cormac come. As we defeated the Coranieid, so we can defeat Cormac."

It was Eithne who voiced a hope.

"Perhaps Cormac will return to Éireann now. He has tried several times to best you and your people, Aonghus. Perhaps he will give up."

Aonghus smiled at her, but he knew Cormac too well to give any credence to her aspiration.

The *Spioróg* sailed on into the darkness, away from the island. Most of the Dési spread themselves on the deck and fell into the sleep of exhaustion. Even Aonghus finally spread his cloak on the stern deck and lay down with Eithne curled in his arms to snatch a few hours' rest.

He was awakened by the piercing cry of herring gulls swooping about the masts in the bright light of dawn. Eithne still lay in his arms, breathing deeply in her sleep. Aonghus blinked and watched the gulls wheeling around and around the ship. Others were already astir. Cairell and Aige were up and standing close together, leaning on the stern rail, heads touching and whispering softly to each other. Maraí was at the tiller, giving instructions to young Teg on how to guide the ship.

Aonghus tried to disengage his arm from Eithne but she stirred, blinked, gazed up at him and smiled.

"Is it morning, lord?"

He grinned.

"It is morning, and there is no need to call me 'lord.' It is not the custom of the Dési."

She pouted.

"I care not for custom. You are my lord . . . until death."

He was about to make a rejoinder when a cry came from the masthead.

"Sail on the starboard, bearing down on us!"

Aonghus was on his feet in a moment, gazing across the rail of the *Spioróg*.

The ship was tall and black like a hawk, skimming the waves as it came out of the receding light.

Maraí recognized it first, although Aonghus knew almost as soon as the cry had rung out.

"The *Díoltas!*"

"Can we escape it?" whispered Eithne.

"She's using rowers as well as sail," Maraí said, examining the oncoming vessel with his trained seaman's eye. "Her warriors are already on deck—bowmen, as well. She means to fight us."

Aonghus shivered slightly in the cold morning air.

"Do we stand and fight?" cried Cairell.

Aonghus gazed at the anxious faces around him before turning back to the threatening shape of the High King's ship as it bore down on them.

"Last night I said that while Cormac Mac Art lives there will be no peace for the Dési. We must fight."

Eithne's hand was imploring at his arm.

"Let us fly, lord."

Aonghus shook his head slowly.

"The Dési have fled too long in the face of this madman's vengeance. No. We must stop and fight . . . one final battle. Now we make an end to constant flight and fear."

He firmly disengaged Eithne's pleading hand and pushed her gently toward Aige.

"Below decks with you."

Then he was looking around and calling orders.

"Teg, get all the women and children below. Cairell, organize our bowmen—and slingmen, too. Each-Tiarna, you organize what spearmen we have on board and form a group prepared to meet with any borders. Maraí . . ."

The sea captain was smiling fiercely.

"Aye, Aonghus. You want me to close with the *Díoltas?*"

Aonghus grinned.

"That I do."

At once all was hustle on board the *Spioróg* as they prepared. Aonghus took up his position by Maraí at the tiller. The High King's ship was speeding toward them now. He could see the oars flashing in the rising sun as the warriors pulled. Fifty blades flashed as one, dipping and feathering white in the blue of the sea, dipping and rising and drawing the dark shape of the vessel closer and closer.

"What's the plan, Aonghus?" cried Cairell, returning to report that his bowmen and slingmen were ready.

"We'll show that our sparrow hawk has a sting," smiled Aonghus. "Make ready the bows and fire on my command."

Cairell had fifty warriors gathered at the sides of the vessel.

Aonghus watched with narrowed eyes as the *Díoltas* came closer.

"Would that I were closing on Cormac with bare steal," he muttered, then turned and yelled to Cairell. "Now!"

The *Díoltas* was less than one hundred yards away. Fifty arrows shot into the air and hissed down on the decks of the High King's ship. There was no break in the forward motion of the great ship, but to Aonghus' ears came the cries of pain and anguish as the shafts found their mark. A moment later and a second shower of arrows was on its way. Then the *Díoltas* was veering aside from her course. The sides of the ships almost scraped each other as they passed. Aonghus had a passing vision of dead and wounded sprawled over the deck as the High King's vessel went by. Even as the ship veered away, Aonghus saw the gaunt figure of Cormac

Mac Art at the stern of the vessel, shaking his fist in impotent rage. By his side, leaning heavily, as if under some disability, stood the bent form of Indech. Indech was not dead! Then *Díoltas* had sped by and was moving off.

A cold determination seized Aonghus.

"Hoist more sail!" he cried. "Bring her around, Maraí, and follow her."

Maraí hesitated. "Why follow? She can't harm us now."

Cairell came running back to the stern.

"I reckon that a third of Cormac's men are dead or wounded."

"Yet Cormac and Indech still live," replied Aonghus. "We will follow until they or I have perished. It is the only way for the Dési to find peace."

Maraí swung on the tiller and begun to yell for more canvas to be spread. The *Spioróg* began to increase its speed as the canvas cracked aloft.

The *Díoltas* was moving off now, back across the open seas. Cormac, or the captain of his ship, was making no attempt to close again. He was running before them. It was obvious that the High King had lost a substantial amount of his men under Cairell's arrows. His ambush had failed.

"Chase her!" Aonghus ground his teeth. "Chase, even though she race across the borders of the Otherworld itself!"

His face was white now. In his mind's eye he was reliving the moment he had arrived at Dún Gorm, visualizing his slain father, his ravished and murdered sister, and the slaughtered members of his clan. Again there came a bloodmist clouding his vision as he stared toward the black silhouette of the *Díoltas*.

"Chase her!" he shouted, his voice rising in fury.

Maraí exchanged a glance with Cairell.

Ahead the *Díoltas* was straining now, the wind filling

its great sails. The survivors had drawn in their oars and were relying on the vast sheets of cracking canvas, creaking and groaning with the timbers, as the freshening wind tugged at them.

"They are drawing away," cried Maraí. "They are the faster ship, especially with this wind behind them."

Aonghus grasped the rail until his knuckles showed white.

"Chase them, I say."

"It's no use, Aonghus," Cairell said. "Cormac will outrun us in this wind."

Aonghus stared toward his prey as if he did not hear Cairell.

"Now Cormac will learn that he, too, can be hunted. I'll chase him across the Plains of Mist before I give up."

There was a cry from the masthead.

"Rocks ahead!"

Maraí glanced nervously at Aonghus.

"Rocks. I can't endanger the ship."

Aonghus swore back at him

"Where Cormac goes, I'll follow," he snarled.

He swung himself up on to the rigging and began to climb upwards. From the higher elevation he saw what the lookout had seen. Way ahead of Cormac's ship, a twin-peaked rock thrust out of the sea, black with sheer sides, like tall cliffs. Around the rock the waters foamed and boiled.

Back on the deck Maraí was worried.

"We'd best give them a wide berth. Who knows what tides run around such rocks?"

Aonghus shook his head.

"The *Díoltas* is heading for them, taking advantage of the wind to increase her distance from us. Wherever the *Díoltas* goes, we will follow."

Maraí protested, but Aonghus cut him short.

"Chase her, I say!"

The madness in his eyes caused Maraí to pause. Before he could say anything further, Aonghus had turned back to observe Cormac's ship. Its captain was obviously sailing close by the rocks in order to keep the wind directly in his sails and so increase his speed. It was true that good seamanship would give a wide berth to the jagged rocks, which surely thrust five hundred feet above sea level. There were also dangers of hidden rocks and rip tides in the area, which ought to be avoided. But there was the *Díoltas*, heading straight into the shadow of the rocks.

On the deck everyone could now see the threatening granite and hear the blustery roar of the seas. Ahead of them the *Díoltas* began to toss. Aonghus pressed forward, wondering whether a new wind was catching her sails. But Cormac's ship was bucking curiously and beginning to swing around, as if it were trying to turn within its own axis.

Then came the lookout's cry.

"Whirlpool! Turn away, turn away, for the love of your ancestors! *Díoltas* is caught in a whirlpool!"

Aonghus hesitated for a moment, but Maraí was already reacting, yelling for the mainsail to be brought down.

Aonghus stood to the rail and watched a moment longer as the great vessel began to toss and tumble. He could hear the roar of the water now. Then the *Spioróg* was caught in the current. The ship shuddered. He could feel the trembling of its timbers as the waters sliced beneath the keel.

Both Teg and Maraí were hauling on the tiller. The bow was turning, but ever so slowly, hauling reluctantly away. The roar of the waters began to increase.

Suddenly all Aonghus' senses returned. The insane bloodmist faded and he ran to help Maraí and Teg.

Miraculously, the bow swung faster, the waters began to grow calmer and the rocks turned behind them.

"Break out the oars!" yelled Maraí.

Twenty of his crewmen took out the oars and began to pull with a will away from the rocks.

"Aonghus!" The cry came from Cairell.

The young charioteer was staring, white-faced, and pointing to a corner of the stern of the vessel.

A figure was shimmering there. It was almost transparent, for the sparkling of the sea could be seen through its misty formation.

Indech's skull-like face glared murderously at him.

Aonghus took an involuntary step forward.

Even in the ghostly half-formed shape, Aonghus could see the pain and hatred on the druid's face, see the blood of the wound in the druid's chest.

"So visions can bleed," Aonghus said slowly.

"Curse you, Aonghus Mac Orba . . ." came a shrill cry.

Then the skull face was flung backward, and the eyes and mouth went wide, gulping as if trying to swallow air. It was the face of a drowning man. The hands waved a moment or two before the face . . . then the vision was gone.

For a moment or two Aonghus stared incredulously at the spot where it had been. Then he climbed swiftly up into the rigging.

He could just make out the top of the masts of the *Díoltas*. They bobbed, twisted and turned in a terrible swift motion as the vessel began its descent into the maelstrom of the awesome whirlpool. To his ears came the sucking sound of the surf and the pounding of the waves against the rocks. Then he could see no more of the High King's ship. There were not even splintered spars or other wreckage floating on the surface of the sea to mark the spot where the *Díoltas* had gone down.

Slowly Aonghus returned to the deck.

He knew beyond a shadow of a doubt that Cormac Mac Art was dead. Dead, too, was Indech, chief druid

of Éireann, in spite of his attempts to project his evil
form away from the vessel in its last moments. Not
even a druid could thwart the will of the gods.

It seemed that a great weight was lifted from Aonghus's
shoulders.

For an hour the *Spioróg* was pulled slowly away
from the rocks by the oarsmen. Aonghus took himself to
a corner of the stern of the ship, to be alone with his
thoughts. Neither Maraí nor Cairell rebuked him for
the danger into which he had nearly precipitated the
ship. They understood. Only when he finally drew back
his shoulders and turned back to the *Spioróg* did Eithne
come forward with a smile and seize his hand.

"All will be well, lord," she smiled. "You'll see."

Teg grinned from where he was now handling the
tiller, allowing Maraí to rest.

"Aye, let us go home."

A troubled look crossed Aonghus' face.

"Home?" His voice was bitter.

"Anywhere that you are will be my home now,"
Eithne said softly.

For many hours the *Spioróg* cut a nor' by nor'east
course through the blue waters. No one spoke much
during this time. A brooding silence seemed to hang
over the vessel. Then the lookout brought everyone
crowding to the rail.

"Sail, sail to port. She's laying a course to intercept
us, Maraí."

The captain stared seaward.

"It's a small vessel, Aonghus," he reported. "Too
small to harm us."

Aonghus grimaced.

"I trust no one. Cairell, prepare your bowmen."

They watched in fascination as the small ship bobbed
nearer. It was Cairell who pointed out that it bore the
royal standard of Éireann. The lighter ship was obviously a fast vessel—it rolled, lifted and pitched in the

heavy seas, but it moved quickly enough. It was not long before it was coming up alongside.

"What ship are you?" cried a voice.

"This is the *Spióróg*," rejoined Maraí.

There was a hesitation. The smaller vessel bumped alongside, and on the stern deck a young warrior stared upwards in astonishment.

"This is a ship of the Dési?"

Aonghus moved to the rail and shouted down.

"And it is Aonghus Mac Orba, chieftain of the Dési, who answer you. Who are you?"

"A messenger out of Temuir. Have you news of Cormac Mac Art?"

Aonghus gave a bark of hollow laughter.

"He has gone to join Manannán Mac Lir, god of the oceans, in the Otherworld," he replied, scarcely keeping the satisfaction from his voice.

The young warrior below shook his head in surprise.

"Great the sorrow in Éireann since Fionn Mac Cumhail's grave was measured."

Aonghus raised an eyebrow.

"How so?"

"I have journeyed several days from Temuir in search of Cormac Mac Art with grave news of Éireann."

"What news?"

"The High King is dead."

"Yes. I have told you, Cormac is drowned with his druid Indech."

The warrior shook his head.

"No. It is of Cairbre Mac Cormac, Cormac's son, that I speak."

Aonghus passed a hand over his forehead, confused.

"Cairbre? High King?"

"Ah, but you would not know," the warrior sighed. "When Cormac left Éireann in pursuit of his vengeance, the old law was invoked. No man shall be High King, nor aspire to any chieftainship, if he is blemished either

mentally or physically. In losing an eye, Cormac lost
the High Kingship. The council at Temuir agreed and,
indeed, Cairbre himself advocated that the Brehons
make a just finding in accordance with that law."

Aonghus made a face.

"So Cairbre became High King?"

"He did."

"And how came he by his death?"

"Simple to relate," went on the warrior. "When Cairbre
was confirmed as High King at Temuir he rejected law
for power. Several times Oscar rebuked the High King.
Then Cairbre began to play on old enmities between
Clan Morna and Oscar's Clan Bascna. Also, since the
death of Fionn, who united them into the Fianna, there
has been no one gifted with diplomacy to keep them
united. Cairbre preyed on their weaknesses and petty
squabbles. His weapons were jealousy and envy."

"What happened?" demanded Aonghus.

"Cairbre finally forced a war between them. Oscar
led the remnants of the Fianna, his men of Clan Bascna,
against Cairbre and Clan Morna. They met at the field
of Gabhra and a terrible battle was fought there.

"Sad that day when the great champions of Éireann
slaughtered each other at Gabhra. And as the sun set,
Oscar slew Cairbre the High King, but was himself
mortally wounded in the affair."

Aonghus' face was sad. If there had been one man in
Cormac Mac Art's retinue who was possessed of honor,
then it was Oscar Mac Oisín.

"So Oscar is dead?"

"And the Fianna with him. It was a terrible day when
Donn, the lord of death, stalked Éireann. Many strange
visions were seen as darkness swept the field. One old
woman swore that she saw the shade of Fionn Mac
Cumhail himself come to the battlefield to lament his
grandson. Then came Oisín, Oscar's father, the son of
Fionn. And with Oisín came Celta, old and venerable—

all who were once the champions of Cormac Mac Art when the world trembled at his name and the Fianna was a byword for honor and valor. They say that Oscar rose and wept at his own death; wept at the shadow that had descended on the land. He passed on to the Otherworld at the fall of night. Oisín and Celta, old as they were, raised a bier of spears and carried him from the field with his battle flag draped across his pierced body."

The warrior paused.

"Oscar's wife, the lady Aidín, hearing the news of his death, betook to her bed and perished of grief. The Fianna are no more and no High King graces Temuir's courts and halls."

Aonghus sighed long and deeply.

"It is a sad tale that you tell, warrior."

"I came to search for Cormac, but you tell me he is dead . . ." The warrior hesitated. "Come back to Temuir, Aonghus Mac Orba. Come back with the Dési. Claim the High Kingship for yourself, for Ireland has needed of you and your kind."

Aonghus smiled softly at the man's earnestness.

"Alas, that is not written. The Dési will never go back to the green rolling hills of Bregia."

"The High Kingship is yours for the asking, Aonghus."

Aonghus shook his head firmly and turned, catching Eithne's hand as she came smiling to his side.

"We will never land on the shores of Éireann again. That is written!"

"And it is also written that I will go wherever you go, son of Orba," whispered Eithne.

"Then we shall go to Dyfed together. There, under the approval of Ludd, the Dési will settle in peace and be free once again."

Teg smiled joyfully.

"All Dyfed will welcome you, Aonghus."

Cairell, arm in arm with Aige, smiled.

"Long life to Aonghus Mac Orba, chieftain of the Dési!"

Maraí, Each-Tiarna and the survivors of the Dési set up a thunderous acclamation.

Below on the smaller vessel, the young warrior smiled sadly and ordered his ship to turn west for Éireann.

Aonghus and Eithne watched it bob away across the waters.

"Set the course for Dyfed, Maraí," he called over his shoulder to the grinning captain of the *Spioróg*. "Let's make haste. The wandering of the Dési has ended."